# Too Many Matchmakers

*by*

*Allison Lane*

A SIGNET BOOK

SIGNET
Published by the Penguin Group
Penguin Putnam Inc., 375 Hudson Street,
New York, New York 10014, U.S.A.
Penguin Books Ltd, 27 Wrights Lane,
London W8 5TZ, England
Penguin Books Australia Ltd, Ringwood,
Victoria, Australia
Penguin Books Canada Ltd, 10 Alcorn Avenue,
Toronto, Ontario, Canada M4V 3B2
Penguin Books (N.Z.) Ltd, 182-190 Wairau Road,
Auckland 10, New Zealand

Penguin Books Ltd, Registered Offices:
Harmondsworth, Middlesex, England

First published by Signet, an imprint of Dutton NAL,
a member of Penguin Putnam Inc.

First Printing, October, 1998
10 9 8 7 6 5 4 3 2 1

Copyright © Susan Ann Pace, 1998

All rights reserved

 REGISTERED TRADEMARK—MARCA REGISTRADA

Printed in the United States of America

Without limiting the rights under copyright reserved above, no part of this publication may be reproduced, stored in or introduced into a retrieval system, or transmitted, in any form, or by any means (electronic, mechanical, photocopying, recording, or otherwise), without the prior written permission of both the copyright owner and the above publisher of this book.

BOOKS ARE AVAILABLE AT QUANTITY DISCOUNTS WHEN USED TO PROMOTE PRODUCTS OR SERVICES. FOR INFORMATION PLEASE WRITE TO PREMIUM MARKETING DIVISION, PENGUIN PUTNAM INC., 375 HUDSON STREET, NEW YORK, NEW YORK 10014.

If you purchased this book without a cover you should be aware that this book is stolen property. It was reported as "unsold and destroyed" to the publisher and neither the author nor the publisher has received any payment for this "stripped book."

# SIGNET REGENCY ROMANCE
## Coming in November 1998

*Mary Balogh*
# The Last Waltz

*Evelyn Richardson*
# The Gallant Guardian

*Carla Kelly*
# Miss Milton Speaks Her Mind

**1-800-253-6476**
ORDER DIRECTLY
WITH VISA OR MASTERCARD

## "May I present the Marquess of Woodvale?"

"My lord." Somehow she kept her voice even, though it felt like every drop of blood had instantly vacated her head.

"D-Diana Winslow!" His obvious shock helped preserve her own control. Never had she thought to see Nicholas Barrington nonplused.

"Lady Bounty," she said, correcting him firmly. "You are Gerald's friend, aren't you? How is he?"

She could not have astonished him more if she had kicked him in the stomach. Or someplace lower. For one long moment, he stared at her, then his eyes blazed in fury. "Gerald's friend?" he snarled. Grabbing her arm, he dragged her into the library and slammed the door. "I'm not stupid, Diana. You cannot have forgotten our last meeting—you vowed to love me for all eternity."

# Chapter One

"Nicholas! When did you get back?"

"Last night." Nicholas Barrington, ninth Marquess of Woodvale, smiled as Lord Justin Landess joined his interrupted stroll down New Bond Street.

"Rather late this Season. We expected you weeks ago."

"Why? You know I've been in mourning."

"Not since Christmas," Justin pointed out, donning his customary mask of *ennui* now that his surprise had faded.

"Perhaps not, but I could hardly return when my status was so uncertain."

"How is the child?"

"Healthy. I cannot say as much for my aunt, though." He shrugged.

Justin fell into a companionable silence, instinctively knowing that the subject of Nicholas's recent difficulties was now closed.

Nicholas let his eyes roam the street, reacquainting himself with London after his two-year absence. Fashion was the most obvious change. Though fops still dressed in a dazzling array of colors, most gentlemen's jackets were darker. Ladies, on the other hand, were wearing fussier gowns, bedecked with ruffles, ribbons, and furbelows.

He grimaced as a small boy tumbled out of the confectioner's shop, nearly knocking him down. A scolding nurse followed, her shrill tones blending with the city's cacophony.

After two years of country silence, he could no longer ignore the noise now reverberating in his head. Wheels and hooves clattered across the cobblestones. Drivers cursed.

Whips cracked. Horses snorted and screamed. People thronged the sidewalks, talking, laughing, and arguing. Venders shouted their wares.

But he shoved the discomfort aside, knowing his ears would soon adapt.

Shelford had a new pair of matched bays, he noted as the Corinthian skillfully threaded his curricle through the usual jam of carriages and drays. And Hartford was riding a high-stepping Arabian stallion—had something happened to Greatheart? But most of the equipage was familiar.

His nose twitched, reminding him of another London reality he had somehow forgotten—the overpowering smell. Smoke from thousands of fires blended with sweaty horses, unwashed people, animal droppings, perfumes from scent shops and flower vendors, aromas from the confectioner's, pungent herbs from the apothecary . . .

And here was another change, he realized as he passed the familiar flower cart on the corner and turned into Piccadilly. The old crone was gone, replaced by a young girl.

His own life had changed far more than London had. Four deaths in sixteen months had brought him his grandmother's wealth and estate, his father's mountain of debts, and finally his uncle's title, including a fortune, vast properties, and uncounted dependents he had never expected and wasn't sure he wanted. The transition had been anything but smooth.

He bit back a sigh. His grandmother's unexpected legacy had turned a long-standing dispute with his father into a serious breach that hadn't begun to heal before the man's own death—which had deepened Nicholas's bitterness by exposing his father's childish retaliation and saddling him with his demanding mother. He had hardly begun dealing with that mess when his uncle, the eighth Marquess of Woodvale, had died. Barely two weeks later his aunt had announced that she was again with child—which suspended the transition and left him hanging in uncertainty.

And not just him. Stewards, solicitors, secretaries, servants, his aunt, and a host of other relatives were left without leadership. His uncle's will had appointed his successor as guardian to any minor children, but no provision had been made for an underage heir. Thus two uncles and a cousin had argued incessantly over which of them should oversee the marquessate if the child was a boy.

For seven and a half months everyone had tiptoed about, staring at the walls while waiting to learn the outcome. But while the birth of a fifth daughter had finally ended that dispute, it had handed Nicholas even more problems.

As the ninth marquess, he was now guardian to all five of the girls, and his aunt's failing health might force him into raising them. He shuddered. Too bad no one was yammering to assume that chore.

But they weren't his only responsibilities. Relatives he had never heard of were crawling out of the woodwork; his mother's demands grew harsher every day; untangling his new affairs promised to tie him up for months—

"Thornhill got himself into a bit of a scrape," announced Justin, thankfully diverting his attention.

"Waite's heir?"

He nodded. "It seems he forgot how to use a key. Dobson slipped away from Cavendish's masquerade to entertain his labybird in what he thought was an empty room, only to find Thornhill and a pair of opera dancers rolling about on the floor."

"Cawker." He suppressed a laugh. Cavendish might host the loosest gatherings outside the courtesan balls, but Thornhill should have known better. "Discretion still counts."

"As you learned from experience?"

"That was eight years ago. I've mellowed since then." In fact, he had more than mellowed. The incident had put an end to his most flamboyant affairs. Six year later, he had given up raking entirely. His only surprise was discovering that he didn't miss it. Occasional visits to a discreet widow were all he really needed.

"You could have made a tidy profit had you been here,"

said Justin. "Bets were running three to one that he would leave town to avoid the scandal."

Nicholas snorted. "Waite's heir run from a minor embarrassment? Fustian! Waite stirred up bigger scandals each and every Season before he wed. As did his sister. It's in their blood. Can you name one member of that family who hasn't caused talk?"

"Like I said, you could have made a tidy profit. You always know how people will react."

"Unless I lose the skill now that I no longer need it." He had supported himself for years by wagering on human behavior, but his various legacies now made it unnecessary.

Justin held the door to Hatchard's bookstore while Lady Cunningham exited, then followed Nicholas inside. "Will you be taking your seat in the Lords?"

He nodded, smiling in anticipation. "I wonder what Porter will say." Porter was a sanctimonious baron who detested rakes in general and Nicholas in particular, in part because he had lost an embarrassing number of wagers to him over the years. It pricked the man's considerable vanity.

"Plenty, and none of it to the point. Of course, you could always claim to be turning over a new leaf. You'll need an heir one of these days."

"You sound like my mother." Nicholas sighed. "She can't utter two words without urging me to set up my nursery." He didn't see the need. The last thing he wanted was yet another dependent who would occupy his time and dip into his purse.

"What mother can?" asked Justin. "Mine is becoming positively loquacious on the subject. But if you don't want a legshackle, you'd best watch your step. The tabbies are already buzzing over your acccession. Once they discover you are here, every matchmaking mama in town will pounce. A wealthy marquess is much different from a charming rake with an empty purse and no prospects."

"I know."

"But do you understand? You've never been seriously pursued—not by the mothers." He caught Nicholas's eye and grinned. "I know the daughters have always loved you. Between that handsome face and your naughty reputation, they can't help themselves."

"It doesn't mean anything," he protested.

"It didn't," Justin corrected. "No father would have approved of you. But it's different now. A title and fortune outweigh far greater sins than yours. Those women are greedy. And they'll pursue you harder than they do me—I might have money and connections, but I'll never sport a title, thank God. Have you any idea how unscrupulous they can be? They will stage accidents in front of your house, fall into your arms in swoons, trap you in empty rooms . . ."

"I get the picture." He had learned that lesson the hard way, almost ten years ago—which was why he had avoided daughters of the aristocracy ever since. But no one knew the tale, not even Justin. And he wasn't about to enlighten him.

"Good." His warning delivered, Justin lightened his voice. "Harrison's heir finally produced a son."

"Really?"

"Just yesterday."

"Which explains why I hadn't heard. Is the child well?" The younger Harrison had been married for five years with nothing to show for it but a series of miscarriages and stillbirths.

"Strong as an ox. They are planning a house party for the christening next month."

"Pass along my regards." The Harrisons were too propriety-conscious to approve of him, though he had known the heir at school. He paused at a table of recently published books.

Justin nodded as Nicholas picked up Thornton's latest collection of poems. "Good choice. It's even better than his last one."

"I thought you disliked poetry." He thumbed through the volume.

"I do as a rule, but Merriweather's illustrations bring his verse to life."

"Is Merriweather one of your artist friends?"

"No, devil take it. Both he and Thornton are obsessively reclusive."

"Still? I've always wondered why they bother. Such talent should be out in the open."

Nicholas had often admired Justin's collection of Merriweather prints. One of his first actions after his grandmother had died was to buy copies for himself. He was also enchanted by Merriweather's oils, finding a pair of stupendous landscapes just that morning. But he didn't mention his interest. He was too accustomed to hiding his financial affairs. And a year of sharing a house with his mother had intensified his secrecy. What she knew, everyone knew, usually in so exaggerated and sensationalized a form that he hardly recognized the tales.

He picked up a volume of war memoirs and added it to his stack.

Justin eyed the eclectic collection and grinned. "If you wish to rehash the late war, you should attend Lady Bounty's *soirée*. Several officers will be there tonight, including that captain."

Nicholas raised a brow. "I understood that she ran a literary *soirée*."

"You know her?"

"No, she arrived in town after my grandmother died. But Fortrier sometimes mentions her."

"He only attends the literary sessions, but she holds gatherings on many topics—art, literature, politics, science. She always includes experts from the appropriate fields." He shrugged. "I attend all her art discussions and occasionally take in others. Anyone is welcome. Why don't I take you up tonight and introduce you?"

"Why not?" Stimulating discussion might divert the blue-devils that had plagued him for so long. And he was curious about Lady Bounty. He had known the earl most of his life, but had never met his second wife.

Bounty had been a cherished mentor in years past. Intelligent and highly educated, his love for debate had inspired

Nicholas's own studies. Nicholas had often researched esoteric topics before one of their meetings, hoping to best him. But not until his second year at Oxford had he actually done it. Bounty had rewarded him with a Shakespeare first edition that remained one of his most prized possessions.

So the fact that his widow now hosted an intellectual *soirée* was hardly surprising. He couldn't imagine the man wedding a brainless widgeon.

But he also could not ignore the charges hurled by Humphrey Reynolds, the current Lord Bounty. They painted a very different picture of the earl's second wife—not that Humphrey's word was particularly trustworthy.

Humphrey was Bounty's nephew. He had long hated his uncle for refusing to fish him out of the River Tick, so he'd openly gloated when Bounty's only son had died of consumption, making Humphrey the heir. With his new expectations, he had embarked on a year of gaming and debauchery that tripled his debts. Thus he had been appalled when Bounty took a young wife at the advanced age of sixty-eight.

Rumors soon circulated, accusing the new Lady Bounty of being a rapacious fortune hunter, a heartless vixen, and a light skirt who would never produce a son of unquestionable parentage. Few doubted the source of the stories, but repetition left many believing the substance. Humphrey's vehemence gradually faded as it became clear that the lady was barren, but it returned in full force after Bounty's death. Humphrey inherited the entailment, which included only the title and an ancient estate that had not turned a profit in nearly a century. The rest of Bounty's fortune, including his town house and other estates, went to his wife.

Furious, Humphrey had barred her from his doors and tried to recover his inheritance. But despite his legal maneuverings, the will had been proven valid.

Nicholas shook his head. Humphrey had ranted against Lady Bounty ever since, but was she really a heartless fortune hunter? He had trouble believing that his old friend could be taken in by such a creature. The man's mind had still been sharp four years after his marriage. And it was Bounty who had taught him to read character, who had expounded on human nature, who had helped him hone the skill that had earned his keep for so long.

He sighed. He would meet the lady tonight and judge for himself. At least he was unlikely to run into matchmakers at an intellectual *soirée*. And conversation would chase away his persistent blue-devils. He hadn't conducted a good debate in years.

His mother was responsible for much of his melancholy. She had been pressuring him for months——to increase her allowance, to take her to London, to avenge a host of slights from this relative or that, to marry and set up his nursery.

But marriage didn't appeal to him. Nor did his mother, he had to admit. Constant quarrels with his father had kept him away from home. Only lately had he realized that her demands had precipitated many of those quarrels. But her nagging was only part of the problem. She was sneaky and manipulative, employing even disreputable tactics to get her own way— which raised the question of whether he was safe from her pressure even now. Before he returned to Woodvale Abbey, he must decide what to do with her. Sharing a roof would never work.

In the meantime, he must figure out what to do with himself. His days of haunting the clubs in search of the perfect wager were long gone. As were the nights of entertaining his latest conquest. He had come to London to straighten out the Woodvale affairs, but that would hardly fill all the hours. Yet attending society gatherings was too dangerous.

"I wish I could come to your *soirée* tonight," exclaimed Chloe Parker as she watched her friend perform magic on a bowl of flowers. "How do you do that?"

"Practice." Diana Reynolds, Dowager Countess of Bounty, laughed at the expression on Chloe's face. The girl looked fragile and delicate, though Diana knew from four years of close acquaintance that she was not. "Don't turn that stony look on me. Your parents will not allow you near the soldiers and politicians who will be here tonight, just as they forbade you to meet the artists I entertained last week. You are only seventeen. They must protect you."

Chloe sighed. "This has nothing to do with protection. They despise anything intellectual and don't even want me reading poetry. If Lord Bounty had not been a neighbor, I doubt they would allow me to visit you."

It was true. And if Lord and Lady Parker had known Bounty well, they would have cut the connection anyway. They distrusted book learning. Bounty had known that, restricting his conversation to topics of mutual interest. Since he divided his years among several properties, he had not seen them often.

But Diana had lived at the Haven since his death. Because she was a known intellectual, she had seen even less of the Parkers. Only the fact that few of their friends were visiting London at the moment made them welcome her here. But if they knew how much time Chloe spent at her house, they would have cut all connections. She rarely asked Chloe if she had permission to call, not wanting to know the answer. Anyone with Chloe's curiosity would suffocate without frequent access to new ideas.

Diana had been in a similar situation before her marriage—awash with curiosity but with no way of satisfying it. Bounty had taken her in hand, opening her mind, praising her mastery of any new subject, and rewarding her when she finally bested him in debate. It was a legacy she was passing on to Chloe.

"What is troubling you?" she asked now. "I doubt missing a discussion of the war put that line between your eyes."

"London is so dull!"

Diana's hands froze in the act of clipping a stem. "Dull?"

"I sound like a spoiled child, don't I?"

"Perhaps, though I know you are not. But few young ladies would describe a London Season as dull."

"True, yet I find it so. At home, it never bothered me that every day was the same, because I expected nothing else. But I thought London would be different. How could it not be?

There are so many things to do and places to see—art exhibits, cathedrals, theaters, galleries. Museums, balloon ascensions, parties, shopping ... Yet Mama insists on following the same daily routine. We start with morning calls, where I must sit demurely while she and the other ladies exchange the same boring gossip day after day. *Who is newly arrived?* Today it was the Marquess of Woodvale. *Who misbehaved last night?* Lord Thornhill did something unmentionable—again. I wish just once they would describe his misdeeds. At least it would enliven the morning. *Who is courting whom?* Lord Rufton is the leading contender for Lady Melissa Stapleton's hand. He waltzed with her twice at two different balls last night." She sighed. "Then we drive in the park and eat dinner before attending one rout and one ball. Mama preaches endlessly about decorum. She nearly went into hysterics when I asked to visit the Egyptian Hall yesterday. If one can believe her, the exhibits would shock a proper lady into the vapors."

Diana nearly choked. "I wonder what she objects to. Napoleon's travel coach, perhaps?"

"Who knows? She would never sully my innocent ears with a description. She also refused to take me to the British Museum on grounds that the Elgin Marbles are lewd."

"Lewd? How odd. Everyone is clothed, and none are writhing with passion. Of course, many of the paintings cannot make that claim." She laughed at the expression on Chloe's face. "My apologies. I shouldn't tease you."

"She would be appalled that I understand the allusion. Or anything else. Papa was furious when I bought that book. Ladies should not read, it seems."

"Thus your comment on poetry. I had forgotten that you purchased Thornton's latest."

"He claims the poems are lewd. They describe wind and water, trees and mountains, power, grandeur, and the majesty of nature. What is lewd about that?"

"Nothing," Diana assured her. Some of Thornton's work *did* evoke an underlying sensuality, but an innocent like Chloe would not recognize it. "You know your parents have very rigid ideas."

"But I did not realize how rigid," she wailed, pacing the floor in agitation. "Why can I not choose my own friends? Why can I not see London? Why must I be shuffled into marriage before I have any chance to live? Could they not at least allow me a say in my own future?"

"Is that what is troubling you? Few girls see more than you have before marriage, Chloe. And you have known all your life that you would wed George. It never bothered you before. In fact, you were quite excited at the prospect only a fortnight ago. What happened?"

"He came to dinner last night."

"And?" she asked when the silence stretched.

"I haven't seen him since he signed the betrothal agreement six years ago. You know he stays on his own estate and never visits his parents."

No one had ever explained why, but Diana nodded. She had known both Chloe's family and George's since her own marriage ten years earlier, but she had met George only during his occasional breaks from Cambridge. She had paid him no heed.

Chloe's eyes shimmered with tears. "He is the most boring man I have ever met," she said on a sob. "And tyrannical. Nothing pleases him. He has no sense of humor. And he is so proper that Papa seems dissolute in comparison."

"Good heavens!" Lord Parker was a staid gentleman who cared for little beyond his estate.

"How can I marry such a man? I will die!"

"Calm yourself, Chloe," she demanded. "You should know better than to judge people on one meeting. Initial impressions are often false."

"How can you say that?"

"Think! Have I taught you nothing? If a gentleman first met you at your parents' table, what would he think?"

Chloe blotted her eyes and sighed. "That I was a boring, comfortable widgeon."

"Exactly. You rarely open your mouth. You never dispute a

statement. You repeat only the most innocuous gossip and never venture an opinion. I fact, I only heard you make three statements during my entire visit to your mother's at-home last week."

"*Sunshine is quite pleasant after a week of rain. Lady Brisbane was overset by encountering Lady Markleigh's poodles in the park. Papa quite properly does not approve the raucous atmosphere to be found at Astley's,*" she repeated in resignation.

"Exactly. And that impression would be reinforced when he saw you making calls with your mother."

"But if I don't remain quiet and demure, she punishes me."

"I know," said Diana soothingly. "I was not criticizing. It is often important to conform to people's expectations. But did you consider that George might also be wearing a social mask?"

"Why would he?"

"He was visiting your family for the first time in six years. He knows their characters, for he grew up on the next estate. He would conform merely to make a good impression."

"Perhaps, but I don't believe it. His eyes tell a different story—you are the one who claims that truth can be found in the eyes and hands."

She nodded. It was one of Bounty's first lessons, and had stood her in good stead many times since. A lady alone had to keep her wits about her, and that meant knowing what her companions really wanted.

"His eyes lit with fanaticism when he disparaged London frivolity—especially modern dancing—and his hands actually twisted his serviette into a noose."

"Was he speaking of the waltz?"

She nodded. "Then he decried the fact that we will not wed until after we return to Wiltshire in July. By holding the wedding here next month, he could remove me from this decadent society before it turns my silly head. He would do it tomorrow if a special license cost less." New tears rolled down her cheek. "I cannot believe he actually berated Papa for bringing me to town. And Papa let him!"

Diana spent several minutes calming her hysteria. Chloe had a history of emotional outbursts, so it was unlikely that George was quite that haughty, but he didn't sound very accommodating. Could his own nervousness have made him belligerent? She didn't like that bit about the noose.

Both the Parkers and the Weymouths were rigidly conventional and old-fashioned, proposing this betrothal just after Chloe was born. When George reached one-and-twenty, they asked him if he objected. He didn't, signing the betrothal contract the same day. Two weeks later he had left home.

There had been no hint of a disagreement, but when years passed without another visit, Diana had concluded that an argument must be keeping him away. Or was it the betrothal? Perhaps George was less willing than anyone believed, not that it mattered. The settlements were signed, the announcement made public. Nothing could change things now.

But it did seem unfair that George had been given a chance to renege on the arrangement while Chloe had not.

Diana suppressed a sigh. Chloe's future was out of her hands. Despite their friendship, she was merely a neighbor. And she already walked a fine line with the Parkers. If she tried to meddle, they might cut the connection, leaving Chloe with no one she could talk to.

Chloe's betrothal chafed at Diana for the rest of the day, intruding into her thoughts even as she welcomed guests to her *soirée*. The girl was so young—and so innocent. Had introducing her to art, literature, and new ideas been wrong? Her curiosity had always been insatiable, but neither of them had considered the consequences of feeding her imagination. Longing for the moon and the stars would bring nothing but pain if her husband did not share her dreams—or at least tolerate them.

Chloe couldn't afford to fight an inevitable future. Instead of throwing tantrums and making threats, she needed to look past the surface to discover George's worth. He might not be handsome or exciting, but he was solidly dependable and probably would be faithful. Chloe would never face unexpected poverty. Her children would not be stigmatized by their father's unethical behavior. The sooner she accepted her marriage, the sooner she would enjoy her new position.

Diana had learned that lesson through experience. Her father had squandered his fortune, forcing her into an arranged marriage that had also seemed quite impossible on the surface.

Dear Harry. She still missed him, though he had been gone for four years. He had ignored her lack of dowry. When he learned that a callous libertine had shattered her heart, he had comforted her, healed her, then helped her to live again. He had honored her intelligence, expanded her education, taught her how to judge people, perfected her social skills, and welcomed her as an equal partner in their marriage. She had missed their frequent debates so much that she had started her weekly *soirées* as a way to recapture his spirit. Debate kept her mind sharp and her grief at bay, filling her need for stimulating conversation.

Grief had now mellowed into contentment. She had good friends and the respect of everyone whose opinion mattered. And even in death Harry made her feel cherished. His will had offered financial security and independence. She split her time between London and the Haven. Life couldn't get much better.

"Lord Justin," she said, offering her hand to the latest arrival. He was a fairly regular attendee, though she hadn't expected him this evening. He usually skipped anything political. "I'm delighted that you could come."

"How could I bypass the most interesting gathering in London?" He openly ogled her, his eyes lingering on her bosom. "Or should I say the most interesting hostess?"

"You never change." She lightly rapped his arm with her fan. An incorrigible flirt, he always tried to fluster her, and she made sure he never succeeded.

"Nor do you. Delectable, as always, my dear. May I present

the Marquess of Woodvale." He stepped aside, providing her first glimpse of his companion.

"My lord." Somehow she kept her voice even, though it felt like every drop of blood had instantly vacated her head. Spots swirled before her eyes. She fought them down, refusing to faint, refusing to give him that satisfaction.

"D-Diana Winslow!" His obvious shock helped preserve her own control. Never had she thought to see Nicholas Barrington nonplused.

"Lady Bounty," she said, correcting him firmly. "You are Gerald's friend, aren't you? Which explains why you look familiar. How is he? I've heard nothing of him since I left Warwickshire."

She could not have astonished him more if she had kicked him in the stomach. Or someplace lower. For one long moment he stared at her, then his eyes blazed in fury.

Lord Justin raised his brows, but prudently moved into the drawing room in response to an imperative thumb.

"*Gerald's friend?*" Nicholas snarled through gritted teeth. Grabbing her arm, he dragged her into the library and slammed the door. "*Look familiar?* I'm not stupid, Diana. You haven't forgotten me. And you cannot have forgotten our last meeting—you vowed to love me for all eternity."

She managed a light tinkle of laughter that drove new flashes of fury across his face. For once her composure exceeded his, though curses screamed through her head and dizziness still threatened to overwhelm her. She had known from the moment she ventured into London that this day would arrive, so she had planned for it, rehearsing the words until they rose automatically to her lips—and that was a blessing, for she had not known that he was now Woodvale. Such ignorance was proof that he finally meant nothing. *Thank you, God.*

"Still as arrogant as ever, I see. Now that you mention it, I do remember you, my lord. But as you pointed out so eloquently at the time, I was suffering from a youthful infatuation that would quickly fade. In fact, my feelings were no more than a girlish fascination with your rakehell reputation. Love feels quite different, as I quickly learned. I married Harry a month later."

"It didn't take you long to find a well-heeled lord and wheedle him out of a fortune."

Pain sliced through her chest, but she hid it. "Does a man of your experience actually believe malicious gossip—"

"Did you think I'd resume our liaison once you became a wealthy widow?" he demanded, cutting through her words as if she hadn't spoken.

Fury engulfed her, overwhelming the pain. He hadn't changed a bit. Money and sex were all he cared about, so he assumed that everyone was driven by the same needs.

*Watch your tongue,* warned a voice in her head. In addition to his lifelong quest for a fortune, he enjoyed a challenge, which explained his reaction just now. Pretending that she no longer recognized him had given her a great deal of satisfaction, but she must be careful not to push him too far.

"Actually, you never crossed my mind after I married Harry," she lied.

"Right!" he scoffed. "A passionate young girl takes one look at an old man and falls hopelessly in love. Do you know any other fairy tales?"

"I should call you out for that! Harry was the kindest, gentlest man I've ever known. You are not worthy to kiss his feet." Tears shimmered in her eyes, and she cursed. Damn Nicholas! He still had the power to destroy her control.

"Do you really expect me to believe that you loved him?" he demanded skeptically.

"I don't care what you believe, though it's true enough." *Make him accept the lie. Please?* She turned aside to hide her trembling lips. Why was he so angry? It couldn't be jealousy after all these years. He hadn't wanted her, so finding that she had married elsewhere could hardly prick his conceit. And his own dishonor was safely buried. Revealing it would expose her naïveté, tarnishing her reputation.

Nicholas stared. Her eyes had filled with tears before she'd turned away. Had she actually loved Bounty? He shuddered.

He couldn't believe it—didn't want to believe it, despite his own fondness for the man. He did not want to picture Bounty bedding a seventeen-year-old—especially *his* seventeen-year-old. But if she lied, then he had forced her into a hideous union. Guilt stabbed his heart.

"Congratulations on your new title." Her voice deflected his thoughts. She again faced him, her face composed. "You must be delighted to have achieved the wealth and power you always craved without having to wed an heiress or abandon your raking."

*Ouch!*

He grimaced, appalled to find his youthful words tossed back at him. "Yes, it was quite convenient," he snapped, temper erasing his guilt.

"I must see to my other guests," she continued dispassionately. "I presume your purpose for dragging me in here was to demand silence about our previous acquaintance. I agree. As far as London is concerned, we first met tonight—though Lord Justin might need some convincing; you made quite a cake of yourself. You are welcome to stay, but I will understand if you prefer to leave."

She was gone by the time he formed a response. Clenching his fists, he stared out the window at her tiny garden. If nothing else, this encounter had disproved every word of Humphrey Reynold's calumny. Despite his taunts, he knew Diana was no fortune hunter. So why had she married Bounty? *Please let it be for love.* He had too many regrets over that summer already.

He had left within hours of their last meeting, already wracked with guilt. And he had cut further contact with Gerald, so he would never see her again. Thus he had not heard of her marriage.

Perhaps he *was* conceited—just a little. He had never imagined her turning to another man, and certainly not to one like Bounty. It hurt. And that made him angrier. She was no more than a youthful acquaintance, of no importance to his life. Her opinion would never influence him. And it certainly should not affect his temper—which he had last lost ten years ago, damn her!

*You must be delighted . . . wealth and power . . .* Not once had he considered the Woodvale title as the fulfillment of his youthful dreams. Nor had he felt more than mild relief when he had inherited his grandmother's money. He would forgo the lot if only he could have her back. She had been his rock during childhood, far more of a mother than his own.

He hated the marquess's duties for which he had never been trained. But he would swallow live coals rather than admit that aloud, especially to Diana. She had lied about forgetting him, but this meeting proved that it was far from her first lie. He couldn't trust her. She had been sweet, loving, passionate, and very innocent that summer, but she had never revealed her intelligence or an education that would be considered extensive even for a man. He had heard too much about the breadth of Lady Bounty's knowledge to believe that she had been uneducated when he knew her. Bounty would hardly have chosen such a bride. So why had she never shared her interests with the man she claimed to love? And how had she put their affair behind her so quickly? Had all her claims been lies?

But this was not the place to contemplate the past. He could not leave without explaining to Justin, and that would never do. His shock had already raised enough questions for one night.

Turning his mind to his old mentor, he moved about the familiar library, noting how many books had been added since he had last studied the shelves. He had passed many an evening here, talking, debating, sharing his studies. Their meetings had continued long after Bounty's marriage to Diana. Why had Bounty never brought her to town with him? That was odd enough, but he had also never mentioned her to Nicholas. Had he known of the connection?

But that was another question for later.

He concentrated on recalling their last debate—on Wolf's contention that more than one hand had written the *Iliad* and the *Odyssey*. The logical flow of point and counterpoint finally allowed him to reassert control over his emotions. Only then did he join the other guests in the drawing room.

But he cursed when he awakened the next morning. He could remember nothing of the *soirée* after he had left the library. Why couldn't he have forgotten the earlier scene instead?

Diana gave up on sleep and stared out the window. Berkeley Square was quiet this time of night. Ladies had long since found their beds, but gentlemen were not yet stumbling home from clubs and boudoirs. Woodvale House loomed directly across the square. She had hardly noticed it before, but now she could not tear her eyes away. It threatened her as no building ever had.

Somehow she had made it through the evening without disgracing herself. Nicholas had stayed, moving from group to group, just as she was, chatting amiably with some guests, debating heatedly with others. His arguments had been clear and concise—and precisely the same ones she herself was making.

Not until she realized that he bypassed any group that included her did she finally relax. Thank heavens he was not interested in further discussion. Her inadvertent challenge had not prompted him to show her up in front of her guests by besting her in debate.

Nor would she challenge him again. She did not need him disrupting her well-ordered life. If he ever learned how badly he had hurt her, he would prod the wound, exploiting any lingering attraction to feed his own conceit. He never ignored a potential conquest. Why else had he pounced on her admiration in the first place?

He was still the unscrupulous scoundrel who had nearly destroyed her, still the answer to any maiden's prayer—at least on the surface. Her eyes had often drifted to him as the hours passed. He had been two-and-twenty in Warwickshire, still gangly with youth. Maturity had broadened his shoulders and developed hard muscles in all the right places. His face was as handsome as ever, but more rugged than pretty now, despite that same black curl draped negligently over his forehead. His green eyes were lighter than she remembered, or perhaps they only darkened with passion. But whatever his emotions, he exuded a presence that was difficult to ignore. No wonder he was so successful a rake.

She sighed, then reminded herself that she was no longer susceptible to his charms.

So why did her safe, cozy world feel like it was crashing around her shoulders? She knew him too well to fall for his blandishments. Thus he could no longer seduce her. And having her ten-year-old misdeeds turn up among the latest *on-dits* was unlikely. For all his faults, Nicholas had never been one to brag about his exploits.

So her discomfort must arise from shame. She should not have lied to him—Nicholas had always been able to see through the slightest prevarication. She had not loved Harry in the beginning, and lying about it revealed how devastating Nicholas's rejection had been. What would he do with that knowledge?

She had accepted Harry out of desperation, needing to escape from her father's estate. By the time he offered, she had no longer been able to leave the house, for Nicholas beckoned from behind every tree. His whispers drowned the gurgling of the stream; his spicy cologne floated on every breeze. But staying indoors did not help. He invaded dreams, his last taunting tirade echoing through myriad nightmares. So she had wed Lord Bounty. He was the antithesis of Nicholas—old, wrinkled, safe, and so very, very kind. And he promised to take her away where maybe, someday, she could forget.

Dear Harry. He had never blamed her for succumbing to Nicholas's wiles. Rakes were experienced at seduction. She had been a sheltered innocent looking for a romantic hero. The results were inevitable.

But she had never accepted Harry's absolution. Despite her innocence, she had known better. Ladies did not talk to gentlemen without a proper introduction. Ladies did not wander about the countryside unchaperoned. They did not make assignations. And they certainly did not allow scandalous liberties.

Her face heated at just how many liberties she had allowed. *Fool!* Many times a fool.

But it was over. Done. Finished. She could not remake the past. All she could do was learn from her mistakes.

And the lesson in this case was clear—avoid Nicholas Barrington.

Wresting her eyes from his house, she collected a book and forced her mind onto reading.

# Chapter Two

Nicholas pried his eyes open and glared at his valet. Stubbs had dragged the draperies back, letting sunlight stream through the window. From the angle, it couldn't be much past nine. He should have changed his orders when he'd staggered in at dawn, but he had been too disgusted with himself to think of it.

Stifling a groan, he tried to push memory aside and concentrate on business. His solicitor would call at eleven, and his man of business at two. Dealing with them would require a sharp mind. Each had clear-cut ideas of what was proper for a marquess. They always argued vociferously over any deviation, but if he remained firm, they carried out his orders to the letter.

Justin had once asked him why he tolerated such disrespect from his employees, but it was merely good business. Open discussion raised questions that might otherwise have been overlooked. He had rarely regretted a business decision. But to be effective, he must be able to think.

That was especially important today, for assuming control of his uncle's title and fortune was proving to be far more difficult than he had anticipated. The Woodvale affairs were a tangled mess of questionable investments and poorly managed properties. Servants ranged from very good to potential thieves. Repairs had often been shoddy or ignored. Today's meetings were only the latest in what promised to be a nearly endless string. Why couldn't his uncle have been as methodical about his affairs as his grandmother had been about hers?

His head was far from clear. Cursing under his breath, he sat up and massaged his temples.

"Have you a headache, sir?" asked Stubbs.

"Not today." If only he *had* overindulged in wine. *That* morning penalty would have righted itself soon enough. What plagued him was a flaw in his character that he had never before suspected.

Settling into a chair so Stubbs could shave him, he faced the truth. Lady Runyon had been as insatiable as ever last evening, but he hadn't enjoyed her. He hadn't wanted her even before taking her home. So why had he accepted her suggestion? It was a question he had asked three mornings in a row. The answer still eluded him.

Though he had abandoned raking two years ago, it had been eight years since he had last indulged in the indiscriminate liaisons he seemed powerless to avoid now. Had a two-year absence from town revived the instincts of a greenling? Or was this symptomatic of a deeper problem?

Giving up old habits had seemed easy, but in truth he had faced little temptation. His own estate was fairly isolated, and the months at Woodvale Abbey had passed in uncertainty over his status. But none of that explained or excused his recent loss of control. Three liaisons in three nights. A courtesan, an actress, and a society matron who could count more gentlemen to her credit than the other two combined. He had wanted none of them. He had enjoyed none of them. That made his behavior all the more frustrating, for his loss of control reminded him too much of his father.

He stifled a grimace, lest Stubbs cut his throat.

Lord James Barrington had rarely curbed his passions, even when they threatened him with danger. He had been a reckless gamester, excusing his massive losses by pointing to the occasional big win. Investments were no different. He had squandered an ample younger son's portion, lost every shilling of his wife's substantial dowry, and died deeply in debt.

In like manner the man had rarely curbed his lust—flaunting a long string of affairs—or controlled his temper, cursing his family for disowning him and flying into rages whenever his will was crossed. He had died when a particularly virulent argument triggered an apoplectic fit.

Nicholas had long disdained the man. He had little tolerance for poor judgment, and he despised wastrels. Which made it hard to admit that his own judgment seemed sadly lacking. Why was he back to behaving like a green cub? The loss of control was terrifying—nearly as bad as that summer in Warwickshire.

It would not happen again, he vowed once Stubbs had removed the last of the soap. He was the Marquess of Woodvale, not some bumbling lad just down from school. He would do nothing without careful thought. No one would ever point to him as an example of a son following in his father's footsteps. Turning his attention to dressing, he snapped orders to Stubbs with all the finesse of a major general.

Sheridan Prescott, Earl of Bankleigh, finally rose from the table and suggested they join the ladies in the drawing room. Nicholas glanced at the case clock in the hallway as he followed his host. Attending this dinner was necessary, but remarkably boring. And it would be at least another hour before he could leave without insult.

Since acceding to the title, he had fielded dozens of requests for money, for favors, and for backing in investment schemes ranging from the dangerous to the absurd. He refused to help anyone he did not know personally. His man of business could check on the soundness of a venture, but he needed to know if the money was likely to be invested at all.

His father's ostracism had meant that he'd never attended family gatherings in his youth, so he knew few of his relatives. To rectify that problem, he was accepting invitations to social affairs that included family. Lady Bankleigh was a cousin, and the guest list also contained other connections—Prescotts and Barringtons had wed so often that their family trees resembled a Gordian knot—which meant that many of tonight's guests wanted favors.

Roger Barrington had regaled him with details of a canal

venture he wished to back—if only he had the money. His brother Dudley wanted Nicholas to meet an inventor who needed a patron. Both had been frustrated when dinner was announced before they had gained his support. Both would pounce the moment he entered the drawing room. Only their position at the far end of the table had prevented them from ruining his dinner.

He sighed. He needed time alone. Surprisingly, he missed the quiet he had found in the country, though he would endure torture rather than admit it to his London friends. Slipping into the library, he settled into a wing chair by the window that by day would offer a glimpse of the garden. What should he do about Roger and Dudley? Or about any of his relatives?

The day had gone from bad to worse. The Woodvale affairs were twisted more than he'd thought. How could an astute woman like his grandmother produce sons who were completely lacking? And the list of distant relatives living on his largess was growing alarmingly. Some oversaw minor properties, occupied vicarages in his parishes, or held seats in Commons that were under his control. Others were elderly, with no place to go. But too many seemed to have no purpose in life. That would have to change.

At least Lady Bankleigh was not one of his dependents. Her husband had a considerable fortune. Her only problem—at least according to her pre-dinner complaints—was their youngest daughter, Sophia, who had reached the advanced age of two-and-twenty without making a match, despite having a dowry of £40,000 and a lucrative estate.

So what should he do about Roger and Dudley? Aside from his own distrust of canal ventures, Roger appeared to be a credulous idiot. Loaning him funds would be pouring money down a rat hole. It would be better to find the lad a position somewhere that would keep him away from temptation. But Dudley was different. Though younger than Roger, he seemed intelligent and astute. Nicholas wasn't ready to promise his patronage, but it might be worth his time to meet the inventor.

Having reached a decision, he was about to rise when the library door opened to admit two ladies.

"I won't countenance rudeness to a guest," stated Lady Bankleigh implacably. "Any guest. Snubbing Charles was unconscionable."

"But he shouldn't even be here," protested Sophia. "What possessed you to invite the Langleys to a family gathering?"

Nicholas sank deeper into his chair. It was too late to reveal his presence. He could only hope they would leave quickly.

"Lord and Lady Langley are friends, and you know very well why we included Charles. But giving him a disgust of you changes nothing. It merely validates your reputation for sharp-tongued arrogance. You have become far too particular, Sophia, which is why your father had to arrange an offer. Charles needs your dowry too badly to allow bad manners to put him off, and he has the spirit and determination to control your megrims once you are wed. You still have a choice, though. If you dislike Charles, then accept someone else. But one way or the other, you will wed this Season."

A sniff hinted that Sophia was on the verge of tears.

"Pull yourself together," commanded Lady Bankleigh. "A proper lady does not display unseemly emotion. You, of all people, should know that. I will expect you in the drawing room in ten minutes. Your behavior will reflect your breeding and your training, starting with an apology to Charles. Is that clear?"

"Yes, Mama."

"If you tarnish your image, you will reduce your chances of bringing someone else up to scratch."

"Yes, Mama."

Lady Bankleigh departed. Nicholas slumped in his chair, hoping to escape detection. But Sophia did not remain by the door.

"My lord!" she gasped, freezing near the window.

"Sorry to eavesdrop," he said with a shrug. "But you gave me no chance to gracefully bow out. Do they really expect you to accept Mr. Langley?"

"Yes." The word sent tears coursing down her face. "How can they be so unreasonable? He is a rake, a rogue, and a wastrel, caring for nothing and no one. And he is naught but another fortune hunter, with no money and seven people between him and a title."

"Then why would your parents force you to wed him?" He was not intimate with the Bankleighs, but they seemed caring. Forcing their daughter into an unsuitable match did not fit his impressions.

"They are not exactly forcing me," she admitted, settling onto an adjacent chair and dabbing at her eyes. "But when I remained unwed after my fourth Season, Papa swore that it would not happen again."

"What is wrong with London gentlemen that you have received no offers?" She was not a beauty, but neither was she an antidote. He did not know her well, but her training seemed impeccable, and her dowry was enormous. Why had the eighth marquess not found her a match if her father was incapable of doing so? As head of the family, it was his duty. Of course, he had already discovered that the man had performed only those duties that required little effort.

"It is not the lack of offers that Papa hates, but the fact that I have turned them down. I despise fortune hunters and am uncomfortable with frivolity. But beyond that, I wish to marry for love. My dearest school friend made a love match. She positively glows, even after four years of marriage and two children. But I've not met anyone I truly care for."

"Have you discussed your feelings with your parents?"

She shrugged. "I've tried, but they do not believe in romantic love, especially in the upper classes."

"But they *do* care for you, so why would they force you into accepting Charles?" he asked again.

"They are using him to pressure me. His parents are their closest friends. He needs money. I have money. So they have decreed that unless I accept another offer this Season, I must wed Charles in July."

"Has he offered for you, then?"

She sighed. "I've not spoken with him since they delivered their ultimatum. In fact, Mother's complaint tonight arose because I cut him in the drawing room. I know of no formal offer. I cannot believe that he likes me, but he must have agreed. How else could they enforce their threat?"

"Is there anyone else you care about?"

"No one. But somehow I must find a husband."

He sighed. "Perhaps I can produce a suitable candidate." He mentally reviewed the list of single gentlemen he knew well enough to approach. Featherstone and Wilkington were dedicated rakes, Linkley drank too much, Oglethorpe would game away every penny of her dowry without a qualm. Did he know no one decent? "What about Sir Francis Pelham? He has a comfortable fortune of his own."

She snorted. "He is a shameless flirt who spends all his time in London, Brighton, or his friends' hunting boxes. I cannot abide living in town."

"Lord Houghington?"

"Surely you jest. He hasn't a thought in his head beyond clothes. Granted he is not a flirt, but the only thing he cares deeply about is cleanliness. Moving to the country would horrify him."

"Lord Albright?"

"A crashing bore. His interests encompass only horses and pugilism."

"Lord Jefferson Janssen?"

"I've already turned him down twice. Have you ever seen his poetry? It is enough to put one off food for a month."

"I can see why your mother believes you to be too particular. Jeff is a very solid specimen and one of my more reputable friends. The verse is actually written by his cousin, who is arguably the worst poet in history."

"It doesn't matter who wrote it. Lord Jefferson quotes it. How can one be serious about a man who can compare my eyes to Scylla and Charybdis with a straight face?"

He was wise enough to keep his mouth shut. "I can see that

your mind is quite made up. Perhaps I can find someone that you have not already met."

"Thank you, but I fear it is hopeless. It would help more if you would convince Charles to withhold any offer." Bidding him farewell, she returned to the drawing room.

Nicholas pondered her situation for several minutes, but could find no real solution. Nor was he certain that the threat was real. Perhaps it was Bankleigh's way of forcing her to seriously consider her suitors. She was, indeed, excessively particular.

But he could not be sure of their motives, so his first step must be to meet Charles Langley. He knew little of the fellow, who was at least six years his junior.

Half an hour later, Langley accompanied him to White's, pouncing on the chance to leave Bankleigh House—not the reaction of a willing suitor.

"You must be relieved to be back in London," Langley commented over a hand of cards. "Country living palls rapidly."

Nicholas said nothing.

"You might want to cultivate Lady Forester, by the way. She likes to play coy, but I've heard she's worth it."

"Is she?" The sparkle in Langley's eyes and the slight curl of his lip hinted at personal experience with the lady.

"So they say. Forester ignores her dallying. He never intended to wed her."

"I heard otherwise."

"Fustian! He was stuck in the country for a few weeks and needed a flirt. She knew from the beginning that he wasn't serious."

"So what happened?"

Langley shrugged. "She must have set him up. If he had known her parentage, he never would have risked it. But he thought she was a daughter of one of the tenants. She led him on for a month, then arranged to have him caught stealing her virtue. Her parents demanded an immediate wedding, of course. And their breeding was just high enough that they made it stick. That was last autumn. They've been in town ever since. He is as licentious as ever, but at least he lets her go her own way."

"Not all husbands are so tolerant."

"The smart ones are. All wives stray once they've produced an heir. Forester already has one, so why should she wait? All she wanted was a title and wealth."

He bit back a sharp reply. Langley was young yet. At that age he had spouted the same nonsense. "Dalliance is hardly universal," he said mildly. "Plenty of husbands demand fidelity from their wives. A goodly number even expect it of themselves."

"Until they spot a trim ankle or a well-endowed bosom." His voice was unusually cynical. "My trick."

Nicholas nodded, shuffling cards for a new game. Was Langley's cynicism real, or was he trying to convince himself that marriage to Sophia would be bearable? If it was the latter, then Sophia would face an even worse future than she feared.

"Hawkins and Bowles are racing tomorrow," said Justin, pausing to watch.

"Where?" asked Nicholas. A crowd was gathering. He rarely played cards in the clubs, so curiosity was inevitable.

"Hampstead to Finchley, Highgate, and back. About ten miles," said Lord Jefferson Janssen.

"Should be a good race," predicted Farley. "Bowles has that new pair of chestnuts."

Langley dealt.

Even as Nicholas focused on his cards, one ear listened to the discussion of the race. It was a habit developed from years of practice. He no longer needed wagers to support himself, but he still filed personal details that might someday come in handy.

"The chestnuts are flashy, but they'll never beat Hawkins's grays," swore Shelford.

Shelford knew horses. He was a renowned member of the Four-in-Hand Club and had set numerous speed records over the years.

"Why not?" demanded Porter. "Just last week they beat Captain Hanson's blacks by more than a furlong over a two-mile course. My money's on him."

Nicholas shook his head when Langley discarded a winning card. "Don't let their talk distract you," he warned, rapidly scooping up the last three tricks to take a resounding victory. Langley's mistake had doubled the man's losses.

"Maybe I'll have better luck betting on the race," Langley grumbled, scribbling a vowel.

"Not if you back Bowles."

"Have you seen his horses? Or Hawkins's?" demanded Farley.

"No."

"Do you know the drivers?" pressed Langley.

"Not personally."

"Then how can you pick a winner?"

"Logic." Nicholas heard Justin's stifled laugh. Old habits died hard. How many times had he been through this routine?

"Care to bet on it?" demanded Langley.

"I never bet against Woodvale," Justin reminded everyone.

"But this is too good to pass up."

"Woodvale's conceit has finally pushed him too far," gloated Porter. "All that philandering has turned his mind. Bowles could offer Hawkins a two-minute head start and still win the race."

Nicholas stared at Porter. "Is that a fact? A monkey says that Hawkins wins. And a side bet that Bowles doesn't finish the course."

"I'll pass," said Justin firmly.

But within minutes Nicholas had ten takers on the first bet and nearly thirty on the second, all for much larger sums. Porter and Langley had been first in line. Despite Justin's warning, few believed that a man who had been out of town for two years could blindly predict a race he knew nothing about.

Nicholas finally excused himself. Langley strongly resembled his own younger self, but the lad lacked the sense to rein in careless impulses. He had fallen neatly into the trap, hedging his bets so that even if Hawkins won the race, he would come out ahead. *Idiot!* He had not once considered the possibility that the first wager was redundant because the second was nearly certain. He wasn't alone, of course. Even Porter had forgotten that Nicholas had long lived on the proceeds of wagers just like this one.

He chuckled. Porter's arrogance never softened. Didn't the man realize that he had supplied half of Nicholas's income for eight years? At least Langley's misjudgment grew from youthful ignorance.

He penned a note asking his secretary to investigate Langley's family and finances, then crawled into bed.

By the next evening, he had a good picture of the Langleys. Charles was the third son, but the family despaired of his future. Now six-and-twenty, he seemed content to laze about town. He had refused all of the paths usual for younger sons. Numerous incidents at school had proven that he lacked the discipline and conformity for an army career. Of course, he also lacked the fortune that would buy a commission in one of the better regiments and allow him to live well once he got there. Officers needed much more than their pay to meet their social obligations.

Studying for the church had never been seriously explored by either side. Given the boy's incessant troublemaking as a youth and unabashed raking since arriving in London, that was hardly a surprise. And his support of the Whigs and of the Regent's estranged wife assured that the doors of government remained firmly closed.

All in all, the lad was much like Nicholas—hanging about the clubs until he found a niche for himself. Where he differed was in overspending his allowance in the meantime. And the Langleys were rapidly losing patience. Appalled by his image as a profligate rakehell, they vowed to bring him under control. Their determination was bolstered by their own recent reverses.

Lord Langley had lost considerable sums during the financial upheaval just after Waterloo. He had lost even more by backing a failed import venture. Then half of his sheep had contracted a lethal hoof fungus. The only way he could weather the shortfall was to bring all his dependents home and cancel their allowances. But Charles had refused, knowing that such a move would turn him into a lifelong estate steward.

Hence the ultimatum to wed Sophia. It would give him an estate of his own, forcing him to abandon the wild London existence that so embarrassed his family. And it would remove him from his father's dependency.

To all appearances, Charles was willing to go along—which hinted at a disturbing lack of substance. Or perhaps he merely wanted her dowry. No one really knew, for the lad had quit speaking seriously with his father years ago.

Nicholas had ignored Langley's flippant licentiousness at White's. His own reputation had long made him an icon among the younger lads, prompting wholesale mimicry. He paid them little heed, though he had twice deflected an especially stupid specimen from serious trouble. Now he had to wonder at Langley's character. Was he another blind disciple, or was he hiding a brain?

He sighed. The last thing Sophia needed was a man who was wedding her only to escape penury. Langley might not be the usual fortune hunter, but the effect would be the same. So he must find her an alternate suitor. But who? He knew of no one she might accept.

Diana moved through Lady Debenham's drawing room, automatically exchanging greetings and gossip. Where was Chloe? She was chaperoning the girl tonight, but somehow they had become separated.

Perhaps she was across the hall. Lady Debenham's house was large, and she always opened half a dozen rooms for her routs. They were invariably squeezes, for no one would risk insulting the gossip by declining an invitation.

She had nearly reached the door when Lady Sophia Prescott deliberately cut Mr. Langley. Diana gasped.

Lady Sophia was proper to the point of priggishness, aiming her cutting tongue at anyone who failed to meet her standards—which were even more rigid than Lord and Lady Parker's. Langley was a London fribble whose reputed dalliances and conscious charm reminded her of Nicholas. She had heard the same comparison from others when she first arrived in town, and so she generally avoided him.

Now she frowned. Had he made an improper advance to Lady Sophia? But that seemed unlikely—unless he had bet he could seduce her.

Or Lady Sophia might be furious at society's tolerance of rakes and be taking it out on Langley. It wouldn't be the first time she had begun a vendetta against practices she considered immoral, although her own standing was not high enough to allow her any success.

Speculation was buzzing on all sides, but no one could offer an explanation. Langley was already gone.

Diana pulled her mind back to her own problems. Drat Chloe! And drat Langley for calling up unwanted comparisons. It was the final straw on a frustrating week.

Why had Nicholas returned to town?

She had long since relegated memories of that summer to a locked corner of her mind, but ever since he had appeared at her *soirée*, they had leaked into her dreams. The restless nights were beginning to show on her face.

How could he have been so unprincipled? Granted, he had been young, but he'd been sufficiently experienced that she could not dismiss his behavior as naïveté. He had deliberately cultivated her, luring her into potentially compromising situations and enticing her into scandalous and nearly ruinous behavior.

Heat engulfed her at the memory of his kisses. Her hands trembled to recall that afternoon when he had bared her to the waist and suckled her breasts. No wonder she had expected him to return her love.

*Beast!* He had merely been toying with her, laughing behind her back at how she innocently allowed him liberties no real gentleman would consider taking. Just as he had laughed in her face after she had admitted her love.

"Love?" he had snorted, thrusting her violently aside. "Girlish nonsense! Forget about trapping a husband. If I had thought you that naïve, I would never have accepted your invitation for a little slap and tickle. Marriage is a long way in my future, infant. And you will always be ineligible. My wife must have impeccable breeding. As the grandson of a marquess, I could never ally myself to a baronet's daughter. My wife must also be an heiress from a powerful family. Money and influence are what I need. You can offer nothing but a moment's reprieve from the boredom of the country."

There had been more—much more. He had twisted her every word and deed into underhanded plots and greedy manipulation. When her tears and choking sobs finally deafened her to that hateful voice, he had left her lying in the dirt. By afternoon he had returned to London, back to the dissolute life he had already begun. She had never wanted to hear of him again, but that was too much to ask. His name appeared often in the gossip columns over the next couple of years. His raking was notorious, as was his charm. It wasn't fair that he was accepted everywhere despite his libertine ways and despite his open admission that he lived on the proceeds of gaming. Society merely smiled indulgently and laughed at his sillier wagers.

But those wagers had tormented her. If he was so good at predicting people's behavior, then he should have known that she would fall in love with him. Had his seduction been deliberate? For God's sake, why? *Please don't let it be for a wager!* The old prayer again whispered through her head. Had he discussed their meetings with his friends? Laughed at her childish infatuation? Disclosed her deepest dreams?

"Disgraceful young men!" snapped the Duchess of Woburton.

"Yes," she agreed before she realized that Her Grace had not been reading her mind. Nicholas had just stepped through the doorway.

"Racing horses around for no reason. Bowles is the one who should have been shot."

"Did he shoot someone?" She had heard mention of yet another race, but hadn't paid much attention. Gentlemen were always racing each other. And Nicholas's name had not been mentioned, so why was the duchess glaring at him?

"His horse," snapped the duchess, which explained her anger. She loved animals.

"Woodvale shot his horse?"

"Bowles."

Bowles shot Woodvale's horse? Her head spun. "What?"

"Bowles tried to push his horses farther and faster than they were able. Idiot boy! No eye for horseflesh. Bought Oglethorpe's breakdowns—all flash, no chest. They were nearly foundered when he whipped them into the last mile. Took a corner at speed, and the leader stumbled. Pulled the other horse down and shattered a foreleg."

"How terrible. Was the leader injured as well?"

"Strained, but he'll recover if Bowles has sense enough to get a decent groom. Doubtful."

Diana uttered soothing noises to the clearly distressed duchess, but the woman refused to be calmed. "His fault, of course," she continued, nodding toward Nicholas.

"Was he the other driver?"

"Stupid question. Hawkins was the other fool. But Woodvale bet Bowles wouldn't finish the course."

Lord Porter arrived and ostentatiously gave Nicholas the cut direct, drawing a gasp from the guests.

"Fool," snapped the duchess as Nicholas shrugged and turned blithely away.

"Woodvale?" Diana was having trouble keeping up with the conversation. The duchess rarely gave voice to more than half her thoughts, often changing the subject without warning.

"Porter. Sanctimonious idiot. Always thinks he knows what's what. Lost two thousand pounds to Woodvale on that race. 'Twas he who urged the lad to whip up his horses. All because of that insane bet."

She continued to mumble about wagers that pushed silly young men into dangerous behavior, but Diana was no longer listening. Inheriting a title and fortune had not made Nicholas less greedy. How sad.

Putting him out of her mind, she resumed her search for Chloe, finally catching sight of the girl in animated conversation with Langley. New uneasiness quickly banished the old. Lady Sophia's cut added to his already poor reputation. The room was too crowded for anything untoward to occur here, but Chloe could not afford association with a man disdained by the high-sticklers. It would give George more reason to press for leaving town.

By the time she managed to detach Chloe, her concern had grown. Langley was dangerous. His charm was more potent than she had expected, explaining why wide-eyed girls fawned over him and matrons vied for his favor. Not that he turned her own head, but Chloe was vulnerable.

His lighthearted tale of his nephew's two dogs had actually made Diana laugh out loud—something no man had done against her will since Nicholas. But Langley had managed it twice, attracting the attention of nearby guests.

They had clearly stayed too long. Drawing Chloe away, she summoned her carriage and left for the evening's ball.

Nicholas avoided Porter by ducking into the next room. The man was furious enough to challenge him. His conceit had grown mightily in the two years Nicholas had been from town.

He sighed. Lady Debenham's rout was not one of his usual haunts, but he had promised Sophia to find her an acceptable husband. But that was going to be difficult if she did not cooperate.

Both she and Langley were here, and gossip claimed that Sophia had cut him again. If she kept that up, she would become a laughingstock and draw comparisons to Porter, whose own cut had merely amused the other guests.

He scanned the crowd, hoping to spot someone who might meet her rigid standards. The sooner he finished this chore, the sooner he could resume his own life. Frequenting Marriage Mart gatherings imperiled his freedom.

All thoughts of Sophia instantly fled.

Langley was laughing with Diana. Nicholas's blood ran cold. She had looked exactly like that—happy, carefree, exuberant—during that summer in Warwickshire. Laughter made her glow and had never failed to affect him. Judging from his heavy groin, that hadn't changed despite her new sharp tongue. The pressing urge to run his fingers through her hair was yet more proof of his slipping control. It had to stop.

Was Langley setting his sights on her? The logic of such a move was obvious. Bounty's legacy had left her very wealthy. She might be a year older than Langley, but with so much at stake, the lad would overlook that trifle. And she had already proven that she was susceptible to charm.

*But Langley wouldn't know that.*

Guilt skittered down his back. He had never told a soul about her—and never would. The tale did not show him to advantage. Why had he been so stupid?

Having survived his first Season in London, he was swaggering with pride by the time he reached Warwickshire. The plans he had devised were already working, offering an escape from the prison of poverty, boredom, and antagonism he had always found at home. Despite his breeding, he had faced many hurdles in that first foray into society—his uncle's opposition, a lack of money, the reputation he must court to support himself.

But he had pulled it off—and without resorting to debt, thanks to Porter's incredible stupidity. Following his father into the River Tick would brand him a failure.

He had spent his school years cultivating a seemingly careless charm, which made him welcome in drawing rooms and ballrooms. His London winnings had paid for an extravagant lifestyle. Opera dancers and London matrons had greatly expanded his education in the bedroom. And several heiresses had cast interested glances in his direction. The future had looked perfect. He could live as he wished for as long as he wished. And when he chose to settle down, he could snag an heiress to guarantee a lifetime of security.

He'd had no intention of starting an affair with Diana Winslow. She was barely seventeen, too insignificant for marriage, and too well-born for dalliance. But he had been so full of his own consequence that he had tried a little mild flirting. After all, she was a budding beauty, whose golden-brown hair, green eyes, and slender grace evoked images of Diana the Huntress. And there were few diversions in the neighborhood.

Damn, but he had been stupid! Despite years of studying human nature, he had ignored the inevitable results of his attentions from the first moment he caught sight of her in the woods.

They had met often after that—in woods, in orchards, along the river. And he was more at fault than she, he admitted for the first time. He had deliberately sought her out. God, what an idiot he had been! Any girl would fall in love with a London gentleman who paid her such determined court. Especially a naïve innocent barely out of the schoolroom.

"Ass!" he muttered, adding several curses for good measure. Nearby people glanced at him, but he flashed a smile and fielded more comments about the morning's race.

No doubt about it. He had played with fire that summer. Only by the grace of God had he escaped being burned. In fact, the tale of Forester's marriage bore an uncanny resemblance to his own summer fling, except that Diana had been too innocent to set him up. But she hadn't needed to. That last meeting had been stupidity personified.

He had been kissing her regularly by then, but all sense had deserted him that day. Kisses weren't enough. He had to touch, to taste, to let her lilac perfume wrap him in its seductive scent. Her dress was nearly off, and he was suckling a breast when she blurted out her vow of love. And he thanked God that she had. It had brought him to his senses. A few more minutes, and he would have had her right there on the ground. From there it would have been a short trip to the altar.

*Stupid!* He should have known better. He *had* known better. But making love to her wasn't the worst of his crimes. Appalled at his lack of discretion, he had lashed out. His cruel mockery still echoed through his ears. Every time he felt the tiniest twinge of pride or the slightest surge of satisfaction, his own voice returned, taunting him with his cruelty and laying bare his basest deeds.

If only he had stopped to think! He could have let her down so much easier. Of course, if he had stopped to think, he would not have found himself in that predicament to begin with.

He had learned a valuable lesson that infamous day. Not once in the ten years since had he given the slightest encouragement to one of society's daughters. Never would he place himself in such jeopardy again. Ironically, his forbearance made him acceptable to even the highest sticklers despite his very public liaisons. Everyone knew he eschewed seducing innocents. He had Diana to thank for removing one of the curbs on his life.

"How did you know, Nicholas?" demanded Justin, thankfully diverting his thoughts.

He raised his brows.

"That Bowles wouldn't finish the race."

"Ah." He smiled. "That one was so easy even a cub should have seen it. Surely you can figure it out. How would you describe Bowles's taste?"

"Flashy."

"Does he know anything about horses?"

"Not really," Justin admitted, his eyes beginning to gleam.

"Exactly. So if he bought a pair of horses, is he likely to get quality?"

"Damn!" He shook his head. "I stood right there while Shelford disparaged his team. But how did you know he'd have an accident?"

Nicholas sighed. "If I'd had any idea he would destroy one of his cattle, I would have done something. I expected him to drop out when he winded them."

"I know that, but why did you expect even that?"

"Think about the race he won so handily against Hanson. How long was the course?"

"Two miles."

"An old campaigner like the captain always chooses stamina over speed. So Bowles probably shot out to the lead, then whipped the team home."

"That's exactly what he did, but I didn't expect the same tactics over a ten-mile run."

"That was your mistake—and everyone else's. Bowles hasn't the brains to consider the course. Whipping up the horses worked once, so why not again?"

"It sounds so simple when you explain," complained Justin.

"Surely you didn't lose money on that race!"

"No, I learned long ago never to bet against you. But I feel for that horse."

He nodded. Justin turned to greet Lady Stafford, allowing his eyes to again stray toward Diana.

She was gone.

Just as well, he decided. He was not ready for another meeting. Even thinking about it set his hand shaking. But he would have to warn her about Langley.

Swearing, he quitted the rout and headed to Drury Lane. One of the actresses could soothe his irritation. Even morning disgust with himself had to be better than the fires now consuming him.

# Chapter Three

Nicholas nearly groaned as he stepped into Lady Hardesty's drawing room. Despite knowing that Diana was now a countess, he had not expected her to be here. In his mind she had remained the daughter of an impoverished baronet. Beautiful, but unimportant.

Ignoring his increased tension, he turned to his hostess.

"Lady Hardesty."

"I am delighted that you could join us, my lord."

The gleam in her eye confirmed that he should have listened to instinct and declined this invitation. Lady Hardesty was a blatant matchmaker.

He had been right to suspect his mother of some devious plot. She had written to several old acquaintances, claiming that he was in the market for a wife. Rumors were already rife, irritating him more each day. The question of what to do with her loomed larger. He wanted her out of the Abbey before he returned.

But at least one of his problems was improving. His aunt was finally recovering from the fever that had consumed her since her last childbed. She and the girls would soon remove to the dower house.

When Lady Hardesty signaled Diana closer, he barely suppressed a new groan.

"May I present Lady Bounty? She is a delightful young widow who shares many of your interests."

"We've met." Adopting an expression of *ennui* that bordered on rude, he toyed with his quizzing glass. "Lord Justin introduced us at her last *soirée*."

Diana shrugged at his lack of enthusiasm, adding another irritation to his day. "Not everyone enjoys them," she said. "Discussing our victory over Napoleon doubtless pales against your usual pastimes."

"What do you know about my pastimes?" He had again awakened in self-disgust. His lack of control was making him defensive.

"Aside from the dalliance—which has titillated the gossips for years—I was referring to your shocking obsession with wagering. I understand Lord Shelford set a new speed record yesterday. Only eight hours to Brighton, or some such. Did you make as much on that as on Bowles's race?" Her tone made it clear that she had no real interest in either him or the subject. She was merely chatting until Lady Hardesty left.

And that was perfect. He had no interest in her, either, and could only be grateful that she had no designs on him. "I find Shelford's incessant racing boring. And I only made about five thousand on Bowles." Those winnings would have supported him for a couple of years in his old lodgings—in opulence. That had been his key to success. He bet seriously only once or twice a Season. The rest of the time, he carefully balanced his wins and losses. A reputation for infallibility would have dried up his income. Only Justin had ever realized that his serious wagers were always side bets.

"Why would anyone risk so much on something so trite?" She could not hide her real curiosity at the question. It gleamed in her eyes, hinting that she shared his interest in human nature.

He had to fight to keep his voice detached and fight harder to keep his hands calmly at his sides. "What risk? The odds that Hawkins was more inept than the little I had heard of Bowles were slim."

"You bet that much on two men you didn't even know?"

"But I knew the course—there are a dozen hills in that ten miles, two of them quite steep."

"Yet people drive them every day," she protested.

"Not at speed. Shelford disparaged the horses, so they must have been short-chested." He grinned. "I supported myself for years on wagers, Diana." He couldn't help himself. When she raised a questioning brow, he plunged into his philosophy of betting. It no longer mattered if people understood his methods. He did not need the income. Besides, few would recognize their peril when faced with their next wager anyway.

"Misdirection," she murmured, smiling. "Astute of you. Do you always make it look like your opponents can't lose, when in fact they can't win?"

Her smile caught him by surprise, punching the air from his lungs and the question from his head. Maturity made her more beautiful than ever. She was dressed in subdued green—which had always flattered her. Though modest for evening, her neckline was low enough to raise his temperature. The color should not have been notable, but somehow the combination of the gown and candlelight made her eyes gleam like shafts of sunlight in a forest. His fingers itched to touch her. His lips recalled how hers could soften with desire.

*Damnation!* Why was he lusting after Lady Bounty? His appetites had raged out of control for days, but it was time to draw the line. She had already burned him once. He would not give her a second chance.

But first he owed her a warning about their hostess. If she knew their peril, she would help by avoiding him.

"How well do you know Lady Hardesty?" he asked, abandoning the subject he could no longer recall.

She raised one elegant brow, but followed his lead. "She was Bounty's goddaughter."

This time it took more effort to hide his surprise. "Then you must know that she fancies herself a matchmaker."

Her smile had all the fondness of a mother for a particularly mischievous child. "But harmless."

"You wouldn't think so if she had her eye on your future."

"What makes you think she doesn't? I've been dodging her candidates since the day I emerged from deep mourning." She looked him up and down. "You're undoubtedly her latest, but you needn't fret. I've no intention of wedding again."

He wanted nothing to do with marriage, but learning that he

was merely the latest in a long time of rejected suitors hurt. What the devil was wrong with him? Prudence failed to keep his mouth shut. "Do you expect me to believe that you would not grab a fortune and title if it were offered? I'm out of short pants. Every lady in London lusts after what I can offer."

"Such conceit. Your priorities haven't changed a bit in ten years, have they?" She sighed, shaking her head almost in sympathy. "Unlike you, I care little for title and wealth—and never have. I could be happy in a country cottage, provided I shared it with a man I loved. Dear Harry. No one can ever replace him."

He didn't understand her at all—and never had, apparently. But Langley's arrival reminded him of another duty. "Perhaps you really are different," he conceded smoothly. "But few gentlemen will see it that way. Have a care with young Langley." He nodded toward the door. "He is desperate for a wealthy wife."

"I see." Her voice had turned to ice. "I'm not sure why you feel this is necessary, as you are neither friend nor relative. Rest assured, you need not concern yourself with my welfare." She turned away, plunging into an animated conversation with Lord Hartleigh.

Accepting wine from a passing footman, Nicholas worked his way to the far side of the room. He should be relieved. Diana no longer cared, confirming that his judgment ten years ago had been sound. She had moved on to a successful marriage and had carved a niche for herself in society.

So why did he feel like the weight of the universe had just been draped over his shoulders? The last of his energy drained out through his feet. Interest in other people rapidly followed. His blue-devils were back, more powerful than ever. But he couldn't find the will to care.

"Who has she got you paired off with?" demanded Justin with a chuckle. He nodded toward Lady Hardesty, who was manipulating Lady Melissa Stapleton into conversation with Lord Rathbone.

"Lady Bounty. She must be slipping. Who did she push on you?"

"Miss Riverton. She does like to see people lined up in twos."

"But few stay that way." Lady Melissa had already turned away. "Besides, the chit's affections are firmly engaged."

"Possibly. But no one knows where. Rufton had eyes only for Miss Rosehill last night." Rufton had been Lady Melissa's most ardent suitor in recent weeks.

Nicholas hid his shock. He had considered Rufton's match a certainty—to the delight of both parties. What had gone wrong? Especially with his judgment. Thank God he no longer depended on it for his living. But if he lost control of anything else, he might need to hire a keeper.

It was a frightening thought.

"Maybe Lady Hardesty is onto something," Justin added as he moved away. Rathbone was gazing after Lady Melissa, his desire almost embarrassing.

Nicholas shuddered. That look elicited an echoing heat in his own loins. He hoped he still had enough control to master his face.

But he dared not look at Diana.

"I need your help, my lord," said Sophia, interrupting his meditations. He hadn't realized she was also here. Lady Hardesty's definition of a small gathering was quite different from his. Fifty people already crowded the drawing room, and dinner would not be called for another half hour.

"With what?"

"Can you please speak to Papa? He must rescind this ridiculous ultimatum. His pressure will land me in Bedlam. Every time I turn around, I trip over Charles."

"I doubt that has anything to do with your father. Langley is under even more pressure than you."

"I hate him," admitted Sophia. "If you cannot dissuade him, I want you to convince Papa to give up this plan and let me leave town. I despise London. This constant frivolity is making me ill. Why can I not move onto my own estate? It would satisfy everyone. I could live my own life, and they would be rid of me."

"You know very well why they will not allow it. Even the most scrupulous chaperon would not do. Setting up your own establishment will destroy your reputation. You are simply too young."

"Too young," she repeated bitterly. "Yet only this morning Mama bemoaned the fact that I am already on the shelf. If I do not wed this Season, she claims, then I will be unmarriageable. No man will take an old maid for a wife."

"It does sound like a conundrum," he agreed. "But that is the way of the world. If you do not wed, you will be shuffled into the spinster's corner as an embarrassment to the family. It will be many years before you could consider living apart from your parents, even with a companion."

"How can they claim to love me when they are forcing me into a distasteful marriage?"

The sheen in her eyes proved how close she was to tears.

"Lady Sophia." He tried to keep his voice gentle, though he was already exasperated with the chit. "You have more freedom of choice than any other girl I know. Your parents have allowed you to dither over prospective suitors for five years. Even now, when you face a choice between marriage and spinsterhood, they are giving you a voice. They could just as easily have signed a nuptial agreement with Langley and saved themselves another Season in town. You will be well served to take a serious look at the new arrivals, because one way or another, you will have to wed."

He watched as she practically stalked away. The Bankleighs had spoiled her. Why else had a girl renowned for propriety entertained even the thought of setting up her own establishment? He would still keep an eye open for possible suitors, but it wouldn't hurt her to believe that she was on her own.

Diana turned her back on Nicholas, praying that she still controlled her face. Why did he have to show up in town this

Season? And why did Lady Hardesty believe that they should make a match of it? The woman was usually more astute.

He had certainly lost no time in warning her not to throw herself at him again.

Humiliation swept her, as it did every time she recalled that scene. Would she ever get over the pain? Not that she still harbored any trace of a *tendre* for him. That had disappeared within a month of her marriage. Nicholas had revealed his true character that day—selfish, scheming, unprincipled, lecherous. Not one minute of that summer had meant anything to him. Every word had been false. Kissing her had filled the time until he could return to London and the women who could satisfy him. Even seducing her held little interest, for she had succumbed to his charms too eagerly to offer him any challenge. So he had discarded her.

But the crowning touch was that remark about Langley. He believed that no gentleman could want her. Only her money made her attractive.

She wanted to scream.

At least she had managed to match his nonchalance. Ignoring him would grow easier with practice. Her heart might leap whenever he walked into a room, but that was merely fear that he would expose her youthful indiscretions.

Wrenching her thoughts back to the present, she went in search of Chloe. Lady Parker's malady, which had begun the day of Lady Debenham's rout, had settled into a chill. It was not serious, but until she recovered, Diana had agreed to escort Chloe.

The girl was laughing with Langley. For the first time in days, she looked like she was enjoying herself. New fears settled on Diana's shoulders.

Nicholas's warning had been unnecessary, for she had no intention of wedding. But Chloe had a sizable dowry. It was not large enough to call her an heiress, but if Langley was desperate, it might do. Legitimate heiresses avoided anyone who smelled like a fortune hunter. An existing betrothal was a minor impediment for a desperate man. It could easily be cured by eloping.

She shivered, recalling Lady Sophia's cut.

Langley laughed again, then moved on to mingle with others. Smooth. Very smooth. Fortune hunters were adept at applying just the right pressure. Had he chosen Chloe because her mother was currently indisposed?

"You should avoid linking your name with his," Diana warned her. "He has a well-deserved reputation as a rake."

"But he's not," protested Chloe. "He cultivates that image because it is acceptable, but his real interests lie elsewhere. He was just telling me the most fascinating tale about Lord Wedgeburn's recent visit to Paris. If only I could go there myself."

"Perhaps George will take you there for your wedding trip."

Chloe snorted. "George won't even allow me back to London once we're wed. He is the most stodgy, unimaginative lout I've ever met. I hate him!"

Alarm knifed Diana's mind. "Quietly, Chloe! Do you wish to create a scandal?"

"It might prompt him to abandon this farce."

"Enough! You know better than to entertain such notions. Betrothals are binding. He could not back out even if he wished to."

"That is the most absurd—"

"Have you honestly tried to understand him?" She interrupted before the girl attracted attention. "He is a good, steady gentleman. And you have no choice. You know very well that your parents will never change their minds. Any display of missishness will only tarnish your reputation."

"I *have* talked to him." At least she had regained control of her voice. "For hours. He ignores most of what I say and rejects the rest. As do my parents. George is a perfect choice in their eyes because he is exactly like them, only stricter. They think of nothing beyond crops and weather. I am surprised they even agreed to bring me to town for the Season. It would have been more in character to schedule the wedding the very day he came to call."

Diana heard the bitterness, but she refused to encourage it. Chloe had always longed for more than she had—more adventure, more excitement, more experiences. This diatribe was a natural case of wedding jitters. The girl devoured books on other lands, and had often expressed a wish to see them, but she could not reasonably expect to actually do so. Few gentlemen took their families farther than Paris, and women did not travel alone—except Lady Hester Stanhope, but she would never again be welcomed into society.

Was Chloe's dissatisfaction a natural reaction in a high-strung girl facing an arranged marriage? Diana felt a wave of guilt. Teaching Chloe to think and act for herself could be making her jitters worse. It hadn't crossed her mind that Chloe might not like her husband.

But Langley's attentions concerned her far more. He was just the sort of rascal who would appeal to a girl facing an unwanted future. The situation was all too familiar. Langley was older than Nicholas had been, but he was a glib-tongued charmer whose intriguing tales were already inciting revolt. If he ever maneuvered Chloe into privacy, he could wreak even more havoc.

Vowing to nip any relationship in the bud, she set out to find him.

"You are aware that Miss Parker is betrothed to Lord Eastbrook," she stated once they had dispensed with greetings and an exchange of *on-dits*.

"Of course, though I cannot perceive why anyone would think them compatible."

"That is not your concern."

"What is your point?" His eyes narrowed oddly.

"Chloe is a dear friend who has little experience of the world. I will not stand for anyone leading her astray, especially a gentleman of your reputation."

"Well, that certainly is blunt."

"Forgive me, but she is under my care at the moment. I do not wish to see her hurt."

"Nor do I. I have no designs on the chit, Lady Bounty. And I am not nearly the loose screw rumor suggests."

"Then why are you under such pressure to set up your nursery? I understand you are in dire need of a fortune."

He flashed an appealing grin. "You don't pull any punches, do you? A most unusual lady. Yes, I am in need of funds—which proves my reputation is exaggerated. I could never afford some of my supposed exploits. My parents are miffed because I refuse to pursue the careers they consider proper for a younger son of the aristocracy. They are rather set in their ways and cannot abide the fact that I wish to go into trade."

Nothing could keep the surprise from her face at so astounding an announcement. "Trade?" she asked weakly.

He stared at her, finally relaxing. "You are merely shocked rather than disapproving. I cannot keep my hand in their pockets forever—we are all agreed on that point. In fact, their largess expired with this quarter's allowance. But I am far too impious for the church."

She joined his chuckle when he flashed a lecherous grin at her.

"The military holds no interest for me. Government has always struck me as intensely boring."

"I expect your politics run against you, as well."

"Of course. What I really want is to start an import business. But the idea so horrified my parents that I had to abandon it. At least for now. I am hoping that my compromise will be acceptable—though opposition will no longer deter me. Their demand that I wed an heiress is absurd. I would wind up in Bedlam if I tried to live as a farmer."

"So what is your compromise?" She couldn't think of anything he had not already rejected.

"I am negotiating a position with the East India Company. It would put me on the other end of the import business. And it would keep me out of sight, which might reconcile my parents."

She nodded. "It might at that. And returning to England as a nabob would remove the taint of trade from any fortune you amassed."

"Lovely mind you have. That thought had crossed mine as well."

"I wish you luck, Mr. Langley."

"Thank you. Have I relieved your anxiety?"

"For the most part. But you should still avoid Miss Parker. She is an impressionable girl who is facing a difficult transition in her life. I don't want to see her hurt."

"You sound grim. I have no intention of hurting her."

"Probably not, but that is no protection. I've seen it happen before. A little innocent flirtation, a few compliments. That is all some girls need to form an infatuation. Don't complicate her life."

"You are an excellent friend and a conscientious chaperon," he said with chagrin. "I won't hurt her."

Nicholas noted the smile Diana bestowed on Langley. She had deliberately sought him out. Had she interpreted his warning as a dare?

It didn't matter, he assured himself repeatedly. He had given her the information to clear his conscience. If she chose to ignore it, that was her business.

So why did the sight of them together drive a stake through his chest? He hadn't believed her claim that she would never remarry. It had been a taunt reminding him that he meant nothing to her.

Or had it? Diana never reacted like other ladies. Perhaps she really had loved Bounty. Granted, the man was older than her grandfather, but stranger things had happened. In that case, Langley was unlikely to turn her head.

Of course, Langley was very much his kindred spirit. So alike that he might have been a young Nicholas. Even their goals sounded the same—enjoy life until money became tight, then wed an heiress. And Langley's charm was legendary. Would history replay itself? Would Diana soon find herself in the same trap that had snared Lord Forester? The same one that she had inadvertently flirted with ten years ago? Only this time the gentleman would not let her escape.

He groaned.

But a new sight drove thoughts of Diana away. Sophia and a stranger were seated in a corner by themselves, holding an earnest conversation. Sophia seemed happier than he had ever seen her. Had she actually found someone she liked?

He stared at the gentleman. Only yesterday the man had been holding an intense—and very congenial—discussion with Lord Porter. Porter might be a sanctimonious fool, but he shared many of Sophia's ideas. Too bad he was already wed. But if his friend felt the same way, he would make a perfect suitor.

Sophia smiled and fluttered her fan.

"Who is the man talking to Lady Sophia?" asked Nicholas, catching Justin as he escaped Lady Hardesty and a young lady. "I've not met him before."

Justin glanced across the room. "Lord Eastbrook—Weymouth's heir. This is the first time he has visited London, though I occasionally run into him in Stafford. He has an estate nearby."

"He looks all of thirty."

"Not quite."

"Why has he avoided town? Money problems?"

"What is your interest in the fellow?"

"Sophia is a second cousin. She needs a husband, but I don't want her involved with a fortune hunter."

"Eastbrook has quite a comfortable fortune of his own. But he hates society—doesn't approve of me, either, which is why we've never been close. You needn't fear he'll entice Lady Sophia, though. He's been betrothed most of his life. The girl is coming out this Season, so he's in town—reluctantly—to protect his interests."

And that was that. He wanted to sigh in disappointment. Eastbrook had seemed promising. He had never seen Sophia this animated.

"I don't suppose you would be interested in her."

"Never thought I'd see you playing matchmaker, Nicholas. Sorry, but even if I were ready to set up my nursery—which I'm not—I would never consider Lady Sophia. Begging your pardon, but she is a prig with a blistering tongue and an exaggerated belief in her own opinions. She would be happier as a Methodist."

Still chuckling, he escorted Miss Riverton to dinner.

# Chapter Four

Nicholas kept his face impassive as he entered Lady Belmont's ballroom. Society events were not his *milieu*—and never had been. He had always preferred less restrictive affairs—like Lord Cavendish's masquerades, with their mixture of *haut monde* and *demimonde* and their opportunities for stealing a kiss or dancing thrice with the same partner without finding himself shackled for life.

But here he was, pursuing duty. He had reluctantly concluded that the Bankleighs were serious about Sophia. They would actually force her into an unsuitable union if she failed to wed. So he had to find her a husband—which meant venturing into the treacherous waters of the Marriage Mart.

The danger lay in that other duty, the one he was ignoring. He had no desire for a wife—and no real need for one. His current heir would make a good marquess, as would the man's son. But his mother refused to accept that. And he was only now learning how tenacious she could be. Her letters claiming that he was hunting for a wife were bad enough. But he had heard new tales just that afternoon that sent shudders into his soul.

He had never been close to his parents. His father cared for no one but himself. His mother hated their estate, their poverty, and their estrangement from Woodvale and the rest of the Barrington family. Her displeasure emerged as rants against his father's weaknesses. Both ignored their only son. By the time he was ten, he had welcomed school because it had removed him from home.

Nicholas's solicitor had brought a fellow solicitor to their afternoon appointment, a man who had secretly served his grandmother by keeping an eye on her second son.

His revelations left Nicholas reeling. His grandmother had paid for his tutor and all of his school expenses. If he had seriously questioned it, he might have wondered where the money was coming from, but he had not. Gratitude for his education had kept him in touch with his parents all those years, for it was the only thing they had ever given him. But it was a lie.

The rest of the tale was all too common. His mother had been the ambitious daughter of a rather boring baron, who had coerced her father into giving her a London Season. There she laid siege to the second son of a wealthy marquess, which was about as high as she could expect to climb. She had assumed that his wealth and standing would propel her into company with London's top hostesses, where she would soon build her own reputation.

But that was not how it worked. She discovered too late that her husband's weakness for gaming had already squandered his inheritance. Her dowry quickly followed. When the old marquess learned that Lord James had turned to theft and partnership in an opium den to keep the cent-per-cents off his back, a family fight erupted that drove James from London. The final agreement gave him an estate and promised silence as long as he stayed there, away from society and the rest of the family. If he broke trust, details of his misdeeds would be turned over to the authorities.

Lady James knew only that they were impoverished and could not return to town. Believing that money would rectify that problem, she drove her weak-willed husband into bad investments and new wagers that ultimately left him heavily in debt. Now she saw her son as her ticket back to society.

He didn't want her in town. Years of bitterness had removed any sign of gentility, all sense of style, and the last vestige of her self-control. He had already dispatched orders that she was to remain on the estate, but her letter campaign was complicating his life. His presence at Lady Belmont's ball was bound to give credence to her claims. And he had no idea what else she might try. He had inherited his determination from her.

Spotting two of the most voracious matchmaking mamas making a beeline in his direction, he rapidly set off the other way. Was his retreat obvious? Dodging behind the knot of sprigs clustered around the Season's Incomparable, he glanced back to gauge his success.

"Oof!"

"My lord!"

*Oh, God!* He had slammed into Lady Hardesty and Diana. His hand shot out to keep Diana from falling. Heat burned through his glove.

"Not even an apology?" demanded Lady Hardesty. Diana was rubbing her arm where he'd grabbed it.

"I beg your pardon, ladies," he managed, forcing his eyes off the peach silk caressing Diana's curves.

"Of course," murmured Diana, but Lady Hardesty overrode her.

"Not at all the thing, to barge about a ballroom with your head in a fog, Woodvale. Lady Bounty might have been injured. Make it up to her by partnering her in this next set."

He really had no choice. Any hesitation would call down Lady Hardesty's censure, creating a scene. The matchmakers again had him in their sights, daughters firmly in tow. "I would be delighted," he said, offering Diana his arm.

The orchestra struck the first note, and he nearly groaned. A waltz. How was he to survive a waltz? Lust already rampaged through his body. If this kept up, he would have to turn fop and adopt those billowing Cossack trousers to hide his reaction.

Diana saw Nicholas grimace and had to fight to keep her own face in check. Proof that he cared nothing for her still hurt, though this went beyond disinterest. Could he not even tolerate one dance? Why did he hate her? He had been at fault all those years ago.

Not that she was thrilled to be waltzing with him. Her arm tingled where he had touched her. It was appalling that her body still yearned for his despite knowing his real character. Appalling and awkward. How was she to remain aloof for an entire set?

Silence wasn't the answer. She needed a distraction from the warmth of his hand at her waist, the firm grip of his fingers on hers, the scant inch that separated her bosom from his chest on the turns.... Heat rolled over her.

*Idiot!* Waltzing was nothing *but* turns.

"I understand you lost your father as well as your uncle," she said, desperate to drag her thoughts away from this emotional abyss.

"And my grandmother and cousin." His voice cracked.

She raised a brow. "You were close to your grandmother?"

He nodded. For a moment she expected him to change the subject, but he surprised her. "I never talked much about my family, did I?"

She shook her head.

"My father had been ostracized before I was born. He was furious when my grandmother accepted me."

"He preferred the *sins of the father* adage, I suppose."

"Perhaps. Or it may have been money. I just discovered that Grandmother paid all my school expenses."

"Rubbing your father's failures in his face?"

"I doubt it, but he would have seen it that way."

He sidestepped another couple, pulling her against him for a brief moment. She nearly gasped, needing all her concentration to keep her breathing unruffled.

"She kept in close touch with me over the years, but was less open than I believed. None of us knew that she had an estate and fortune of her own. She left it all to me." He shook his head. "Even if my cousin had survived the carriage accident that killed them both, I would have gotten it all."

"You don't sound happy about it," she said lightly. "Isn't that what you always wanted?"

"Yes, but she left too many questions along with it. Why the secrecy? If I was her heir, why not help me openly before she died? There were times when I was down to my last shilling. And why cut my cousin out?"

"That's easy enough. He was in line for the Woodvale fortune."

"I suppose so. But she left me in quite a bind. My father was incensed, of course. His need was far greater than mine, and she was his mother. His ranting destroyed our last vestige of affection. And he deliberately ran up debts during that last year that he knew I would have to pay."

"Do you honestly believe that was in retaliation?"

He nodded.

"Fustian! You still think the world centers on you, don't you? Once your cousin died, who was next in line for the title?"

He sighed. "Father. But Woodvale's second wife was still young."

"I expect he ignored that—especially given her history of producing daughters."

He grunted.

"Put yourself in his shoes," she suggested. "I don't know why he had been ostracized, but he had probably begrudged his brother the heir's privileges long before. He had been kicked out and forced to live in poverty. Now fate had put him in line for the fortune his family had denied him. Why should he live frugally when he would eventually inherit money? Many a man lives on expectations. And even if his brother outlived him, his debts would be paid from the marquess's coffers."

"All right. Perhaps I overreacted."

Despite the harsh grumble, his face looked lighter. Diana moved the conversation onto a less personal topic while she pondered his words. Growing up in an impoverished household filled with hatred and resentment had left a mark. Perhaps his obsession with amassing a fortune was not as selfish as she had thought.

It was difficult to imagine such heartless parents. Her own had showered her with love and support. Even thrusting her into marriage with Harry had been based on love. How would she have lived without it?

But Nicholas had. His father was a bitter wastrel who would have resented his grandmother's support. No wonder Nicholas had avoided going home that summer.

Sophia cornered Nicholas in the refreshment room half an hour later. "Are you going to Lord Harrison's house party?"

He nodded. The fortune hunters and matchmakers were growing bolder. He needed to get out of London for a week. A brief hiatus from town would also allow him to regain some control over himself and his life.

How had he been trapped into dancing with Diana? She had a most unsettling effect on his mind—from guilt, of course. She revived memories of a disreputable interlude and reminded him that he had always had a penchant for willowy women with green eyes. Such truths were unwelcome just now.

On the other hand, she had just done him a great service. He had never discussed the pain his father's profligacy had caused, not wanting to air his family's dirty linen in public or to risk sounding greedy—he ignored the fact that he had just willingly done both with a woman who already held him in low esteem. But she had unerringly cut through his pain to expose the truth. Of course his father had ignored the possibility of a new heir. He was too much a gamester to be prudent.

While his own inheritance had caused arguments, it was his cousin's death that had changed his father's conduct—goaded on by his rapacious mother, no doubt.

Which cast his grandmother's secrecy into a different light. If his parents had known of her wealth, they would have plagued her with demands for money. And if they had suspected that Nicholas was her heir, they would have found a way to place him under obligation to them. Her silence had protected him.

Had Bounty known? He had been so sure that Nicholas would eventually have the security he sought—

Sophia laid a pleading hand on his arm. He had developed a dangerous habit of woolgathering in public. What if a matchmaker had sneaked up on him? He shuddered.

"You must help me," she begged. "Flirt with Miss Chloe Parker. Convince her to release Lord Eastbrook from that absurd betrothal."

"What?" He recoiled, leaving her hand dangling in space.

"Please? George is the man of my dreams. He is exactly the husband I need—kind, considerate, sober-minded. He shares both my love of the country and my disgust of London society. I love him, my lord. That betrothal is something his father dreamed up seventeen years ago—it is ridiculous that parents can be so feudal in this day and age!"

He grimaced. Sophia was old-fashioned herself, when it suited her. "He signed the settlements after reaching his majority," he reminded her, revealing that he had already checked on the match.

"He was forced! He didn't even know her! For heaven's sake, she was only eleven at the time. Now he is trapped. He is far too proper to back out."

Propriety had nothing to do with it, of course. No gentleman could break a betrothal if he ever wished to be received again. "Encouraging you to form an unsuitable attachment does not sound at all proper. And you know this is unsuitable, Lady Sophia. Betrothals are binding. Turn your eyes to eligible gentlemen."

"I can't." Tears glistened, one of them trickling down her cheek. "Why should a betrothal be binding for men and not for women? George was barely ten when it was proposed, and Miss Parker only a babe. But their parents insist on it, though she will make him miserable."

"Sophia—" he warned, but she refused to listen.

"He needs a wife who can share his interests. Miss Parker is far too wild. You wouldn't believe the radical ideas she has picked up from that awful Lady Bounty! She actually claims it would be fun to explore the wilds of America or heathenish lands like Egypt and China. And she lacks any hint of decorum. I saw her galloping in Hyde Park only yesterday!"

"Control yourself," he ordered sharply. "Do you wish to become the latest *on-dit?*" The refreshment room was empty at the moment, but that would not remain true for long. The day had been unusually warm. Someone was bound to come in search of lemonade.

She sighed. "Forgive me. The way they manipulate George is criminal. He will be miserable—and she will surely be just as unhappy."

"If they wish to end their betrothal, they can do so merely by speaking with their parents," he pointed out.

"But George would never consider it. He is far too proper."

"If he is so proper, why has he discussed his displeasure with you?"

"Of course he has never put it into words! That would be quite—"

"—improper," he finished for her. "So what makes you think he wants to terminate his betrothal—or that he would turn to you if he did?"

Her shoulders sagged. "I just know. We have often talked at length—he dislikes dancing, though he is obligated to escort the Parkers to balls. He is irritated by Miss Parker's persistent flirtations, wishing she was of a more sober mien. He pays lip service to her parents' claim that she is merely enjoying her introduction to society, but I know he does not really believe it."

Nicholas bit back a sarcastic retort. How had he gotten himself into this mess? Sophia was usually rigidly proper, but her parents' pressure had made her desperate. Did Eastbrook have any feelings for her, or was she imagining him as a white knight because she was so eager to escape Langley?

He frowned. There was a darker explanation for her behavior. Sooner or later, most girls developed a *tendre* for one of society's rogues. No one knew that better than a man who had been the recipient of more than his share of coming looks. Only his bleak prospects had spared him from worse. Was Sophia attracted to Charles? Not that she would ever admit it, for he was the antithesis of what she claimed to want. But she was now in a position to win that prize. By pursuing a man who was unavailable, she could drift through the Season without another offer, then tearfully accept Charles in the end.

Not that it mattered. Whether she truly cared for Eastbrook or was simply using him to win Langley was irrelevant. He could not get involved with Miss Parker. The girl had grown up expecting this match, and had probably convinced herself that she loved Eastbrook. Flirtation could only hurt her.

"I will have nothing to do with Miss Parker," he announced firmly.

"But you must!" Again that entreating hand touched his arm.

"Absolutely not. Have you considered what jilting Eastbrook would mean to her? Aside from tarnishing her reputation—if not outright ruining it—she and I would both be harmed if we did not immediately wed."

She frowned. "I had not considered that, though she seems far more suited to be your wife than George's."

"No." He set his face into an intimidating glare. "I have no intention of setting up my nursery just yet."

"But everyone claims you are looking for a wife."

"My mother's doing. She has been pressing since I came into the title. Her mistake was in wanting a grandchild so badly that she convinced herself that I agreed," he lied. "Are you making the same mistake? Eastbrook has never admitted that he is dissatisfied or that you are more than a friend."

"Just because his manners are impeccable does not mean that he likes his situation. I know him far better than you think. He may not have admitted it, but he loves me just as much as I love him."

He sighed. "Perhaps I can talk to the Parkers," he agreed at last. "If their daughter is unhappy, they might reconsider."

"Thank you." Both hands now gripped his arm. He could feel the excitement thrumming through her fingers, and it gave him pause. Perhaps she really did love Eastbrook.

"No guarantees," he said soothingly, covering her hands as he loosened her fingers. "You may have to accept his betrothal." Pressing a cousinly kiss to her forehead, he turned to go.

His eyes clashed with Diana's. She stood just inside the doorway, the hint of a smile curling one side of her mouth. That half smile had always weakened his knees, and today was no different. Lust was becoming a constant companion.

Anger followed. She was a witch. She had to be. How else could she continue to attract him long after he had learned to despise her for leading him astray? Their dance had been infuriating. An hour later he could still feel her breasts pressed into his chest.

Her sensuous mouth widened into a full-blown smile before she turned away to accept a glass of lemonade from a footman. His hand trembled—with fury, he assured himself grimly. She had deliberately provoked him. Driving him crazy was her way of retaliating.

Well, it wouldn't work. He would be leaving in the morning for the Harrisons' house party. Perhaps when it was over, he would visit Meadowbrook. It wasn't far away, but he had not checked its condition since acceding to the title. His secretary claimed that all was well, but he preferred to see for himself.

Diana nearly choked on a very unladylike gulp of lemonade. So the rumors were true. And Nicholas had stuck to his vow. Now that he needed a wife, he was pursuing the wealthiest heiress. She almost felt sorry for him. He would be miserable with Lady Sophia, who in five Seasons had gained a reputation for sharp-tongued disapproval. But in light of his heartless pursuit of money and power, he deserved no better.

And she didn't care. His life had nothing to do with her.

Yet the image of that parting kiss—reasonably chaste in deference to the audience of servants—was burned into her mind.

She needed to get away for a few days—especially since Lady Hardesty was determined to throw her into Nicholas's company. For some reason seeing him was resurrecting all her old reactions—purely from habit, of course. A week would allow her to reassert control. And a short holiday would spare her from watching him make a fool of himself.

But she was *not* running away, she insisted, appalled at the direction her thoughts had taken. Never before had a Season weighed so heavily on her shoulders. Usually she thrived in town, mixing light entertainment with the stimulating discussions favored by her closest friends. But this year she could not relax. Nicholas moved in the same circles, so she never knew where she would find him. Even such innocuous activities as shopping did not spare her from his company. And every meeting resurrected the pain of his cruelty. Since revealing that would award him more importance than he deserved, she fought a constant battle to keep her face indifferent. Success required that she expect him around every corner. The strain was too much.

Finishing the lemonade, she returned to the ballroom. Perhaps she should accept Lady Harrison's invitation to a house party. That would give her enough time to regain her equilibrium.

It would also let her keep a friendly eye on Chloe. The girl had been flirting with Langley again. Nothing could come of her growing *tendre*, so it was best to sever the connection. So far the Parkers remained ignorant—but only because Lady Parker had spent the last week recovering from a chill. A few days in the country would allow her to talk some sense into the girl.

She tried to figure out how to make Chloe see reason, but her mind kept returning to that image of Nicholas kissing Lady Sophia. Was he really courting her?

His raking grew more scandalous every day. He had abandoned all restraint and was making little effort to conceal his liaisons. Some of the higher sticklers were already looking at him askance. Was this the behavior of a man ready to settle down?

She doubted it. Yet his attentions to Lady Sophia had to be serious. She was not his usual target for seduction. The rest might be no more than a last wild fling before marriage. He could even be using indiscriminate sex to balance having to ingratiate himself to someone so straight-laced. Not that it mattered.

Putting him out of her mind, she went in search of the hostess. It was time to go home.

Nicholas paused in the shadow of a potted palm, sighing in relief as Mrs. Turkell gave up the pursuit and forced her daughter onto Lord Rufton. None of his goals had been reached tonight. He'd found no gentleman who might interest Sophia. After their chat, he had hoped to speak with Miss Parker to determine her thoughts on her betrothal, but she was again escorted by a rigidly proper mother. Not only did that prevent him from approaching her, but her apparent contentment cast doubt on Sophia's claims.

"You must help me convince dear Diana not to leave so early," declared Lady Hardesty, making him jump in surprise.

"Perhaps she has a headache," he suggested, cursing himself for allowing the woman to sneak up on him. *He* was the one who ought to leave. Dodging the machinations of multiple matchmakers drained any enjoyment he might have derived from the evening. Contacting Miss Parker was best postponed until the Harrisons' house party.

"Nonsense. Take the girl out and dance with her—or would you prefer to partner Miss Willowby," she added, nodding toward the approaching lady.

"We'll dance." He dragged Diana onto the floor. *Damn!* Another waltz. But at least he had escaped the Willowby chit.

"Shouldn't you at least have asked me?" she snapped, fury plain in her eyes.

"Take pity on me, Diana," he begged. "Miss Willowby would find a way to drag me outside, where her mother would appear and scream compromise."

"Have you no will of your own?"

"I thought so until tonight. Lady Hardesty is nearly as bad as Mrs. Willowby."

"Hardly. She creates opportunities, but does not use force. If you fear her so much, why go along with her?"

"Perhaps I enjoy playing with fire," he responded lightly, relaxing into social repartee.

"That would account for the frequency with which your liaisons have entertained society's drawing rooms of late," she agreed. "Mrs. Drummond-Burrell's brows disappeared into her hair when Lady Beatrice revealed your carriage mishap the other night."

"That incident has been grossly exaggerated," he swore hiding chagrin. Unfortunately, it hadn't. He had been accompanying Lady Alston home when her carriage had partially overturned in Berkeley Square. She had tumbled out, her hair in disarray and her gown pushed down to expose her breasts. Despite the late hour, several gentlemen had witnessed the scene. And not all of them had had their eyes glued to her bosom when Nicholas slipped out of sight.

He twirled Diana into a dizzy sequence of turns, cursing himself for succumbing to Lady Alston's advances. He felt unclean.

"Or do you give in to Lady Hardesty because you know you are safe with me?" she demanded, apparently not caring that he had been caught in an embarrassing indiscretion.

"Neither," he snapped, unaccountably hurt. "The lady is as devious as any other matchmaker. I plan to avoid her in the future."

"Scared?" she taunted, her smile clearly malicious.

"Never." He smiled back. "As disinterested as ever, my dear. And far too old to succumb to implied dares." He noted a flash of pain in her eyes and again cursed. He hadn't meant to hurt her.

"I issued no dares, implied or otherwise. Inferring one can only be a defense against admitting that I don't care."

This was clearly getting out of hand, he decided, setting aside his anger. Adopting a glare to hide his own pain, he quitted the conversation. He should not have danced with her again. And he certainly should not be raging with lust. But lust was inevitable just now. He ran into her nearly everywhere he went, keeping his nerves on edge and giving him no chance to regain his composure. A few days of calm would restore his balance. Thank God he was leaving town in the morning.

Diana suppressed a shudder as his hand burned into her waist. Every reaction to his touch irritated her more. No wonder she was turning into a sharp-tongued shrew. How else could she protect herself from his wiles?

She cursed Lady Hardesty. In the past, the woman's antics had been mildly amusing, but no more. She was becoming dangerous. Thank God for the Harrisons. They offered the perfect chance to escape both of her problems for a few days.

# Chapter Five

"They hate me!" Chloe waved her arms as she paced Diana's room at Harrison Court.

Diana sighed. Her maid had barely finished unpacking before Chloe rushed into the room in near hysterics. She still didn't know what had happened—and wouldn't until she could calm Chloe enough so the girl made sense.

"Of course your parents don't hate you," she said soothingly. "They only want what is best for you."

"Hah!" Tears trembled on her lashes. "If they cared, they would never force me to wed a man who will make me miserable."

"Sit down." Handing Chloe the tea she had not had time to drink, she waited. By the time the cup was empty, the girl had calmed. "Now, tell me what has overset you."

Chloe dabbed at her eyes. "Papa rode down from London, so Mama and I were alone in the carriage. I told her that I disliked George and asked that the betrothal be set aside so that I could find a more congenial husband. You would have thought I had admitted to murder. She ranted and raved for the rest of the journey. George has every virtue known to man. I am displaying too many vices. But they will forgive me, as I am suffering from wedding nerves, which makes me incapable of rational thought. Forgiveness is conditional, of course. I must set aside my fears and thank them for providing such a responsible husband."

Diana sighed. "That was not a very good place to begin an argument. You knew you would be confined for at least two hours."

"Which was why I chose it. I thought that would give me time to convince her. She usually ignores anything I say. If I persist, she either sets me some urgent task or recalls a chore needing her attention."

"You still have much to learn about people, Chloe. That is not a criticism," she added, cutting off an indignant protest. "I was just as ignorant at your age." She paused to swallow a sudden lump. If only she had known more when she'd met Nicholas. But it was Harry who had taught her about human nature.

"What don't I understand?"

Diana sighed. "George is a sober, responsible gentleman who cares for little beyond his estate—exactly like your father. Your parents' match was arranged, but your mother has grown to love him. Why would she expect you to respond differently?"

Chloe wiped a tear from her eye. "I should have figured that out, especially since Mama believes that I am exactly like her. But our argument did not end the discussion. The moment we arrived, Mama told Papa that I was being missish, and he threatened to fetch a special license if I did not behave myself. He wants to be rid of me as quickly as possible." She broke into sobs, burying her face in Diana's shoulder.

"Hardly. He wants to see you settled. And he despises scandal. Jilting George would cause scandal—and would call his judgment into question for arranging the match. Unless you can produce very convincing evidence that George is a frivolous loose screw who is both dishonest and dishonorable, he will never consider voiding your betrothal."

"Then what am I to do? I won't wed George."

"He is a decent man, Chloe. Have you given him a chance? Are you sure that your disillusionment doesn't arise from your parents' pressure?"

"I'm not an ignorant child!" she spat, recoiling from Diana's side. "Are you turning against me, too?"

"Of course not!" She paused to control her temper. Chloe was too upset to think rationally, but one of them must stay calm. "I am merely trying to decide what to do. Is George really so impossible?"

"More than impossible!" She made a visible effort to rein in her emotions. "He is far worse than Papa. Dull. Boring. Stupid. And he thinks I am an infant."

"If you treated him to one of your temper tantrums, that is hardly surprising." A raised hand stopped Chloe's protest. "You know that you are prone to emotional outbursts." She gestured to the door, reminding her of her entrance only a quarter hour past.

"But I am usually restrained. With you, I can be myself, because you understand and accept me."

"So you have not lost your temper with George?"

"Never. I have been perfectly behaved—even more than usual. But he cares not. All he wants from me is an heir. He even had the audacity to tell me not to make any changes to his household because my taste is appalling. His housekeeper knows what he likes, so I'm to leave her alone and not meddle. And I am not to make a scandal by flaunting my views about the neighborhood. To make sure I don't embarrass him, I will not leave the estate without his escort. It will be like living in a prison!"

Diana sighed. George did not sound any more enthusiastic about this match than Chloe. "What prompted those comments?"

"He had escorted us to Lady Stafford's at-home, where I admired her drawing room."

Lady Stafford was a very proper matron with impeccable taste. She had redecorated the room several years earlier in what was now being called the Regency style. It was restrained, elegant, and universally admired, unlike the flamboyant Egyptian decor used by Lady Debenham or the spare Greek designs to be found at Mrs. Bassington's.

But George's comments might mean nothing. Perhaps Chloe had misinterpreted his intent. Or perhaps he had been deflecting any possibility of redecorating his house. That was not an uncommon expectation for new wives, but many men balked at change—or at the cost.

Chloe gave her no chance to pose that question. "I won't marry him," she stated firmly. "I love Charles."

"What?"

"I love Charles."

"Langley?" She froze in shock.

Chloe nodded. "He shares my interests, my hopes, my dreams. He would never force me to be something I am not. And he loves me."

"He has admitted that?" She knew that they had spoken on several occasions, but this seemed suspiciously sudden. And quite improper. Nicholas's warnings echoed. She should never have believed Langley's denials.

"Yes. Oh, Diana, he is so wonderful! He understands my need for adventure. He shares my interest in faraway places. He doesn't care whether I can stitch elaborate tapestries or rival Catalini's voice." Lady Parker had long demanded that Chloe master every possible female accomplishment. "I have to see more of the world, Diana. Do you realize that this trip to London is the farthest I've ever been from home? Even school was only a two-hour drive. Mama chose one nearby so she could keep a close eye on the headmistress and make sure I wasn't learning anything that she disapproved of."

"I know."

"Charles understands me even better than you do. He wants to marry me."

Diana fought down a wave of dizziness. "He actually discussed marriage with a girl already promised to another?"

"Don't sound so prim and proper. He knows that I had no say in this betrothal. He is sure to get a position with the East India Company. We will elope and wed at sea."

"And how will his superiors react? Have either of you considered that? He has a reputation as a profligate rakehell. That has to be affecting his negotiations with them. The East India Company does not tolerate scandal."

Chloe's face fell. "They would likely disown him."

"Exactly. Eloping will leave him with no means of support—and I doubt your parents would give you a dowry after such an escapade."

Chloe sighed. "He knows that—which is why I spoke to my parents. My next step will be talking to George. Eloping is the last alternative."

"But it will ruin you both."

"Then what am I to do? I cannot marry George."

"I will talk to your parents. Perhaps I can convince them to reconsider the match. Since the wedding itself is to be a small country affair with only the family in attendance, they could quietly drop it. But you need to be honest with yourself. Charles has dazzled you—in part because he is offering you excitement and the fulfillment of a dream. But many dreams prove to be painfully sordid in execution. Have you considered the discomfort, the primitive conditions, and the disrespect you would receive as an outsider? Have you truly listened to those who have been to India? They describe enervating heat, debilitating diseases, and the very-present threat of violence from native populations that despise everything English. That is not the stuff of which dreams are made."

"Yes, I have listened. I know that travel is not all wonder and excitement. But it is what I want."

Diana sighed. "At least make an honest effort to like George. Grab every opportunity this week to spend time with him. Demonstrate that you are trying to accept the situation. If you can prove that you've done everything possible to like him, but still cannot bring yourself to do so, they may be more receptive. He is here, I presume."

Chloe nodded. "But I had hoped to avoid him. I would rather talk to Charles."

"He is also here?" She could not hide her surprise, for with his reputation, she had not expected to find him on the guest list. She had trouble imagining him in the same circle as the propriety-conscious Harrisons.

"His parents are close friends of the Harrisons. They insisted he be invited because they are trying to force him into marriage with Lady Sophia. Their ultimatum is what pushed him into approaching the East India Company."

"Avoid him this week, Chloe," she warned sharply, almost groaning at the image of yet more matchmaking parents. Who, in his right mind, would imagine that Langley and Lady Sophia might suit? "I will explain your predicament to him. If your parents think you harbor a *tendre* for him, they will fetch that special license and have you in church in a trice. His reputation is wild enough that they will suspect him of attempted seduction. Immediately wedding you to George would protect your reputation." And they wouldn't be far wrong, she reminded herself. Langley's actions were indeed suspect. Was he using Chloe to escape his parents' pressure? Away from his mind-numbing charm, she had trouble believing his claims—one of which was already revealed as a lie.

Chloe groaned. "Very well. Talk to him. And speak with my parents. I will pretend to like George, but I will not wed him. We'll take our chances with eloping if you can find no alternative."

"Maybe you can discover what caused the rift between George and his parents. If we mend that, they might be more receptive to ending this betrothal."

Diana waited until Chloe was gone before dropping her head into her hands. What a mess! Chloe was showing more backbone than usual. The girl had always accepted whatever her parents suggested. The very threat of an unpleasant confrontation was usually enough to force compliance.

Which proved that she felt very strongly about Langley. Diana could not yet decide if it was love or merely infatuation intensified by an opportunity to live her fantasies instead of settling down, but it was powerful enough to fuel rebellion.

Langley's feelings were even harder to gauge. Their earlier discussion had suggested that he was more responsible than she had thought. Now she had to wonder. Though he was nearly her own age, his actions were imprudent at best and downright juvenile in some respects.

He had flirted with a girl already betrothed to another, drawing her into compromising situations—she had spotted them walking in dark gardens twice—and introducing topics that were far out of line. And how could he suggest eloping, knowing it would sever their ties to the only society Chloe knew and endanger the career he expected to support them?

But sitting in her room would accomplish nothing. Smoothing her gown, she headed downstairs to find him.

"I've just spoken with Chloe," she said bluntly, having run him to ground in the bookroom. "How can you seriously suggest eloping?"

Shock flared in his eyes, but he quickly controlled it. "I had not realized how deeply you were in her confidence."

"We are closer than most sisters. I will not stand by and see her hurt—which is something you swore you'd never do."

"I love her." He glared at her, but relaxed when she did not contradict him. "I never planned on this, Lady Bounty. But I cannot ignore it."

"What a mess." She took a turn about the room.

"Are you going to tell her parents?"

"That depends on whether you are stupid enough to actually try it. Have you any idea of the effect of such a scandal?"

"Yes," he growled, running his hands through his hair as he paced the other way. "But if that is our only choice, we'll do it. You must know her situation. The Parkers are adamant. They will not change course now that the betrothal is public. Nor will they admit that Chloe shares none of their interests. Eloping is far from ideal, but I will not give her up. And frankly, I hope it won't come to that."

"Did you expect her to succeed in her confrontation?"

"What confrontation?"

By the time she finished recounting Chloe's actions, he had dropped into a chair with his head in his hands.

"Damn! *Damn! DAMN!*" He grimaced. "Pardon the language, but she just made a bad situation worse. If I'd suspected her plans, I would have stopped her."

"You understand their character." It was not a question.

He nodded anyway. "I had hoped that an elopement would blackmail them into supporting the match."

"Your wits are addled. They are far too proper to ignore society's censure."

"I wasn't planning on making it public."

She pursed her lips. "Just what do you have in mind?"

"A very quiet false elopement. We would notify them of our intentions, but no one else. I can prevent Lord Parker from catching us until morning. Eastbrook is too proper to accept a soiled wife, which would leave marriage to me as the only way to retain Chloe's respectability. The wedding would cause talk, but our immediate departure would quiet most of it. Eastbrook would never reveal the elopement, to retain his own credit if for no other reason."

"You've thought it out, I see, though there is no guarantee that it would work. You do not know the Parkers and Weymouths as well as I do. They are more apt to immediately force Chloe and George to the altar. Appearances are all that matter to any of them, so Chloe's feelings and George's wouldn't count. A rift exists between George and his family. A promise to mend it would exert considerable pressure if he balked."

Charles grimaced.

"If you truly love her, give me a chance to change their minds about George."

"Considering what you've just said, I can't imagine that anything you could do would make a difference."

"Possibly not, but if I make the effort, then you will know that your scheme is truly the last resort, though I suspect you will need a bona fide marriage to succeed. They could save face by performing a second ceremony in church, thus hiding the first. But stay away from her this week. If her parents think you are sniffing around her, they will have her wed so fast your head will spin."

"How can I remain aloof?" he demanded in irritation.

"Really, Langley! You know very well how you've treated marriageable misses in the past. You look right through them, and if you are ever forced to actually greet one, your voice could freeze water. Treat Chloe the same way you treat Lady Sophia. If leaving her alone chafes too badly, come complain to me. If the Parkers believe you are courting my fortune, they won't fear that you might harm Chloe."

He immediately took offense at the implication, but she ignored him.

"Your reputation will hardly endear you to parents of a young innocent," she reminded him brutally. "Especially to propriety-conscious high sticklers like the Parkers. Some people don't even condone sowing wild oats before settling down. And frankly, your image long ago passed wild oats. Never mind whether it's true," she added, stopping his protest with a raised hand. "These people care for nothing beyond appearances."

"You are right, of course," he agreed on a long sigh. "How could they produce such an adventurous daughter?"

"Reaction. They pushed Chloe into longing for freedom by hemming her in with too many restrictions. But enough of this. You will avoid her and let me try to influence her parents. She will avoid you by seeking out George and making an effort to like him. Perhaps that will prompt her parents to listen to her."

"I should have stayed in London," he growled.

"It would have been better."

He sighed. "Thank you for your support, Lady Bounty."

"Try Diana. I have a feeling we're going to be close friends before this is over."

"It wouldn't surprise me, Diana." Lifting her hand to his lips, he bade her farewell and left.

Before she could follow, Nicholas stepped through the door. She swayed. "I hardly expected the Harrisons to include a hardened libertine among their house guests," she said, fighting to keep her voice steady. It was surprise that set her heart racing and made her dizzy. This was one time she was not prepared to see him.

She fisted her hands to keep her fingers from smoothing his hair. It had a raffish look today, as though he had repeatedly run his fingers through it, which recalled that summer all too clearly.

He sneered. "Still a naïve innocent, aren't you? A title covers a multitude of sins, my dear." Sarcasm dripped from every word.

"Which is why you always lusted after one. Who would dare criticize a wealthy lord?"

"Still annoyed with me, aren't you?"

"Not at all." She shrugged. Obviously, he had wangled an invitation so he could continue his pursuit of Lady Sophia's fortune. At least Lady Hardesty wasn't here. "I merely know you too well."

"You know nothing!" His face twisted into a ferocious scowl, sending chills down her spine, but she hid any sign of trepidation.

"Very good, my lord. You've added to your repertoire since Warwickshire." She made her voice approving, even as she seethed. "Intimidation forms such a useful contrast to charm. It gives you mastery over an even larger circle of credulous fools. Too bad I no longer qualify. I *do* know you well, my lord. You do nothing unless it furthers your own interests. Your every action is dictated by selfishness. You went after money, because you thought money would confer power. Even when you believed you would never accede to Woodvale's title, you toyed with ways of getting your own. Again, for power. You always expected that power would give you *carte blanche*, removing all public censure for your deeds. Perhaps you've actually reached that point—why else would Harrison invite you to his home? But I doubt success has made you happy. Such ruthless determination must have cut you off from would-be friends." Her hand reached for the door handle. "And you still get that tic in your left eye when you're tense."

Without another word she left the bookroom, barely making it to her room before bursting into tears. Devil take him! How had he provoked that outburst? And why did she care how he passed his time? She hated him. She despised him. If he tied himself to Lady Sophia, she would laugh for the next forty years at his discomfort.

*Stupid!* chided the voice, and she had to agree. Adding that last observation put her claims of indifference to the lie.

Nicholas stared at the door long after Diana had left. What had brought that on? And why did he care? She belonged to his past. Her words had not hurt. Of course not! He was merely piqued that a near-stranger would dare criticize him to his face.

He ignored the spectral hand that squeezed his heart when he called her a stranger. And he refused to think about why she had been shut in the bookroom with Langley—or how long they had been here. Langley's face had reflected both longing and fury when he left. And Diana had looked the same. Had an assignation ended in a spat? Langley had addressed her as Diana, making it clear that they were closer than he'd thought.

He cursed the icy chills wracking his body. Langley was poison, preying on an unprotected heiress to fund his own debauchery. But Diana's affairs were none of his concern, he reminded himself sharply.

The only reason he was even thinking of her was to give his nerves a chance to settle after that humiliating encounter with Lord and Lady Parker. Searching out the bookroom had been a quest for peace.

Damn Sophia for embroiling him in her affairs!

He had found the Parkers in a small salon shortly after his arrival. In retrospect, he must have caught them at a bad time—Miss Parker had passed him in the hallway, her face alight with fury; and the tension in the salon had been thick enough to cut. But he had not noticed, attributing the discomfort to his own nervousness. He hated intruding into affairs that were clearly none of his business.

"I understand that Miss Parker's betrothal is of long standing," he had said after indulging in mutual inquiries after their health and the health of their families.

"Was settled seventeen years ago," confirmed Lord Parker shortly. "Good match. She'll be a countess one day, and Eastbrook's a steady lad. Obvious even at age ten."

"It is rather unusual these days for settlements to be signed so early," he had commented. "Most parents wait to make sure that both principals are agreeable."

"Modern nonsense!" snorted Lord Parker. "Raising the bride to conform to the groom's expectations assures a comfortable match. None of this newfangled air dreaming for my girl. She's always known exactly where she was going."

"What is your interest in the matter?" demanded Lady Parker, her eyes narrowing in speculation.

"Mere curiosity. One rarely sees such arrangements these days, and I wondered if the participants truly approved."

She straightened, boldly meeting his eye. "They are in perfect accord. Chloe has been trained from birth to be his wife. George does not like argument, so she has learned never to contradict him. He prefers to live in the country, so her training has concentrated on estate duties rather than London entertaining."

So if Chloe had been raised to mimic George's ideas, where had Sophia gotten the idea that the girl would make George miserable? "Yes, I can see that lifelong training can work to advantage," he said noncommittally.

The hint of a smile touched her lips. "Indeed. Her governesses were carefully chosen, and she spent only one year away at school. The mistresses were very strict. The girls could not even sneak novels into their rooms."

"Heathenish books ought to be banned," grumbled Parker. "Putting ideas into girls' heads."

He had tried to return to the topic of Chloe's betrothal, even going so far as to explain that he had just become guardian to five girls and was looking for hints on raising them, but Lady Parker obviously suspected his motives. Despite the fact that he had never even met Miss Parker, they acted as though he were trying to seduce her.

He finally gave up and excused himself. He could do Sophia

no good if the Parkers left London to protect their daughter from unsuitable influences.

Which brought his thoughts full circle to his reputation. The Parkers must believe every exaggerated tale about him. As did Diana. While it was true that he had cut an impressive swath through the *demimonde* in his youth, it had never been as wide as rumor reported.

Of course, since returning to London, he had been every bit as wild as during the first months after leaving Warwickshire. He frowned. There was no connection. Granted, his earlier excess had been a reaction to Diana's attempt to lure him into parson's mousetrap. But his recent lapses were merely habit triggered by his mother's pressure.

*Fustian!* scoffed a voice in his head. *You want her and always have*.

"That's absurd," he muttered. But it wasn't. How many times had he prevented his hand from reaching out to touch her? He had awakened night after night, stiff with longing despite liaisons only hours earlier.

Lust.

It burned hotter than ever, sharpening his senses until he could barely refrain from ripping off his clothes. And hers.

But what was wrong with that? His brain was still mired in Warwickshire. She had been young, chaste, and too high-born for dalliance. But that was no longer true. She was a widow in a society that ignored discreet liaisons.

He had been stupid to avoid her, stupid to hold her at a distance. He needed her too badly—in his arms, in his bed. And she needed him. He could see it in her eyes.

She would fight him, of course, but he would win in the end. He'd seduced her before. And this time nothing stood in the way. Her widowhood removed all the barriers. An affair would put an end to his unsatisfactory public liaisons, allowing his reputation to return to something more dignified. She would be able to put her marriage behind her and learn the joy of making love with a young, virile man. And the fact that she was barren would be a blessing.

It was perfect. So perfect that he could hardly wait to begin. But he must, he admitted even as his groin strained for release. Discretion was mandatory. He could not draw attention to them—which meant waiting until they returned to London to actually bed her.

But he could set the stage so there would be no delays. An apology for his ham-handed behavior would be a good starting point. It might be enough by itself to make her fall into his arms.

# Chapter Six

Diana arrived in the drawing room just in time to see George administer an unobtrusive but deliberate cut direct to Charles. Did he know that Charles and Chloe were in love? Or did he object to sharing the room with a reputed rake? In that case, he should be even more incensed to discover Nicholas's presence.

Charles opened his mouth as if to protest, but quickly shut it, apparently realizing that discretion would serve him better in the long run.

Chloe was not so even-tempered, though. She was already heading for George, the fury in her eyes evident to anyone who chose to look.

Diana glanced around as she hurried to cut Chloe off, relieved to see that the other Parkers had not yet come down. Fewer than half the guests were present. Most had missed George's actions, and none were yet watching Chloe. "Don't make a scene," she hissed.

"But—"

"Your cause will not be served by drawing attention either to yourself or to George's behavior. And it will be ruined by linking your name to Charles's. Take a deep breath, then tell me what happened. I only caught the end of it."

"There was no end." Another hiss made Chloe lower her voice. "George walked in, spotted Charles, and deliberately cut him dead."

"Could Charles have done something to annoy him?" murmured Diana. "They've not met in town that I know of. Did they quarrel at school?"

"I doubt it. George attended Harrow and Cambridge; Charles went to Eton and Oxford. And I can't imagine where they might have met in town. George stays home unless he's escorting me."

Good heavens! The man sounded even more boring than Chloe had claimed. Did he not visit his clubs? Weymouth must be delighted to have an heir who avoided every conceivable vice while assiduously carrying out his duties. She shuddered.

"Could he have learned of your intentions?"

"I doubt it. He walked with me in the gardens this afternoon—at Mama's insistence. He surely would have said something if he suspected—especially considering our discussion." She blushed.

"What did he say that was so embarrassing?" She guided Chloe into a corner where they would be less likely to be overheard.

"I found out why he despises his parents."

"He is the one who began the feud?"

"I think so. He was quite vague about the details, so much of this is guesswork."

Diana nodded.

"It started last time he visited home."

"Why did he sign the betrothal agreement, then?"

"He had already done so. You might recall that he had planned to remain at Hutchings Park with his parents until our marriage, and only then move to Eastbrook Manor."

"There was some talk of that, but when he left, we all assumed that the gossip was wrong. After all, he had just inherited the Manor and had never seen it. It made sense to ready it for his bride. Of course, we also expected him to visit home occasionally—to see you if nothing else."

She nodded.

"His failure to do so started tales of a family feud."

"For once, speculation was right."

"So why did he leave so suddenly?"

Chloe again blushed. "His parents have always seemed as straight-laced as mine, but they are not. He heard his mother entertaining a family friend in her bedchamber."

"A male friend, I suppose."

"Yes. Incensed at her disloyalty—and appalled at her sinful conduct—he rushed to the village to fetch his father, expecting that Lord Weymouth would properly chastise her and call the friend out."

"He didn't?"

"George never spoke to him. Weymouth was spending the afternoon with his mistress. It must be a long-standing arrangement, for the woman has lived in the village for thirty years and has half a dozen children."

"Not Mrs. Landers!"

She nodded. "George fled. He could not reconcile his parents' behavior with their lifelong exhortations on honor and duty, so he left home. He swears he will never return to such an immoral house, but he still intends to honor the contract his father forced him to sign." She sighed.

"What a prude." Diana was shaking her head, unable to understand how George had survived ten years in public schools if he thought like a Methodist.

"Surely you don't advocate infidelity!"

"Not at all." Chloe had that much in common with George. She was still young enough to believe in absolutes. "But my own standards do not prevent me from understanding other people. Until recently, all marriages in our class were arranged." Chloe cringed. "My own was arranged, you might recall. Like your parents, I came to love my husband, and would never have considered breaking my vows even if I had not. But the Weymouths are different. Their relationship never warmed beyond common civility. And neither pays more than lip service to fidelity—like most of society."

"George will never condone such behavior. You called him a prude, but that is too mild. He believes his mother should be incarcerated and his father shot. He also thinks that no woman of any age or status should spend even a moment alone with a man. We are far too weak-willed to resist temptation."

"Heavens! Does he plan to lock you up?"

"Who knows? But do you see why I cannot wed him?" Chloe wailed, only barely keeping her tone soft enough to remain private.

"Yes, he is certainly not the man of your dreams. But perhaps we can use his rigidity against him. Your mother was singing his praises during tea, so I doubt I can change her mind. George is so like your parents, they already view him as a son. But if he were to take you in disgust, they might reconsider."

"Eloping would certainly assure that."

"But it would also damage Charles's career and ruin both of your reputations. I think we should start with something less drastic. Teach George that you will be a constant source of annoyance. Let him see your real character—though not all at once; too big a shock could have unpleasant consequences. Start by letting him know how much you love London society."

"That will merely convince him that he should remove me from town as soon as possible."

"Not if you do it right. I am not suggesting that you suddenly start raving about town. But we are currently in the country. Remark that the Harrisons are wonderful hosts, then temper your words with a more favorable assessment of one particular London gathering. The next time you talk, say something like, 'I can't wait to escape Mama's censorship. I look forward to reading *Glenarvon*.' Or name the intellectuals you wish to entertain, or the lectures you've missed on scientifics and inventions, or mention how fascinating you found Lord Harrison's discussion of Greek tragedies, but that you personally prefer Shakespeare."

"Greek tragedies?"

Diana chuckled. "If you haven't yet held such a discussion, hie thee to Harrison's side right now. He is obsessed with Greek drama. I doubt George paid any attention to the subject in school."

"I see what you mean. I should introduce one of my interests into each conversation, then gently disagree when he criticizes my words."

"Exactly. Prove that you are not the meek, silent girl your mother has demanded you be. But be careful not to push him too far. You want to gradually increase his fear of wedding you. But he sounds quick to judge and even quicker to punish. Don't make him determined to whip you into line."

Chloe moved off in search of Lord Harrison.

"Lady Bounty! I had not realized that you were to be part of this group."

Diana smiled at Lord Justin. "You skipped my last *soirée*."

"Not from disinterest. I was devastated to miss speaking with Constable, but my aunt fell down the stairs that afternoon. She will recover, though it was rather uncertain at the time."

"Lady Wembley?"

He nodded.

"I had heard, but I didn't realize you were with her."

"It is fortunate that I was. My uncle is worthless in a crisis. Will Constable remain in town for a while?"

"Not at this time."

He sighed. "I had hoped to commission a painting. But enough of that. I've wanted to ask for weeks and can no longer resist. How do you happen to know Woodvale? And why did you never mention it before?" The complications and uncertainties surrounding the Woodvale title had been *on-dits* for nearly a year.

"I hadn't made the connection until I saw him, and I never really knew him anyway. He spent a summer with one of our neighbors many years ago."

"Your first youthful *tendre* perhaps?" He was smiling, but his curiosity was obviously piqued. What interest did he have in their acquaintance?

"Sorry to disappoint you. I was little more than a child in those days and had too much else on my mind. My father was very ill and died soon after. We didn't socialize much."

"Forgive my curiosity, my lady. His shock on seeing you again was more than a minor meeting many years ago should warrant."

She forced a light laugh. "We all know his reputation. I suspect that he had planned to seduce the new widow, but was surprised to recognize someone he last saw as a child. Perhaps it reminded him of the passing years. Why don't you ask him?"

He frowned, obviously dissatisfied with her response.

"Has Harrison introduced you to his grandson yet?" she asked, ruthlessly changing the subject.

"The moment I arrived. He's prouder than the father."

Diana kept talk on the upcoming christening until she could move on to another guest. Chloe had finished with Harrison and was now speaking animatedly to George, whose forehead was creased deeper than she had ever seen it. Charles was flirting lightly with Lady Harrison. The Parkers and Weymouths were chatting seriously in one corner. Were they discussing Chloe's dissatisfaction?

"The Parker chit is delectable," Nicholas said from just behind her shoulder. "Half the gentlemen here have their eye on her."

"Including you, of course," she snapped, turning to meet his gaze. "Stay away from her, Woodvale."

"Innocents never interested me—except one I met in Warwickshire. Miss Parker pales in comparison."

Danger signals screamed in her head. He'd gone from angry to smooth in the course of an hour. His intent was clear even before she noted the heat in his eyes. He'd decided to seduce her—again.

*Over my dead body.* She deliberately let her gaze wander over his physique—from the broad shoulders under Weston's superfine jacket, down the tight gray pantaloons that blatantly displayed his purpose, to his highly polished evening shoes. The emeralds glittering on his quizzing glass made his green eyes glow even brighter.

"I got all I wanted from you ten years ago, my lord. I find I've grown more particular with age."

His eyes darkened dangerously, but she ignored them, turning away without another word.

Only then did she curse herself for issuing an open challenge—in more ways than one. A surreptitious glance verified that the tightening she'd felt when her gaze reached his groin had peaked her nipples. He would not have missed so telltale a sign.

Her mental expletives exhausted the collection Humphrey had uttered when Harry left him nothing but a title and a worthless estate. Then she added a few new ones.

Nicholas glared at Diana's retreating back. That certainly had not gone as he'd imagined. She had not allowed him time to apologize.

On the other hand, she clearly felt the same lust as he did. He could not have mistaken that reaction. The next time he approached her, there would be no audience. They needed to discuss this openly, like adults.

She might think she'd had the last word, but she was wrong. One way or another, he would get his fill of her. Only then could he sleep at night.

Sophia interrupted his planning.

"Did you talk to the Parkers?" she demanded the moment she had drawn him into a quiet corner.

"Yes, but it did no good. They suspect me of having designs on the girl myself. If I try to push, they will rush her into marriage. I think a better plan would be to talk to Weymouth. If he learns that she is likely to make Eastbrook miserable, perhaps he will pressure the Parkers into calling off the wedding."

"When pigs fly!" She clamped her mouth shut, fighting for control. "They think George is too sober. Not ten minutes ago, I heard Lord Weymouth criticize him for being aloof. He claims that Miss Parker's youthful gaiety will draw George out, and her enthusiasm will force him to enjoy society. He is furious that George eschews the clubs—which are nothing more than glorified gaming hells—and that he prefers sober conversation with people like Coke to socializing." She sniffed.

"Didn't I see you talking to Coke yourself?"

"Probably. His agricultural experiments are fascinating, as George agrees. So does Lord Weymouth, for that matter. But what business is it of his how George spends his time and money? What is wrong with disliking town?"

Nicholas raised his brows.

"Forgive my outburst. I am too frustrated for words. Talk to Weymouth if you think it will serve, but don't be surprised if it does no good. I still think the best course is to convince Miss Parker to jilt him. She would do it if you flirted with her. Every other chit finds your reputation appealing. Why not her?"

"From all appearances, both parties approve the match," he pointed out gently, nodding across the room where Chloe was laughing with Eastbrook.

Sophia sucked in a sharp breath. "She cannot possibly like him. They are nothing alike."

"Many people form odd attachments," he reminded her. "And even more mistake their true feelings, eschewing good matches out of pride, or chasing bad matches because they offer a challenge. Perhaps you should examine your own feelings. Why do you believe Eastbrook might return your affection?"

Pain filled her eyes. "I just know."

*Women!* "I have done as much as possible for today. I will watch Miss Parker and Eastbrook before I make any further moves. I would suggest you do the same."

The butler announced dinner, giving him a chance to slip away from her.

He spent the rest of the evening observing his fellow guests. Miss Parker was seated next to Eastbrook. He was too distant to overhear their conversation, but their demeanor validated Weymouth's assessment. Miss Parker spoke animatedly to both her dinner partners, drawing Eastbrook out of his shell several times. Lady Weymouth appeared pleased.

Lady Bankleigh had forced a clearly reluctant Langley to partner Sophia. They were seated across from him. Langley showed no interest in her, confirming his doubts about whether an offer would ever be made—Langley was capable of finding his own solution to the family money crisis. Sophia did not appreciate his disinterest. Was it pique or was she secretly hoping to wed him? The question simply would not go away.

Langley's own intentions surfaced when the gentlemen rejoined the ladies in the drawing room. He immediately approached Diana, talking, laughing, and flirting. Lady Langley said nothing, but speculation blazed in her eyes. He clearly had no personal attachment to Sophia, and Diana was a better prize. His parents wouldn't care who he wed as long as they didn't have to support him.

Nicholas bit back a growl. Langley would have to wait. No one would walk off with Diana before he'd gotten her out of his system.

Diana nearly groaned when Nicholas appeared in the stables. She had hardly slept—all his fault—and had hoped a brisk ride might blow away the cobwebs.

He had sought her out more than once the previous evening—before dinner, after dinner, in the music room, where she had joined several singers in an attempt to escape his attentions. Since he had never enjoyed music, his presence there could only have been deliberate. He was pursuing her with relentless determination. The question was why.

Yesterday had confirmed that he wanted her body. Did he also want her fortune? He was ready to set up his nursery. The only people he had sought out were her and Lady Sophia—the two wealthiest unwed ladies at the house party. But his purpose was irrelevant. She would not allow his charm to seduce her again.

She was no longer a naïve child who accepted a rake's words at face value, especially one who had no heart of his own and wanted no one else's. He would not fool her a second time. Since her arrival in London, more than one gentleman had developed a virulent case of calf-love after considering her inheritance. Others had hoped to console the young widow. Nicholas would fare no better than his predecessors.

Maybe it was time to let the world know exactly how Harry had left things. She had gotten only one third of Harry's fortune—Humphrey had been unwilling to admit that the rest had gone directly to his own son, Jeremy—and she had not inherited it outright. It had been left in trust, with her as both sole trustee and beneficiary. She could pass that position to an heir, but a husband would have no control of her fortune. The fact that Bounty had left control to a woman angered Humphrey even more than losing the wealth. Jeremy's portion was in a second trust, guaranteeing that the lad's death would add nothing to the Bounty coffers. Harry had not trusted Humphrey one little bit.

But that was beside the point just now. She feared Nicholas even more since last night. He exuded a virility that raised responses in her body. Avoiding him in company would be impossible, but she must guard against ever being alone with him.

Using a block, she mounted her horse before he could help her, then galloped away.

Nicholas watched Diana leave, impatient because his own horse was not ready. If he knew her—and he did—she would veer off her present course the moment she passed the first line of trees. Probably to the right.

He bit his lip as he mounted. She knew exactly how well he knew her. Setting his horse to a gallop, he headed left, suppressing a satisfied smile when he intercepted her half a mile away.

"You were always an intrepid rider, but you've improved, my lady."

She glared. "If you remember anything, you should know that I prefer to ride alone." She turned sharply aside.

He followed. "What I recall is that you only prefer solitude when I am not the one accompanying you."

Her face burned. He could almost see the memories parading through her mind. Their rides had usually ended with warm embraces in secluded clearings. As the days passed, the rides grew shorter and the embraces longer. And warmer.

"Tastes change," she said shortly.

"Sometimes," he acknowledged.

"Good day, Nicholas. I'm sure you can find your way back."

"Diana!" His hand shot out to grab her arm, preventing her from leaving. Both came to a standstill as they stared at each other. "We need to talk, but without the audience one always has in the house."

"Release me." Her voice was icy.

"Not until you agree to stay."

"Release my arm, or I'll cry rape so fast you won't know what hit you. You'll be a pariah, Nicholas."

He let his lips curl into a smile. "No one would believe you."

"Not even when I describe that mole near your manhood?"

He shook his head. "You're not an innocent miss anymore, Diana. No one expects you to forego the pleasures of bed. They would conclude that you were pursuing a lovers' spat. It is you who would become the pariah—for exposing common practice to the light of day. Discretion is society's watchword. Once you cease being discreet, others will avoid you for casting guilt on their own activities."

She blushed. "Just let me go. We really have nothing to say to each other. I am no longer an awestruck schoolgirl mooning over a London rake. You are no longer a bored libertine making do with a country chit."

"I've never forgotten you," he admitted quietly.

"More lies?" she said on a sigh. "You had no idea who I was until you actually faced me again."

"It's true that I had not kept in touch with Gerald, so I did not know who you married. But I never forgot you, Diana. You were special, snaring me before I realized what was going on—you know that is true," he added as she shook her head. "Why else would I have gotten so deeply involved with an undowered innocent when I had no means to support even myself?"

"It doesn't matter, Nicholas." She pulled her arm free of his grasp, but made no attempt to leave. "That girl no longer exists. You cannot resurrect your own youth by looking for her."

"Is that what you think I'm doing?"

"In part. Plus I inadvertently challenged you by making my disinterest clear."

"Disinterest? Do not take me for a flat. You want this as much as I do. But I can be as discreet as you wish. We can set up a meeting place removed from both our houses. Your reputation as a virtuous widow will remain intact."

In the early morning light, it almost seemed as if she'd paled. "Still the same despicable cad you were ten years ago," she said softly.

Her virulence slammed through his chest, robbing him of breath. "I must have explained bad—"

"I don't believe in secret lives and false reputations, my lord," she continued, ignoring his protest. "Nor do I believe in dalliance."

"A nice speech, but your body doesn't agree."

She laughed, scraping his nerves raw. "Unlike you, I am not a slave to my appetites. Don't try to change my mind. Begging makes you look foolish. And nothing can twist so ignoble an offer into something remotely enticing."

"Diana—"

"Nothing, my lord. I despise affairs and those who wage them. Nor will I ever wed again. Independence is too precious."

Casting him a look of pure loathing, she set heels to her horse and left.

*Damnation!* He had hurt her far more than he'd thought. It was the only explanation. Why else would an intelligent, beautiful woman eschew all men—he finally had to admit that she was serious. It was her way of avoiding further pain. He closed his eyes on another wave of guilt.

At seventeen she had been an irresistible combination of innocence, beauty, and passion. He had been hooked before he even realized it. And the temptation had been impossible to ignore—at least until her vow of eternal love made him recoil. Only then did he remember his position and the grimness of his prospects.

The thoughts that had flashed through his mind had been stark. He had nothing but his winnings. While they kept up his appearance in London, they would never support a wife, and the chances of inheriting his father's small estate were remote. The man would likely lose it to his creditors. Thus the only way to assure his own future was to marry money. Diana didn't have it. Her father was barely keeping his own head above water, and his heir had little more.

He had panicked at the threat she posed to his plans. And in panic, he had lashed out, examining none of his words before uttering them. His sole purpose had been salvaging control of his life and his future. Not until later did he realize how cruel he had been. And not until much later did he admit that he could have achieved his purpose without destroying Diana in the process.

She still carried the scars. He could see them in her distrust, in her acceptance of an elderly husband who had been unlikely to hurt her, in her determination to avoid all male entanglements. He must heal the damage he had caused.

*You only want an excuse to bed her,* whispered a voice in his head, but he shook it off. Yes he wanted to bed her. He couldn't come near her without a physical response. She was even more delectable than she had been as a girl. But he had to slow down. First he had to win her trust. That would be even more difficult now that he'd made his intentions clear.

*Idiot!* His brain ceased functioning near her. He had meant to start with an apology, clearing away the past before moving on to the future. Now he'd messed even that up. She was still furious over the past, had a new grievance in the present, and had rejected any dealings in the future. He'd never before had to dig himself out of a hole this deep.

Where could he start?

# Chapter Seven

Diana stopped in her tracks, turning to gaze intently at the portrait of some long-dead Harrison ancestor that hung in a dark corner of the hallway. She had been heading for the library, but Nicholas had reached it first.

Their morning confrontation had been the most humiliating experience of her life. Not that he had been the first to offer her *carte blanche*. She'd turned down a dozen overtures in the last two years and deflected several others. But it hurt badly to receive one from a man she had once loved—a man who had never seen her as more than a temporary diversion, she reminded herself brutally. Not even her fortune tempted him into considering marriage. His assumptions belittled her youthful emotions, and taunted her because her body still responded to him.

*Damn him!*

But even as she railed against him, her conscience railed back. She also bore responsibility for the pain of that summer. She had been far too free with her favors. Given her conduct, any man would have assumed she was his for the asking. Her behavior had demanded no respect. His impressions had not changed in ten years.

Nor would they. But he could think what he liked. She would hold her head high and behave like the principled lady she was. He was unimportant, of no more consequence than any other lord. So she would treat him no differently.

She frowned. Unfortunately, he was not behaving like other lords. It should have been easy to avoid him in a place the size of Harrison Court, with its sprawling park and hundred-odd guests, but he was stalking her. No matter where she went, he was there. More than once she had turned tail and fled.

No more. Her back stiffened. Such cowardice was unworthy of her and implied that he disturbed her. She wouldn't give him that satisfaction.

Marching into the library, she headed for the shelves that held Harrison's books on other countries.

"Planning on leaving England?" drawled Nicholas when she selected one on North America.

"Not at all. I'm merely checking something Lord Justin said just now." She flipped pages. "As I thought. Purple coneflower is American, not Chinese."

"How did *that* question arise?" He looked startled.

"We were discussing the treatment Dr. McClarren prescribed for his aunt. He was sure the herb was Chinese, but McClarren once mentioned it at one of my gatherings. Lady Broadbanks had originally brought it to his attention, having learned of it from an American brother-in-law."

"Raeburn?"

She nodded.

"I know the lad. He waxes so eloquently about the New World that I almost want to see it for myself."

She laughed. "Not I. While I enjoy reading about other places, I like my comforts too well to ever enjoy traveling."

"You did not used to be so bookish, Diana." A smile tugged the corners of his mouth, sending shivers down her arms.

She ignored them. "People change." She moved to a shelf of novels—undoubtedly purchased by Harrison's daughter-in-law—and picked up a copy of Peacock's *Headlong Hall*.

"People grow. They mature. They broaden their horizons. They don't change." He pulled her around to face him.

"Release me." She glared into his face, suppressing the tingles radiating from his fingers. "I am not one of your playthings, my lord."

His eyes narrowed.

"Nor will I be," she added, brushing his hands aside. "Surely I made myself clear enough this morning."

"Quite clear." He clasped his hands behind his back, but his eyes never left her. She could read them easily enough—hot, feral, and greedy. He would bide his time, but eventually he would press her again.

He stepped back a pace, easing the tension. "I never knew the extent of your education. Why?"

She shrugged. "You were interested only in dalliance that summer, so the subject never arose. Besides, I had only a basic education, for we had few books at home. Harry was the one who expanded it, tapping a curiosity I hadn't realized was there. My *soirées* continue the learning process."

"Why bother? Most women are incapable of understanding the world. You set yourself apart when you try."

She laughed. "You sound threatened. Most women are capable of mastering any lesson you set them. But they lack the training that would develop their abilities, and they lack the incentive to try. Look around you, my lord. Many women are well educated—Mrs. Baillie, Lady Hartleigh, and Lady Broadbanks, for example. And surely you met Madame de Staël when she visited London. Other women run successful businesses, like modiste shops, employment agencies, and even inns."

"But those are from the working classes."

"Madame Celeste is the daughter of a French nobleman," she reminded him.

"But—"

"Do you honestly believe that the aristocracy produces women of less ability than is commonly found among tradesmen and peasants? If that were true, then only marriage to a commoner would preserve your own intelligence and talents for future generations. Does one breed a fast stallion to a slow mare and expect their offspring to win races?"

He choked. "If women are so intelligent, then why do I see no evidence of it?"

"Perhaps you are afraid to look." She sighed, but debating was a long-standing habit. Even her nervousness over Nicholas's nearness could not dim the exhilaration of making a point. "When one is taught from birth that education is only suitable for males, that subjects beyond deportment and needlework are too complex, that one's only purpose in life is to produce an heir, and that rational thinking destroys femininity, then it is difficult to believe otherwise. Questioning one's assigned role courts censure, threatening the comfortable life that conformity promises."

"That hasn't stopped you."

"But the credit goes to Harry. He needed debate the way most men need food and drink, but his closest friends had died. So he encouraged me to think."

"And did you no favor in the process. He turned you into a freak."

Pain stabbed at her heart, but she thrust it down, shaking her head in exaggerated sadness. "Tsk, tsk. My point, I believe. Switching to personal attacks when your argument is bested is bad debate form." She smiled at his glare. "I have many friends among the intelligentsia—of both genders. And an interest in politics and philosophy does not preclude enjoyment of more traditional activities. If gossip were a mindless pursuit that could be enjoyed only by the uneducated, then why do so many gentlemen indulge in it?"

"Point to you. But sooner or later you will get lonely living by yourself, Diana. What then? A reputation for rebellion—or even eccentricity—is cold comfort in the dark reaches of the night."

"I wondered how long it would take to bring up your disreputable offer," she said, all trace of affability gone. "The answer is still no. Some of us manage to feel good about ourselves without having to prove our prowess on a new partner every day."

"You don't know everything, Diana." His eyes darkened with anger. "Most people wouldn't twist genuine concern into sexual innuendo."

"Nice try," she spat. "But wasted. You've been doing exactly that for years. Save the protests for someone more credulous. I know you too well." Clutching her book, she strode from the library.

Nicholas watched her go. Damnation! She didn't believe a word he said. Lust did not preclude genuine caring. Despite her claims, she would eventually decide to remarry, but her choices would be limited to fortune hunters if she acquired a reputation as an outspoken advocate of changing the way society worked. Blurring the lines defining women's roles would create chaos.

*She bested you. Your points lacked logic.*

He snorted, suppressing the ignominy of losing a debate—something that hadn't happened in years. Bounty had done her an immense disservice by educating her like a man. It had been one thing to teach Nicholas how to debate, but forcing Diana to learn the technique was intolerable. He'd left her unmarriageable. No man would put up with her sharp-tongued impertinence.

At least not in a wife. But that played into his hands. She would accept his proposition. It was only a matter of time, for her passion still simmered.

He had removed his gloves when he had returned from observing the games Lady Harrison had organized on the lawn. Without them, grasping the bare skin below her sleeves had sent a jolt up his arm that still burned. And his fingers still felt the ripples that had shaken her at the contact. It had taken considerable determination to back out of reach.

He should have taken advantage of their privacy to tender his apologies. But she had caught him off guard. He had managed to avoid her since their morning ride, retreating whenever she appeared. His cowardice was unworthy of him, but he had needed the time to regain his composure before beginning his campaign to earn her friendship.

Only now did he realize how often they had nearly met—far more than chance would dictate in a party of this size. Was she stalking him? Was rubbing his nose in her supposed indifference her way of exacting punishment?

She stared deeply into his eyes, her own troubled.

"That is why I made sure to lose as many bets as I won, Diana. I could not afford to influence the important ones. And I swear that wagering had nothing to do with you. I've never told a soul about that summer."

"Perhaps." But her eyes had softened just a little.

"Think about it. And about being friends."

"That is not possible." She turned to leave, but he blocked the path.

"Set your justified anger aside, and use that logic you are so proud of, Lady Bounty. We are going to keep running into each other. I refuse to avoid your *soirées* just because you are the hostess. Reports of them fascinated me even before I returned to town. And we have so many friends in common that we are bound to be at the same social gatherings. Then there are Lady Hardesty's maneuverings."

"What is your point?"

"We need to get comfortable with each other. You must stop jumping when I appear, and you should banish that scared rabbit expression whenever we speak."

"Scared rabbit!" she growled, glaring into his eyes. "What an imagination! You can't stand the idea that I didn't spend the last ten years pining for you, can you? So you've come up with this ludicrous idea that I don't want you around. You are as welcome as anyone at my *soirées*. And I'm not going to fall into a swoon if you enter a ballroom. If anyone has a problem, it's you. Every time you come near me, you act like I'm a feast and you haven't eaten in six months. Pull your tongue back into your mouth before people decide you're finally ready for Bedlam."

"Wha—"

"Don't deny it. You are as obvious as a stallion scenting a mare in heat. Do you enjoy cultivating the image of a slavering fool? Or are you so incensed that I'm not falling worshipfully at your feet that you are truly blind to your appearance?"

"You are the one who needs Bedlam." He was quivering with rage.

"Hardly. Ask Lord Justin if you doubt me. But don't expect me to take you seriously. Your apology is either the first move in a new seduction scheme or a weak attempt to assuage your guilt. The same is true of this demand for friendship. I'm not interested."

Well, she had certainly turned that effort against him. She had refused to forgive him, enunciated crimes he had never considered, revealed more pain than he had ever imagined she had suffered, seen through every statement to his real purpose, and rejected everything he offered. How much slower could he go without ceasing to see her at all?

Another sleepless night sent Diana riding before dawn. At least Nicholas did not join her this time.

He had avoided her in the drawing room last night, too. It was what she had asked for, so why did his attentions to Lady Sophia annoy her?

It didn't matter. He was a hypocritical libertine who was unworthy of her attention. And she had plenty of other problems.

Chloe had been near tears last night, discouraged and dismayed because George was not developing a disgust of her.

Diana sighed. She had not made it clear that success would take days—possibly even weeks. George was very stubborn, and Chloe could not push him too hard without triggering a response no one would like.

It had taken half an hour to calm the girl. And George *was* reacting, she noted later. Chloe's exuberance tightened his mouth and strained his eyes.

Charles was also champing at the bit. His love for Chloe was plain to anyone watching him closely—as she had tried to warn him more than once. He must keep his eyes off her. With luck, he would spend the day hunting with the rest of the men.

George would not be with them. He despised blood sports. Perhaps she could talk with him and paint a clearer picture of Chloe's interests.

The path she was following emerged into a small clearing along the bank of a stream. Early sunlight filtered through the leaves, picking out the wildflowers scattered across the ground. Clumps of shrubs and a large rock hung over the water. A bird sang in the trees. It closely resembled a clearing at home that she had last seen ten years ago.

She dismounted, tying her horse to a low branch. Nicholas's words in the rose garden had been nipping at her mind all night. Relief that he had not seduced her for a wager had lightened her heart—his shock had been too genuine to question his disclaimer. And he was right about the rest as well. Unless she was prepared to abandon London, they would meet often. Only mourning and the uncertainty of his accession had kept him away this long. She had pushed him so firmly into the past that she had not noticed his absence. Which was good. Surely she could do it again.

She sat down on the rock and stared into the water. More birds added their voices, though without the territorial squabbling common earlier in the year. The stream burbled over rounded rocks, forming a counterpoint to the sounds of dawn. The first rays of sun warmed the back of her hand where it rested beside her.

This clearing was too familiar. A robin swooped in to deliver food to a nest across the stream. Way too familiar. There had been robins then, too. The third time she had seen him . . .

Walking through the woods, they had come on the clearing unexpectedly. It was a little later in the day, for most of the fog had burned off. A robin had been chivvying her babies out of the nest and onto a branch near the top of a large shrub.

She sighed.

Nicholas's hand had rested comfortably on her shoulder as they settled in to watch the nestlings' first flying lesson. Their meeting had not been arranged—none of them ever were—but both had expected to spend the morning together. Even that first day, they had been able to read each other's minds.

*Stupid!* She had been so naïve in those days. He had probably created that impression by spying on her.

But she hadn't felt naïve that morning. The sun warmed the air. The tiniest of breezes swirled the fading mist into wisps and wraiths. And the baby birds showed every sign of wanting to stay in their cozy nest, pretending that the larger world did not exist. Venturing out where they would be responsible for themselves was not attractive.

The mother bird had patiently coaxed—and finally insisted—that they try their wings. She could still hear the surprised chirps as the babies tumbled one by one off the branch, could still feel their exhilaration as frantic flaps slowed their falls and even gained them some height.

Something about their foray had seemed magical. Nicholas's hand had moved slightly, his touch changing to a gentle caress. She had turned surprised eyes to meet his and found his lips only inches away. That gap hadn't lasted long. Like the bird, he had chivvied her out of childhood, into a grown-up world of wonder.

She shivered, again feeling that first kiss. He had barely brushed her mouth, but the touch had exploded sensation throughout her body. He had felt her response—no surprise there—and increased the pressure. But he had kept himself firmly under control, touching her only with the one hand and his lips.

After he pulled away, he had met her eyes. His held confusion, and a look that she had interpreted as awe—but which was probably only satisfaction. That was the moment she had fallen in love.

Poor naïve fool.

So how was she to put him behind her once and for all? This time she had no Harry to comfort her tears, no new home to occupy her time and energy, no grief at a father's death to overwhelm her senses. All she had was a man whose appearance affected her more strongly than before, a routine that required little thought to continue, and a taunt reminding her that no bevy of friends could assuage the loneliness that had gnawed a hole in her heart for ten years.

But she must. Nicholas was now open about his goals. She might be lonely, but she was smart enough to know that no liaison, however satisfactory, could fill that desolation. And he had no interest in permanence. Even setting aside his own words, lords looked for youthful virgins when choosing a wife.

Nicholas opened his eyes when a bird's shrill call made his horse snort. He must have dozed off. A second horse was cropping grass off to his right. He cursed another sleepless night as he brushed leaves from his coat. If he couldn't sleep in his bed, why could he do so here?

He was reaching for the bridle when he spotted the other early riser—Diana—and everything clicked into place. No wonder this spot had relaxed him. The clearing closely resembled that other meeting place, where morning mist had so often cloaked their encounters.

Never once had they made specific assignations. But there were many things they knew without resorting to words. Any morning without rain would bring him to the clearing. Sometimes he arrived first, sometimes she did. But neither had ever waited more than five minutes. In the afternoons they met other places, but mornings were for the clearing.

He stared at her now, again feeling the enchantment. Diana, so beautiful, so different. The forest and the early mist made this meeting feel inevitable.

"Peaceful, isn't it?" he murmured, coming up behind her.

She jumped, exactly as he had accused her of doing yesterday. He watched the realization and chagrin chase across her face. "You startled me. Where did you come from?"

"I've been here for an hour." He nodded toward a second rock that jutted over the water beyond a large shrub. "This reminds me of another wood, another stream." Already he was falling into her eyes, swept back to the wonder and excitement of those summer days. Lilac reached out, drawing him into a sensual web.

"I wonder if the clearing is still there," she whispered.

"Why wouldn't it be?" He joined her on the rock, careful to keep a small distance between them.

She shrugged. "My uncle disapproved of everything my father loved. I've not been back to see if he cut down the wood."

"Not once in ten years?"

"We were never close. And Harry stopped traveling toward the end."

That put a period to that topic. And just as well. He didn't want to learn that she had become estranged from her family; didn't want to hear tales of watching her husband die. Bounty had been showing his age badly the last time he'd come to town. The end could not have been easy. "Why did you start your *soirée?*" he asked instead.

"Harry. I missed our debates."

"So you re-created them on a larger scale. I wish we had spent our time talking. I would have enjoyed awakening your mind, and things might have been different."

"Or they might not. You were too young to question what you had been taught about women's abilities, and you were too full of your own consequence to ignore your desires."

"Are you implying that I forced you?"

"Not at all. I am pointing out that intellectual debate with a schoolroom miss was not a high priority when you were two-and-twenty. Nor does it matter if it might have been. We cannot remake the past. We can only learn from it."

"And what have you learned, Diana? To stay out of the forest in the early morning? To lock yourself behind rigid propriety lest temptation again sway you?" He had always associated her with the dawn. It was when they had first met. Like today, she had worn green, a simple gown that clung to slender legs and youthful breasts. She should carry a bow, he thought again, as the rising sun cleared a tree, bathing her in golden light. "I know what you haven't learned," he whispered. "Your passion still lives. For all your claims of contentment, you have not learned how to banish it."

Her eyes darkened, their gold specks blazing with desire. Her lips parted—perhaps to speak—but no sound emerged. It was there, as always, the cord that drew them together.

His lips touched hers softly, a butterfly caress, here and gone in a trice. But the fire exploded into a conflagration that consumed him. He returned, touching, brushing, and finally molding his mouth to hers. Her moan chased the last thought from his head. One hand tightened on her neck, drawing her closer. The other pulled her into his lap. His tongue plunged, ravishing her mouth, claiming it for his own.

Diana tried to think, tried to remember something important, but her mind would not function. Her arms had wound around his neck where her fingers already sifted through his hair. It was shorter now, but just as soft, just as silky.

The rest of him was not. Muscles clenched in his shoulders as he tightened his hold. His manhood pressed urgently against her thigh. Before she could register thought, he surged to his feet, pulling her hard against him. Her mind shut down, and she was left with nothing but sensation . . .

The smooth caress of his tongue, teasing, taunting, arrogantly demanding possession, flushing her skin with heat that pooled deep in her stomach . . . Shock stabbing through her soul as he touched the hard tip of one breast, rolling it between a thumb and finger, melting the bones in her knees . . .

Twin moans echoed across the clearing. Their kisses grew hotter, deeper, wetter—plundering kisses that ravished both her mouth and his. Not until she felt a matching wetness between her legs did she recoil.

"No!"

"You want this as much as I do," he gasped, pulling her hips tight against him. Passion and need swirled through eyes blank of any intelligence.

"No!"

She pushed frantically against his shoulders, terrified that he was too absorbed to stop. Dear God! How had she let him seduce her again? Her own need was betraying her. Never had it been this strong. He had gained much experience in ten years—to her detriment.

"No," she sobbed. "Please, no."

He stilled for several seconds. His breathing was as ragged as hers, but he stared into her eyes and sighed, reluctantly dropping his arms to free her. It cost him. She could see it and was grateful that he complied, but it boded ill for the future.

Backpedaling toward her horse, she scrubbed at the tears rolling down her cheeks. He was more dangerous than ever, because it was true. She wanted him. But he was the one man who could breach the walls around her heart. She couldn't take that chance. So she must avoid him.

"No more," she begged brokenly. "If you care even a little, leave me alone. An affair would destroy me." She scrabbled about for a rock she could use as a mounting block. The one she had sat on was too close to where he still stood.

"Let me help, Diana," he said. His voice was huskier than usual, but he had regained control of everything else. "You're safe enough. I've never yet taken an unwilling woman, and I won't start with you."

She had no choice. Steeling herself against his touch, she nodded. And for once he spoke the truth. He lifted her easily into the saddle, then released her and stepped back.

"This isn't over," he promised. "None of it."

She said nothing, galloping toward the stables, tears again wetting her cheeks.

Nicholas stared at the path until he no longer heard her horse's hoofbeats. Then he returned to the rock, dropping his head into his hands. What the devil had happened?

He should have slipped quietly away and left her in peace. But she had stirred so many memories that he hadn't been able to do it. Not that he had intended to touch her. He had only wanted to talk, to share a moment of friendship.

*Right!* Like everything else in recent weeks, the situation had rapidly escalated out of control. Within moments he'd been kissing her senseless.

To say nothing of himself. He was still quaking.

He grimaced. She had destroyed his reason. Again. Just as she'd done in Warwickshire. He had never intended to get involved with her. She'd been a pretty girl who shared some of his interests. Funny to remember that now. Their liaisons had started because both enjoyed watching the birds. She had not originally affected him sexually.

But it hadn't stayed platonic for long. He could no longer remember why he had kissed her the first time, but that one act had changed everything. Never had a simple kiss felt so good. That had been the start, of course. One kiss had turned to two, then more. He couldn't get enough of her—touching, tasting, smelling the lilac she always wore.

Was that what had triggered his reaction today? Her perfume had reached out to draw him in. It still lingered faintly around the rock.

Answers eluded him. What should he do next? Somehow, he would have to keep his hands to himself, letting her settle down and get used to him again. She was as skittish as a newborn colt right now.

But the one indisputable result of the morning was his renewed determination. He *would* have her. His reaction was too powerful to ignore. He still hurt.

# Chapter Eight

By the time Diana descended for breakfast, she had stopped shaking. Allowing his kiss had been the height of stupidity. And *allow* was exactly right. He hadn't forced her. There had been a moment when she had known he would kiss her if she didn't turn away. She hadn't. A tiny voice inside her head had wondered if it would be the same.

*Fool!* It was not the same. She could have controlled her reaction to his old kisses. But this was beyond her wildest dreams—so far beyond that she doubted she could have controlled herself even if she had known what to expect.

Worse was the admission that he made her feel alive in a way she had not been for ten years. Even arguing with him left her glowing for hours. But his goals had not changed. He had no use for her beyond sex. He could still seduce her, she admitted in despair. Somehow she must prevent that from happening, for accepting his attentions would betray Harry.

"How I wish you were here, Harry!" she whispered.

But he wasn't. And she was too weak. So she must avoid Nicholas—and if that meant avoiding London, she would do it. Let him think what he would. It no longer mattered. She could not handle another broken heart.

It had been Harry who had repaired her last one. She doubted her father had even known.

All the old guilt returned. She had been so wrapped up in Nicholas that she had paid little attention to her father beyond gratitude that she was able to slip away so often. Her mother had died four years earlier, and her governess had left in May. Only the two of them remained at home, but he spent most of his time dealing with estate matters, seeing her only at dinner. Not until a week after Nicholas left did she learn the full truth.

Sir Walter Winslow had made a series of bad investments that had put him on the verge of ruin. He had hoped to convince a distant cousin to bear the expense of presenting her to society, but that was not to be. So there would be no London Season.

In her grief over Nicholas, she had actually been glad. Seeing him in London would have destroyed her. But his next statement had driven even thoughts of Nicholas away.

He was dying.

She had really looked at him then, shocked to see how thin he had grown, appalled at the waxy pallor that underlay remnants of tan. She had hardly taken in that reality before he announced that Lord Bounty had offered for her. When he pressed her to accept, she could only agree. Shock and grief had made thinking impossible.

But she knew she could not go to Bounty without admitting that her heart was engaged. And so she had bared every detail of that summer to the near-stranger who asked for her hand. She could still feel his comforting arms close around her as he gently dried her tears.

"There, there, child," he had murmured as she cried on his shoulder. "Time will lessen the pain. I've known the lad since he was in leading strings. While he is often heedless and impulsive, I've never known him to be deliberately cruel. It pains me to find that he hurt you, but I will help you forget."

And he had, though their marriage was nothing like she had expected. He had showed her more respect than any man she had ever known—including her father—starting in that same interview, for he refused to wed her under false pretenses.

Her father would be gone within months. Knowing his brother and heir all too well, he had tried to find her a husband, but the hundred pounds he could scrape together for a dowry brought no acceptable suitors. So he had approached his good friend Bounty.

Bounty had no real need for a wife. His only son had recently died, but he was already grooming a grand-nephew to take his place. The boy's greedy father would get the title first, but little of the property was entailed, so it could be passed directly to Jeremy.

But he owed Winslow several favors. Caring for Diana would repay them. He was no longer capable of consummating a marriage, but he would protect her, and he hoped they would become friends.

And they *had* become friends—even closer than friends. He had taught her much—how to judge people, how to handle money, how to run an estate, how to hold her own in debates on any subject. When he died, she mourned him far more deeply than she had mourned her father. And his will had surprised her, for she had not expected more than a jointure.

Sighing, she smiled at the quartet of ladies in the breakfast room. Ten minutes later she had to subdue a ridiculous spurt of pique when Nicholas appeared. He included her in a general greeting, then joined Lady Sophia.

She was acceptable for private dalliance, but he was still courting the virgin heiress. Had that interlude by the river meant nothing to him?

*All he wants from her is money and an heir,* reminded that voice. *He'll take his pleasure elsewhere. He can't know that you could give him all three.*

Appalled at where her thoughts were heading, she ruthlessly suppressed them. She had never corrected the popular misconception that her failure to provide Bounty an heir proved that she was barren. Nor would she now. Revealing his condition—which had existed for thirty years—would tarnish his memory, even among his friends. Gentleman placed inordinate importance on sexual prowess. It was yet another reason she must avoid Nicholas. Despite understanding his motives, she was weak around him. Eventually he would breach her controls and seduce her, uncovering her secrets and dishonoring Harry.

Tamping down the lingering pain, she averted her eyes from the sight of Nicholas laughing with Lady Sophia, finished her unwanted breakfast, and retired to her room.

\* \* \*

Sophia strolled aimlessly through the gardens, vainly trying to believe that Woodvale would free George from Miss Parker's clutches. His report at breakfast had been even more pessimistic than his earlier ones. Lord Weymouth had secured a wife for his heir, and that was that. Whether they cared for each other or merely rubbed along together was irrelevant. A wife's only use was to produce an heir. Chloe would do that quite well.

With every passing hour, her hope faded further. Weymouth didn't care. The Parkers were adamant. George was too proper to cancel the arrangement. Miss Parker seemed resigned—though Sophia still believed the girl could not wish to marry George. And Woodvale refused to consider the only approach that might work.

Her own situation seemed worse every day. Despite her parents' claims, Charles did not want her, so any offer he made would be under duress. His feelings should be obvious to any observer. He avoided her whenever possible and missed no opportunity to deride country living. He wanted nothing to do with running an estate. With luck he would refuse to offer for her, but she couldn't take chances. If he decided that her fortune was too attractive to pass up, he would use it to set himself up in town, keeping her with him until she produced an heir. He might even sell her estate to raise more cash.

She shuddered. It was all too much. Aside from her hatred of London, she had plans for that estate—and for a good portion of her fortune. She could not accept anyone who might disapprove of those plans.

But even if she avoided Charles, her parents would resort to the same ultimatum with a more willing suitor next Season. So she had to free George. No other husband would do. George shared her ideals and her love for the country. He would support her projects and take pride in her efforts to counter the modern laxity that produced flighty, novel-reading girls and rakish, wastrel boys. She would serve as a model of propriety for neighboring children and a voice of reason for their parents.

She rounded a corner and gasped. A picturesque Grecian folly overlooked a lake. Protected by trees and shrubs on two sides, it was nonetheless open to view by anyone on the lake or approaching from the formal gardens. Yet its current occupants were indulging in a heated embrace. Scandalous! Precisely the sort of conduct that must be stamped out if society was to endure in any civilized manner. The very fabric that had made England great was threa—

Identifying the culprits deflected her outrage—Charles and Miss Parker.

What a perfect opportunity to end George's betrothal! And to get rid of Charles. She could solve both problems and teach the other guests a lesson about loose morals, all with one stroke.

Ducking out of sight, she rapidly retraced her steps. In response to her prayers, God had provided the ideal solution. Lord and Lady Parker were in the garden. All she need do was to invite them for a walk around the lake. They were such sticklers for propriety, that finding their daughter compromised by a gentleman would lead to an immediate marriage.

George would be free.

Diana strolled through the knot garden, forcing her mind onto Chloe's problems so she wouldn't think about Nicholas. Talking with Lady Parker had accomplished nothing. The woman was convinced that Chloe shared her every interest, and nothing would dissuade her. She looked at her daughter and saw herself.

Even worse, she accused Diana of corrupting Chloe with unladylike ideas. George was still pushing to move the wedding forward. Lady Parker had balked lest the change raise questions about Chloe's chastity. But she was reconsidering her opposition. Lord Parker was anxious to leave London, so he would readily agree that the Season was doing Chloe no good.

Diana sighed. After that diatribe, she had not dared push. The Parkers would forbid further contact if they decided she was leading Chloe astray. It was clear that they were on the verge of that decision already. Her reputation as an intellectual was far stronger in London than in Wiltshire, so they were only now discovering the full range of her interests. They would never believe that by teaching Chloe to think for herself and offering reading material beyond innocuous improving literature, she had channeled the girl's restless yearning into positive activities. Chloe had so chafed at her parents' restrictions that Diana had once feared she would run away and come to harm.

Lady Sophia rushed toward the gardens from the direction of the lake. She looked disheveled—and quite rattled. Diana frowned. Had Nicholas been taking unwelcome liberties with her? His kisses were enough to rattle even the least propriety-conscious miss. But she couldn't picture him overstepping the bounds with a potential wife. He reserved that for prospective mistresses.

And Sophia's distress might not arise from advances. She was so prim that even finding herself alone with a gentleman would rattle her.

But the problem could not be serious. The girl spotted other guests, instantly dropping her pace to an elegant stroll as her hands smoothed her gown and tucked a wayward curl under her bonnet.

Diana was turning back to the house when Lady Sophia stopped to speak to the Parkers. They seemed surprised, but a gesture urged them to accompany her to the lake. Her words were unintelligible, but her tone carried an undercurrent of spite—or possibly cunning.

*Chloe!*

Dear Lord, the girl had wandered toward the lake twenty minutes earlier. Had she arranged an assignation with Charles? Despite his honorable intentions, Charles was little different than Nicholas when it came to getting his own way. She should have expected him to meet Chloe even while they were supposed to be ignoring each other.

If the Parkers found them together, Chloe would be wed to George before the week was out. They would never countenance giving her to a rake. Nor would they tolerate the slightest tarnish to her reputation.

Shortsighted, hedonistic idiots! Couldn't they think beyond the moment? With prissy misses like Lady Sophia about—to say nothing of the Parkers—they could not afford to take chances.

Racing along a servants' shortcut through the shrubbery, she prayed she could find the pair before their indiscretion ruined any chance of marriage.

The path emerged next to the folly, but the scene that greeted her was far more intimate than a kiss. Charles held Chloe in his arms, his head resting atop hers as they silently communed. They presented an image of such perfect amity that Diana blinked back a tear. But there was no time for sentiment.

"Your parents are headed this way," she said, appearing so quickly that they both jumped in alarm. "Chloe, take that path through the trees, get back to the house, and pretend you've been there all afternoon. Hurry!"

Chloe grabbed her bonnet and bolted.

"You had best head around the lake," she told Charles. "If they spot her, you cannot be anywhere nearby. I'll remain here and admire the view."

"Surely if other guests found us together, they would have to accept me," he protested.

"Idiot! They are the most pigheaded fools alive. I don't care if the Regent and the Archbishop of Canterbury found you naked in bed! The Parkers would see her wed immediately—to George. Now, go."

"Thank you." He gave her a quick hug. "I didn't know the risk I was running."

"Appalling!" snapped Lady Parker.

Charles stiffened.

"Indecent!" added Lady Sophia.

"What is the meaning of this?" demanded Lord Parker. "I

thought better of you, Lady Bounty," he added as he stepped into the folly and identified her.

Charles's eyes filled with panic.

"Do it," whispered Diana so only he could hear. "It's your only hope. We'll straighten it out later. You needn't fear I'll hold you to it."

Charles pulled himself together and grinned. "Wish me happy. Lady Bounty has accepted my hand in marriage." He gallantly raised her fingers to his lips.

Something akin to horror flashed in Lady Sophia's eyes, but it was gone too quickly to identify it. More likely it had been surprise. She had expected to find Chloe here—though why she had sought to get her in trouble, Diana did not know. The two girls had never met, so there should be no reason for enmity. Now she would assume she had been mistaken. Chloe's gown was nearly the twin of her own. It was the first break of the day. Without seeing their faces, a distant observer would not differentiate them.

The Parkers' shock instantly changed to delight, for they had long urged her to remarry. Despite her demonstrated expertise, they did not believe a woman was capable of running an estate. And her refusal to hire a chaperon offended their strict propriety. If they had known that she also directed her own investments—through the offices of Harry's man of business—they would have gone into hysterics.

Thus they welcomed the news. By the time the party returned to the house, nearly every guest had been apprised of the betrothal.

Nicholas ducked into the woods. He had successfully avoided Diana since she had left the clearing yesterday. Now he wished he hadn't. Less than three days after swearing off both dalliance and marriage, she had been caught in the former and forced into the latter.

The force had been obvious. He had reached the edge of the trees just as the Parkers had arrived. Langley's embrace had hurt, though even a casual glance detected no passion in the gesture. But Langley had stiffened when Lady Parker spoke. Panic had flashed across his face. Diana's had been turned away, but she must have been equally surprised. Had she willingly met Langley, or had the man cornered her in the folly and pressed attentions on her?

The very thought that she might welcome Langley left him reeling. Leaning against a tree, he fought for breath. But she must have, he admitted. He had caught a glimpse of them fifteen minutes earlier. Distance had blurred the image enough that he had not recognized either party, but that passionate embrace had been two-sided. So perhaps Langley's face had reflected surprise rather than panic. And pleased surprise at that. He had been courting Diana's fortune since receiving his parents' ultimatum.

Nicholas drew in a deep breath. Had he driven her into Langley's arms? Sliding to the ground, he laid his head on his knees and swallowed the hot tickle in his throat. He had lost control by the stream. She had responded, hotter than ever before, though retaining a hint of the sweet innocence that had always driven him wild—so despite her love, Bounty must have used her sparingly, he realized in a pleased aside.

But he had pushed her too hard. Her own response had shocked her. She had been unwilling to give up her anger—and probably hatred; in ten years, she would have convinced herself that she hated him.

Damn! Why did he always cease thinking when he was with her—at least with his head; his groin was doing just fine, devil take it. He shifted to ease its discomfort. He knew he should have moved slower. Yet even after losing control of what should have been a simple kiss, he had made things worse with that parting shot.

*This isn't over. None of it.*

A threat. That's what she would have heard. A bloody threat to force her into his bed.

Her resistance arose from pride, but discovering that she still responded to his touch would have horrified her, impelling her to find a way to avoid him.

Why hadn't he seen it earlier? Preferably before finding her in the clearing. She had loved him once, but he had behaved like an insensitive brute. Now that he had proven that she remained susceptible, she would fear him. And so she had sought protection from Langley, who would offer honor rather than dishonor.

*Idiot!* All of them were idiots. But he took the prize.

If he had held off until they were back in London, she could at least have found someone respectable. Langley was no good—certainly not for Diana. She deserved so much more than a glib-tongued libertine in desperate need of cash. After a loving marriage with Bounty—he suppressed another surge of guilt over pushing her into that one, never mind that she had come to love him—how would she survive life with a womanizing scoundrel?

And it was all his fault. He was no good, ruining her life and stripping her of any hope for happiness. She would be stuck with Langley forever. He was far too young to be sticking his spoon into the wall any time soon.

He suppressed a stronger twinge of pain as he pictured Langley making love to her. It should be him in that bed! And if he had only controlled himself a little better, it would have been. Where had his finesse gone? Two years away from town should not have destroyed his technique. But he had behaved even worse this time than he had as a young man.

Logic finally began working again. Perhaps Langley had not forced her. His own vanity preferred that she was blindly walking into an intolerable situation, but that did her an injustice. She was smart enough to know Langley needed cash. Aside from his own warnings, she had recognized Graffington's penury before anyone else even suspected he was floundering in debt.

Yet he also hoped Langley had trapped her. Nicholas sighed. He did not want to admit that she preferred a man who was even younger than herself. He did not want to admit that her youthful love had been reduced to hatred and lust. And he never wanted to admit that her vow of eternal love had been what he had claimed—a passing *tendre*.

Her words had warmed him for years, though he had never consciously recalled them. But even as he had hurled her proffered heart back at her feet, he had grasped the words and tucked them safely away. When he had met her again, he had remembered that vow and expected her to fall into his arms. But she hadn't.

He climbed to his feet. There was nothing he could do now. Diana had made her choice. And she deserved the permanence of marriage. Hopefully, that was what Langley had offered, but even if she had only meant to use Langley to avoid his own attentions this week, she could never escape him now. Not if she wanted to remain in London. The Parkers and Harrisons would make sure that the wedding took place—soon. One of the servants was probably already riding to London for a special license. Backing out would destroy her.

Dusting himself off, he set his face in a proper social mask and headed for the house, ready to offer congratulations to the happy couple. Once he managed that, he would visit the village and drink himself into oblivion.

He should never have come to this house party. He knew betrothals were binding. If he had not tried to interfere with Eastbrook's, this would not have happened. He would not inquire into her true feelings, for discovering that she was trapped might tempt him into interfering yet again. And that could only lead to new trouble.

At least Sophia had part of her wish. Langley couldn't marry her now. She could drift through yet another Season unwed. He no longer cared. And perhaps by next year, she would have come to her senses and be ready to settle down.

For himself he had had enough of society for now. He could wind up his business within the week. Then he would embark on a tour of all his properties. By the time he returned to the Abbey, he would have decided what to do with his mother. Only then would he consider his own future.

## Chapter Nine

By the time Nicholas washed, changed clothes, and finished some correspondence, he was calm enough to face Langley and Diana. He found them in the drawing room, still accepting congratulations from house guests.

"Have you set the date?" Lady Weymouth was asking as he entered the room.

"Autumn," said Langley.

"We need to check with St. George's before we'll know the exact date," explained Diana, naming the most fashionable church in London. "But it will be during the Little Season. Will you be in town?"

Nicholas ignored the response, his eyes narrowing as he stared at Langley. Though the man was gazing rapturously at Diana, his eyes were cool. Was he seeing Diana, the educated hostess, fascinating conversationalist, and most seductive woman alive? Or was he seeing Lady Bounty's bottomless coffers?

Red mist obscured his vision. Diana deserved more than life with a dishonorable rogue. But he would not question her betrothal, he reminded himself strongly. He would play the role of gracious loser. Since he had never offered her more than a lusty affair, it should be easy. Only he knew how much he still wanted her.

But he couldn't stop his mind from asking questions. Why were they waiting until autumn? Langley needed money now. Was Diana hoping to wiggle out of the affair? His heart pounded. But she would never get away with it—especially in the country. She lived too close to the Parkers.

It was not his affair, he reminded himself again as Lady Weymouth left to change for dinner. He was a minor acquaintance of both bride and groom. Touring his estates would give his groin time to remember that. All he had to do was maintain his dignity for a few more days.

"I hear congratulations are in order," he said lightly.

"Thank you, my lord." Diana's voice was calm, but pain flashed deep in her eyes. It resonated in his chest, robbing him of breath. Raising her hand for a brief kiss covered his inability to speak.

"Langley," he managed finally, shaking hands with her intended even as the man's voice echoed in his mind. *You might want to cultivate Lady Forester. She's worth it.* Langley's mouth had been curled in a reminiscent smile that any libertine would recognize. And now his eyes looked at Diana with false affection. And hers hid pain—and determination.

*Oh, God, Diana! What have you gotten yourself into?* Had Langley taken a page from Lady Forester's book and set her up?

Excusing himself, he called for his horse and went in search of an inn with a well-stocked taproom.

Diana finally escaped the drawing room. Chloe must have heard by now. Everyone else had.

Nicholas's eyes had been the worst. Other guests had wished them well. Some believed the betrothal was planned; others suspected she had been caught in an indiscretion. But none really cared.

Except Nicholas. His eyes had bored into her head, searching for the truth. And he had found it. He had blinked when he registered that she did not want this match, and blinked again when he noted that Charles's enthusiasm was an act. Her only success had been convincing him that she would make the best of it. But she feared what he might do with his knowledge. And knowing that they could still communicate without words was terrifying.

She had never been sure whether the mind-reading was

real—especially after he repudiated her love. Over the years she had convinced herself that it had been imagination—a few coincidences born of similar tastes coupled with the deliberate deceit he had employed to seduce her. Now she had to wonder.

They shared no experiences these days. Not even friendship. They had not seen or heard from each other in ten years. Yet he had looked into her mind and been furious at what he found. And hurt.

She pushed that impression aside. Later. For now she had to concentrate on Chloe.

What a mess! If it had been difficult to help Chloe and Charles before, it was worse now that they had two betrothals to undo. She would release Charles as soon as possible, of course, but how were they to escape with everyone's reputation intact?

"How could you?" demanded Chloe, admitting Diana to her room. Her eyes were puffy from the tears that still rolled down her cheeks. "Traitor! Did you plan this so you could have him yourself?"

"That is utter nonsense. I don't want him."

"Then why are you now betrothed to him?" Her voice cracked.

"I could not refuse without destroying my reputation. Is that what you want?"

"So you will wed a man you don't love just to keep up appearances. For heaven's sake, you're nearly thirty! How could Charles even consider marrying someone older than he is?"

"That is quite enough, Chloe," snapped Diana, tamping down her own anger with difficulty. "Sit down. This is as much your fault as anyone's. Instead of wasting time spewing insults, why don't you pull yourself together so we can figure out what to do?"

"*My* fault?" Shock dried her tears.

"In part. I warned you to stay away from Charles this week. You knew what would happen if your parents suspected your intentions. You chose to ignore that warning and allow a moment of pleasure to jeopardize your future. Now we have a bigger imbroglio on our hands than before. You are lucky it is no worse."

Chloe sighed. "What happened?"

Diana sat on the couch. "As near as I can figure, Lady Sophia spotted you and Charles in the folly. She is a very priggish high-stickler who wouldn't dream of ignoring anything she considers improper. This is not the first time she has exposed someone's indiscretions." Nor was it the first time she had precipitated a betrothal. At least one scheming fortune hunter had already used her to trap a lord into marriage—not that Sophia would ever admit to being a pawn for an unscrupulous, greedy mushroom. But she had appointed herself guardian of public morality, and no voices to the contrary would dissuade her.

"So she told my parents."

"Of course not. Carrying tales is bad *ton*. Her code of conduct is far too rigid to allow such gauche behavior. She simply led them to the folly so they could discover your sins for themselves. If you had not made your escape before they arrived, you would now be meeting George in church. And don't think you could have escaped. Your parents would have locked you up under guard until the license arrived."

Chloe shuddered.

"Charles was not so lucky. He made the mistake of pausing to thank me. Thus your parents and Lady Sophia found us together. If we had not immediately announced a betrothal, I would have been ruined. He would have been forgiven, of course, for rakes are expected to seduce widows. I can only be thankful that he is gentlemanly enough to protect me." His response had not been quite that altruistic, of course. Confirming his rakish reputation would never win the Parkers' approval.

"So he will marry you, which leaves me no choice but to wed George." New tears trickled down Chloe's cheeks.

"Fiddle-faddle. I have no intention of wedding anyone. If we cannot find an acceptable way to dissolve both these betrothals, you and Charles can elope. Being jilted will harm me less than it would an innocent. I can cope with being thought fast, though it would be better if I didn't have to. A temporary betrothal will allow the immediate scandal to die. By the time you and Charles sail, most people will have left London. Next Season's scandals will push memory of this aside."

She did not address the problem of country memories. The Parkers would not let her perfidy rest—they would know that she had encouraged Chloe and Charles. Since their estate ran with hers, she would have to live with their animosity for a long time.

Chloe dried her tears and blew her nose. "I should have known you would not abandon me. Few people would risk their place in society for a relative, let alone a neighbor, but you have always helped me."

"Enough." Embarrassed, she made her voice brisker. "This may actually be a blessing. Since Charles is tied to me—he is quite good at acting the besotted suitor, by the way, so don't be shocked by his demeanor—you will be able to speak with him in company. He is no longer a threat, so your parents should not object. Just remember to control your face and keep the meetings brief. You must continue spending time with George, but this gives us time to convince everyone that you and he are not suited. Work on him and your parents. Forget the Weymouths. They are not in a position to release you, and they don't really care whom he weds. Once we break your betrothal, I will gracefully step aside so you and Charles can be together."

Leaving Chloe to erase all signs of tears, Diana retired to her room to prepare for dinner. Going into battle could not be more nerve-racking.

She and Charles were again the focus of attention in the drawing room. But this would be the last time. By morning their sudden betrothal would be old news. Talk would shift to tomorrow's christening and grand ball.

This time they separated, speaking individually with the other guests. Chloe and the Parkers arrived. When Chloe approached Charles to apparently offer her congratulations, her parents showed no concern. But when she remained with

Charles for a full five minutes, a line appeared in Lady Parker's forehead.

"That's long enough for now," murmured Diana, joining the couple. "Congratulate me, Chloe. Your mother is watching."

"Is she upset?" She complied.

"Just anxious. Be very careful. If you show undue interest in each other, this whole scheme could fall apart. Talk to George, Chloe. Charles, look like you're glad to see me." His face had fallen into a frown.

He turned his adoring admiration in her direction, but his eyes were looking at Chloe.

"Clever," Diana murmured. No one else could see his eyes. "Just don't outsmart yourself."

"Relax," Charles advised her once Chloe had left. "You look like you are ready to swoon."

"I will be fine. After tonight, people won't watch so closely."

He nodded, escorting her to dinner. And she did relax—as soon as she confirmed that Nicholas was absent. Curse the man. He affected her even when he wasn't there.

Nicholas leaned against the wall of Harrison's ballroom and let his gaze wander over the other guests. Thank God he could return to London in the morning.

He had gotten just as drunk as he had intended last night—and had paid for it with a pounding head and churning stomach. He had forgotten just how rotten the aftermath always felt. Even Stubbs's magic elixir hadn't done much good. Thus the morning's christening had seemed interminable. He had skipped the drawing room afterward, choosing to sleep until he felt slightly more human. But he was unable to skip the ball without insulting his host.

So here he was. Harrison had greeted him, so his presence had been duly noted. He would prop up this wall for another set or two, then leave.

Diana and Langley stepped into the first set together. That gaze of false adoration was looking a trifle pinched.

Nicholas swore. Time to go. But the door was across the room. Lady Bankleigh accosted him, then Lord Warfarin, and Mrs. Beasley.

Two sets later he led Diana out for a waltz.

Why was he doing this? Her touch raised heat far more intense than the last time they had waltzed. But only because he acknowledged his lust, he assured himself. He couldn't help but react when he wanted her so badly.

But he would never have her now. And not just because custom put matrons off limits until they had produced an heir. He had done some serious thinking while drowning himself in wine. Diana's loyalty was one of her attractions, but it would prevent her from even considering infidelity. So she was lost to him.

Accepting that had been bad enough, but his reflections had been brutally honest for once. Until now his entire life had been sordid. He had used people for years—always for selfish purposes. While it was true that he had never accepted a wager his opponent couldn't afford to lose, he had often misled men into placing bets—and had taken advantage of inebriation more than once. He had seduced any number of women merely for the sport of it. But the most ignoble act of all had been trying to seduce Diana.

He couldn't get that flash of pain out of his mind. She did not want this marriage, but she would make the best of it, turning all her warmth, her caring, and her loyalty on Langley. Never mind that the man didn't deserve it and wouldn't appreciate it. He would continue living as before, with mistresses and affairs at every turn. But she would smile and make the best of it.

And he would have to bite his tongue at every insult, swallowing the knowledge that it was all his fault.

So why was he torturing himself even more by dancing with her? And why had he chosen a waltz? *Idiot!* He should have asked for an innocuous country dance or a sprightly reel. Holding her was weakening his control. Again.

"Who will be the guests of honor at your next *soirée*?" he asked, more to divert his attention from her narrow waist and that mindnumbing lilac perfume than because he was interested. And because she had not spoken a word to him since yesterday afternoon. Even when he had asked her to dance, she had merely shrugged and accepted his arm.

"Thornton, the poet." Her secretive smile sent new heat racing through his body.

But this time, he easily ignored it. "Talk about a coup! People have wanted to meet the man for ten years. His latest book was exceptional."

"I know."

"So how did you convince the elusive Thornton to appear in public?"

"I didn't." Again she flashed that cat-in-the-creampot smile. "He decided it was time to reveal his identity."

His jaw dropped. "Thornton is a pen name." It was not a question. His mind raced at the implications.

She nodded.

"Your *soirée* will be overrun once word of this gets out."

"Actually, this will not be one of my regular *soirées*. It's invitation only." She pursed her lips. "I'll send you one."

He shuddered. Those pursed lips recalled every one of their kisses—especially those by the stream. "Thank you." Somehow he kept his voice level.

"He's bringing his illustrator," she added.

"Merriweather?"

She nodded.

"Another recluse. I've got every one of the man's prints and two of his oils. He's remarkable."

"You will enjoy an introduction, then." Again she flashed that secretive smile. "Are you more interested in meeting the poet or the artist?"

"That's difficult to say. They are both extraordinary. I've heard Thornton criticized for making readers uncomfortable, but I cannot agree."

"That sounds like something Lady Catkin would say."

"It was." He swung her into a complex series of turns. "Perceptive of you."

"Hardly. She does not like baring her emotions—you have noted that her theatrics are quite contrived, I presume?"

He nodded.

"She hides her real self behind a flamboyant shell, but Thornton wrests emotional control from his readers. The poetry is as elemental as the forces he describes, reaching deep inside to pull out pain, sorrow, wonder, or life-affirming exuberance. One's reaction is both powerful and spontaneous."

"But other poets draw an emotional response, too," he protested.

"Certainly, but not in the same way. Melancholy, appreciation, affection—they lack that intense, visceral quality that Thornton taps. Even strong reactions are usually on behalf of the characters rather than oneself. I nearly swooned from laughing at an excerpt from Byron's *Don Juan* last month. He was so incredibly absurd. But laughing at another's foibles is far different than expressing joy on one's own behalf."

He frowned. "*Don Juan?* I haven't seen that one."

"Not surprising. He hasn't finished it, but Shelley brought a page to one of my *soirées*. He met Byron in Geneva last year." She bestowed one more smile as the music drew to a close.

He watched her take the floor with Lord Harrison, then slipped out of the ballroom. That smile bothered him—as if she was enjoying a huge joke. But he pushed the feeling aside. Her observations were remarkable—and matched many of his own. He couldn't remember the last time he had enjoyed a conversation more. He should have returned to town after Christmas. Her *soirées* would have been far more entertaining than listening to his mother's complaints and his uncles' quarrels. Stimulating discussion made life enjoyable—a lesson he had learned from Bounty. As had Diana.

How the devil had she gotten Thornton for her *soirée?* The man had been an enigma for years. Absolutely nothing was known of him beyond his desire for privacy. He had never even heard a suggestion that Thornton might be a pseudonym.

He grinned as he helped himself to a glass of wine from the refreshment room, then wandered toward the main block of the Court.

Lady Debenham would be furious when she heard that Diana would hold the gathering of the Season. She had long prided herself on being the most talked-about hostess in town. Now she would not only lose that distinction, but she would lose it to an intellectual *soirée*. Even people who eschewed reading bought Thornton's books. He was the most celebrated poet in the country—doubly true now that Byron had sacrificed his fame on the altar of scandal. Pride at Diana's achievement warmed his heart.

Pausing in an alcove to gaze over the moonlit gardens, he shook his head. Not even Lady Beatrice, the best-informed gossip in town, had heard about Diana's coup—which could only mean that she had not yet sent out the invitations. Had she shared her plans with him first?

The idea started a treacherous glow in his more private regions. To distract himself, he tried to guess Thornton's real name. He would bet his last shilling that the man was part of the *ton*. Why else would he hide his identity?

Ten minutes later, his only progress was to decide that Thornton was more likely a government leader than a society figure. His thoughts were interrupted by voices in the hall— Lord and Lady Bankleigh, Sophia's parents.

"Of course Langley will approve Charles's betrothal," snapped Lord Bankleigh. "All he wanted was to get the lad's hand out of the family purse. Lady Bounty is a much better match than Sophia."

"How can you say that?" demanded his wife. "She may have married an earl, but her father was merely a baronet."

"Easily. Her fortune is ten times Sophia's dowry. Her estate is larger, and she owns that town house. Charles has always preferred lighthearted women and London pastimes. Sophia is sober, straight-laced, and prefers living in the country. You must know that I never seriously expected an offer from him. Langley's pressure pushed him into choosing a wife, but he would have suffocated under Sophia's implacable propriety. She is not a comfortable chit to live with, and won't be until she learns the art of compromise."

Lady Bankleigh gasped. "I went along with you, Sheridan, because you convinced me that presenting a united front was important. But I would never have done so had I known that you were proposing a union you knew she would despise."

"Come now, Harriet, it would have served nicely." He sighed. "Now I must find her another suitor. Unless she weds this Season, she will be relegated to the shelf. I won't allow her to become a spinster. The ignominy would be intolerable. People are already speculating what is wrong with us that we have been unable to find a match for the chit. Nor will you discuss this with her. It is your mollycoddling that has encouraged her excessive particularity. I hope to find a new alternative by next week. That will leave her ample time to choose her own candidate if she does not care for mine. You will remind her that Charles's betrothal changes nothing. She will wed."

They retraced their steps toward the ballroom.

Nicholas sighed.

There went his plans to tour his estates. Diana's *soirée* would have kept him in town a few days longer—nothing would keep him away from that one—but now it looked like he would be stuck there for the rest of the Season.

Sophia must take the same hard look at reality as he had done last night. Eastbrook was unavailable. Bankleigh was going to find the worst alternative he could, so she must consider other suitors. The man's determination was obvious. As was his thinking. He wanted to give her a say in her future, but she had to make a decision.

Even Sophia should be able to see that Eastbrook and Miss Parker were rapidly building rapport. Whatever uncertainties had plagued them earlier, they were now comfortable together and spent much of their time in each other's company. He saw no evidence of love, but acceptance was there.

\* \* \*

Diana relaxed when Nicholas abandoned the ballroom. Talking to him was always taxing—though she had enjoyed this last conversation immensely. But knowing that he could see past her chosen facade made him dangerous. She had managed to mask her reactions this time, but it had been difficult.

His touch had swirled heat through her body, recalling their meeting by the stream. The dizzying motion of the dance had intensified her lightheadedness. Thank heaven he had decided to talk, or she might have melted.

But he was gone. And he would not return. She didn't wonder how she knew that. She just did.

So she was free to work on George.

She found him in the refreshment room. "Both Chloe and I are counting the days until your marriage," she said after the ritual exchange of greetings. "She longs for the freedom to pay morning calls on her own friends. Lady Parker chooses to visit only the most staid dowagers."

He grunted.

"The poor girl is bored to tears by the endless gossip in such drawing rooms. She prefers to discuss ideas, which is why her mother's restrictions are so onerous. She can participate in few activities of interest."

"What could she possible want to do that they would forbid?" His glare was quite off-putting.

But she merely smiled. "Attend my *soirées*, for one. Shelley was featured last month. He is quite a remarkable young poet. Chloe was devastated at missing him."

"Absurd. She's no business filling her mind with such tripe."

"His odes are charming," she countered. "And he is quite harmless—there are some men I wouldn't dream of introducing to a young girl; but Shelley dotes on his wife. The *soirées* are dedicated to civilized conversation, so there is no risk that she might fall into bad company."

Again he glared.

"If only you would speak to the Parkers. Surely they would allow you to escort her to next week's gathering. She is anxious to see His Grace of Wellington and Lord Castlereagh. You will also wish to meet them. Such connections will be indispensable once you assume your father's honors."

"You overstep yourself, Lady Bounty. I've no interest in politics and no intention of allowing a credulous young girl near a man like Wellington. He is worse than a flirt. Nor will I condone your insidious influence. Once we retire to the country, you will be barred from further meddling."

"Do not blame me for Chloe's character. She will be bored to tears without intelligent company."

"Her current fits have nothing to do with character. She is merely mimicking a disreputable neighbor. Since girls invariably mature into copies of their mothers, you waste your time trying to corrupt her, Lady Bounty. Fortunately, Lord Parker agrees that bringing her to town was a serious mistake. The first banns will be called on Sunday."

Having shocked her into silence, he turned on his heel and stalked away.

# Chapter Ten

A week later, Diana and Charles welcomed guests to her special *soirée*. They had become good friends since their betrothal, though neither felt the tiniest spark of anything more. His intelligence, interests, and manner reminded her of Nicholas. What he lacked was the overpowering masculinity that never let her relax. He also approached his poverty differently, and he could befriend a lady without trying to seduce her.

Chloe was resigned to watching Charles escort Diana. The betrothal had produced several benefits, one of which was the ease with which the lovers could now meet at Diana's house. And the masquerade would soon end. Charles had a firm offer from the East India Company and planned to press for Chloe's hand as soon as he knew his departure date.

Diana had abandoned hope of an honorable resolution. The Parkers were blind fools, and George was worse. He passed off Chloe's most frivolous statements as youthful exuberance or excitement over their upcoming marriage, believing that she would become sober, quiet, and obedient the moment they left town. And his success in rescheduling the wedding increased the pressure on everyone.

Thank heavens he had told her about the new date. She had broken the news to Chloe that same night, throwing the girl into hysterics. Fortunately, the Parkers did not observe that. By the time they brought the subject up themselves—after returning to London—Chloe had been able to respond with equanimity.

The three of them had been discussing alternatives ever

since, but until Charles received his orders, they could make no real plans. Diana hoped it was soon. Chloe's wedding was barely three weeks off. The closer they came to the date, the bigger the scandal would be for canceling—and the more impact it would have on Charles's position with the Company. Announcing a London wedding also made it impossible to change grooms quietly. Had Lady Sophia hinted at Chloe's liaison? That might explain the Parkers' capitulation.

But this was not the time to be fretting over Chloe, Diana reminded herself, turning to greet the latest arrivals. Word of her coup had swept Mayfair within an hour of dispatching the invitations. Society had talked of little else for a week. She had been approached in dozens of ways by people wanting to be included on the guest list, but she had refused, citing space and Thornton's desire to keep the crowd small. Which wasn't exactly true. They both knew that he would be mobbed the moment he left her house. Even those who usually derided bluestockings waited with bated breath to see him.

She suppressed a grin. Thornton loved crowds and often courted attention. She had heard outrageous tales from his younger days. Now he was deliberately building the suspense, focusing attention where he wanted it. There were aspects of his career he wished to hide, so he was carefully orchestrating his disclosures so no one would suspect that he hid further secrets. Shock had a way of numbing thought. By the time it wore off, his identity would be old news, supplanted by the next scandal, and people would think no more about it.

"You have surpassed yourself," said Nicholas, reaching the head of the line. "There has not been a more coveted invitation in years. Why did you issue so few?"

"You, too? We wished to avoid a squeeze," she said lightly.

"Inside, at least." The square was already filling with people who hoped to be the first to carry the news elsewhere—if other gatherings had anyone in attendance.

"Not my doing." She smiled.

"Sly. Very sly. I always suspected you were."

Offering Langley a cool smile, he joined the other guests in the drawing room. His eye swept the gathering, intrigued by the people she had gathered. It was not the selection he had expected. Was that a clue to Thornton's identity?

He had made no progress in his personal quest to unravel the mystery. Every name that seemed possible had equally strong arguments against it. But he had eliminated all the known intellectuals. None of them had a reason to remain secretive. He had also reluctantly decided that government leaders were out. If Thornton had remained hidden to protect a political career, he would not be here tonight. No one who had recently retired from government service seemed likely.

Which had returned his thoughts to society figures. Who, of the forty-odd people gathered, might be Thornton?

The crowd included several poets and writers, two well-known artists, and the core of regulars from Diana's weekly *soirées*. None of them seemed reasonable candidates.

Lady Chartley had an oddly shuttered expression on her face. She was another of London's intellectual hostesses, whose *soirées* rivaled Diana's. Was Thornton a female? It was the one possibility he had not yet considered. He reviewed his favorite Thornton poems. Some, especially the recent ones, seemed softer than he would expect from a man. But he couldn't imagine Lady Chartley writing them. He had heard some of her poetry, and it bore no resemblance to Thornton's. Besides, revealing a female identity would hurt Thornton's popularity. So Lady Chartley's expression probably hid pique that Diana, and not she, was hosting this affair.

What about the Earl of Hartleigh? He pondered the man and his wife briefly before dismissing them. Hartleigh was too busy with government business to write, and his wife was too involved with her charities.

The Hartleighs joined their friends, Lord and Lady Blackthorn. Now there was a surprise. Nicholas had not expected to encounter them here. Before his marriage, Blackthorn had been an outcast, suspected of crimes ranging from seduction to murder. His wife had proven the charges false, but they still avoided many social functions. And Blackthorn was no poet. He was now one of the more vocal leaders of the reform movement. But what about Lady Blackthorn?

He frowned. That was possible. Exposing a woman's success in a man's business might be calculated to bolster her husband's claim that women should have more control over their own lives. But he doubted she was old enough to be Thornton. She couldn't have been more than eighteen when the first book was published. Besides, he had always detected an underlying sensuality in Thornton's work, though the subjects dealt solely with the grandeur of nature. That alone cast doubt that they were written by a woman.

He sighed. This was pointless. But he couldn't seem to help himself. And others were doing the same thing. Eyes ceaselessly scanned the room, trying to identify Thornton. Some even rested briefly on him.

He absently accepted a glass from a footman, then joined Justin. They had hardly finished greetings when a gasp drew his eyes to the door.

Lord and Lady Bridgeport were entering. Nicholas carefully swallowed his wine. The earl's reputation as a rake had far surpassed his own until the man's unexpected marriage five years earlier.

Justin nudged him. "Why did Lady Bounty invite him? He hasn't a thought in his head beyond his wife and sporting."

"I suspect it was the countess who was invited. I've run across her a few times. She is amazingly well-read and loves Thornton's poetry."

"Ah. So who do you think is our elusive poet?"

"I've narrowed the field to you and Lady Blackthorn." He grinned when Justin choked. "Not you, I take it. In truth, I've no idea, but I expect you are more interested in meeting Merriweather."

"True. Ackermann's has a new set of his prints—village craftsmen. Marvelous pieces. He makes the most ordinary workers look like artists. The weaver is a wonder, evoking almost mythological magic."

Nicholas nodded, but didn't mention that he also owned the set. His own favorites were the blacksmith and the baker. Somehow Merriweather had conveyed the blistering heat of forge and oven without any of the usual gimmicks.

Justin sighed. "I almost got one of his oils yesterday—powerful painting of the Cornish coast. But it had already sold."

"Too bad." It was on its way to the Abbey, with orders to hang it in the library in place of his uncle's favorite horse.

He let Justin's comments wash over him as he again scanned the crowd. There wasn't a single guest he didn't know. But the poet and artist might not have arrived yet, he admitted, directing Justin's attention away from Merriweather's art with a question about his aunt's health.

Giving up on his guessing game, he turned his eyes to Diana and Langley. He had had to work hard to remain aloof during that brief greeting. Langley's attentions to Diana hurt. Much as he hated to admit it, they shared a rapport that he had not expected, and a very genuine affection. Whatever had precipitated this betrothal no longer bothered them.

Perhaps he had been wrong, he admitted as Diana laughed at something Langley murmured in her ear. And that was good. He wanted her to be happy. If Langley cared, then he would return her loyalty. God knew she harbored enough passion to keep any man from straying.

Memories jostled for attention, blinding him to the room. He could not rid himself of guilt—for his youthful cruelty, for his recent attempts to seduce her, for any number of gaffes that might have forced her into Langley's arms.

Not until Justin jostled him did he set aside his bitter soulsearching.

Diana was poised to make the expected introduction. Most of the guests looked around in surprise. No strangers had arrived. Unless Thornton and his illustrator were waiting in another room, they were already here.

Nicholas was one of the few who kept his eyes turned to Diana. She was beautiful this evening, her slim figure draped in green silk. Emeralds sparkled at ears and throat. The curve of her mouth sent tremors into his hands. He should not have come. Lust still burned—hotter than ever.

"My friends," Diana began, seeming to look straight into his eyes. "You all know why we are here. As lovers of poetry and art, we have long debated why Thornton insisted on anonymity. Many of you have wished to tell him how much you enjoy his work. Others have expressed awe that Merriweather's illustrations so perfectly capture the essence of his poetry. Now is your chance to be heard. Please join me in welcoming Mr. Thornton and M. E. Merriweather."

She held out her hands. A collective gasp filled the room when the Earl and Countess of Bridgeport joined her. The earl's face had reddened, but Nicholas lost sight of them as the crowed surged forward, the babble of voices nearly deafening.

"Bridgeport?" he stammered, turning to Justin.

Justin gave his head a quick shake as if to realign his brain. "Unbelievable! And Lady Bridgeport? I thought you were joking when you suggested a female."

"But Bridgeport? My God! I've known him since Eton. Not well, admittedly, as he is several years older, but I would never have pegged him as an intellectual. Between sports and women, he filled every hour."

"Perhaps not," said Justin slowly. "Raintree once complained that life was unfair, for he could not function on less than nine hours of sleep, while Bridgeport needed only three or four."

Nicholas frowned, adding numbers in his head. If that was true, then even at the height of Bridgeport's rakehell years, he had probably spent four hours a day writing.

He let out a long breath. Diana had escaped the mob around Bridgeport.

"Quite a shock," he said, moving to her side. "Congratulations. Lady Beatrice will gnash her teeth when she hears."

She grinned. "She knows by now. She only lives two doors away. My butler was listening, and one of her footmen has been loitering around my servants' entrance all evening." She laughed. "Lady Beatrice always gives generous vails for information. Norton should be quite satisfied with the evening."

"So why did Bridgeport decide that you should have the honor of revealing his secret pastime?"

"Writing is far more than a pastime for him," she said seriously. "Mark has two great loves—his family and his work." She stared into his eyes and must have seen his objection even before he formed the words. "His public pursuits kept him fit, but they were never more than a cloak for his real life. I've known him for ten years—one of his estates adjoined Bounty's seat—and I've known of his writing since his marriage. He ceased caring about secrecy several years ago, but maintained his silence until he was sure that Elaine would not suffer from the exposure."

"She is a formidable talent."

"With an even more formidable intelligence. Just like Mark. Neither of them forgets anything. They can quote entire books and repeat conversations from months past. But she is still female."

He shook his head, awed by such mental power, but he knew what she meant. Bridgeport must have decided his clout was strong enough to keep the publishers from retaliating. Women never got the prestigious illustration jobs and were rarely paid more than a pittance.

"She was another example I could have cited during our little debate that day."

"On the abilities of women." He shook his head. "Another point to you. Is that why you invited me?"

"In part. And because you admire her work." *And because you meant to leave town.*

He could almost hear the words. Mind-reading again. No one knew of those plans, which had since been put on hold. He suppressed a shiver. But there was no point in belaboring the subject. "Have you and Langley set a date yet?"

"I've been too busy setting up this evening to begin arrangements, but sometime next autumn."

"You are content?" He probed her eyes, though he could not have said what he was looking for.

"Of course. As is Charles. All our plans are falling into place." She seemed puzzled by his interest, but he detected no fear and no unhappiness.

"I suspected that you were being coerced," he explained.

"No one will ever force me down a path not of my choosing, my lord. And you have no right to judge me in any case. I refused your offer and would have done so again."

"I would not have made it again," he lied, though the moment the words left his tongue, he knew that he spoke the truth. She deserved far more than life as a man's mistress—even his. "I admire your integrity—and your loyalty. It is something I should have recognized sooner. Langley offered you more than I ever have. I can hardly blame you for accepting."

"No, you cannot. I can only rejoice that you recognize my character at last."

Nodding briskly, he went to meet Lady Bridgeport. Would anything be different if he had recognized it earlier? Pain had again flashed in her eyes. So it must be him that was causing it. That damned proposition. Offering her a post as his mistress had insulted her. As well it should.

News that Bridgeport was Thornton echoed from every drawing room and club in London, overshadowing even the most scandalous gossip. Speculation was rampant that he used other aliases. Recalling Diana's comment on Bridgeport's intelligence, Nicholas was unsurprised to learn that the man's political commentary appeared in several highly respected newspapers and his well-reasoned arguments favoring reform showed up in others.

His own interest in the tale rapidly waned, pushed aside by renewed pressure from his mother. She was determined to see him wed, and had blatantly enlisted Lady Hardesty's help.

The matchmaker pestered him until he wanted to scream. He was trying to find a suitor for Sophia, but every time he spoke to a gentleman, Lady Hardesty would appear with one of her brainless protégées in tow. More than once, he dragged Diana into a set just to escape the woman. Dealing with unfulfilled lust was better than being trapped into marriage.

"Who are you avoiding this time?" she asked at the Barkley ball. It was the second set he had claimed that evening.

"Miss Hardcastle. She is even more determined than Lady Hortense. Why won't they leave me alone?"

"Society knows you need a wife. Despite all your protests, you are here. Since you have decided to frequent the Marriage Mart rounds, you cannot blame people for assuming that you are shopping. Either admit the truth or leave town."

The dance separated them.

But despite the dangers he ran, he couldn't leave, he realized as he smiled at his new partner. Sophia was stubbornly ignoring all suitors. She refused to believe that her father was serious, spending much of her time pining for Eastbrook. Every day her social mask came closer to cracking. She often sought Nicholas out, railing at fate and grieving over a man she had never had. But even that outlet failed to relieve much pressure. And pointing out that Eastbrook was so anxious to wed Miss Parker that he had moved up his wedding date did no good.

"Charles mentioned that wagers are running ten to one in favor of you being leg-shackled by summer," said Diana when the dance again brought them together. "No one agrees on who will win with your hand, but at least half the *ton* expects you to be compromised." She raised her brows. "Watch your back."

"You sound concerned." But he knew she was right. The Season had passed the midpoint. Girls who had no serious suitors were growing desperate. Talking about it made his skin crawl worse than usual.

"I dislike force."

"You wouldn't like my mother, then." He met her eyes. "I'm not enamored of her myself."

"Because she is pushing you to marry?"

"Not entirely. I only recently discovered that many of my

father's excesses—including the crimes that got him banished to the country—resulted from my mother's pressure to rebuild his fortune."

"Not an uncommon story."

"Now she's trying to run my life."

"But you have more backbone than your father." She smiled.

The dance separated them. He certainly didn't feel like he had a backbone. He felt more like a leaf caught in a breeze, batted about by events, with little control of his destiny.

Yet Diana looked into his eyes and saw strength. Why? He had no answers. And despite their growing friendship, he could hardly ask her. She was just beginning to relax with him. He dared do nothing to change that.

"Is Bridgeport sorry he revealed himself?" he asked when they came together again, uncomfortable with how personal their conversation had gotten.

"He expected a furor, but it is only a nine-days wonder. Already it is blowing over as people speculate on why Heflin is limping." The baron had arrived in town two days earlier but refused to discuss his injury. "Bridgeport is satisfied. There will be no more questions, for people understand that his body of work is larger than most writers manage, even without the additional duties of his title and position."

"My God! He's also—"

Her eyes stopped his words, but he had already made the connection—and saw verification in Diana's face. Merriweather had illustrated other volumes over the years, one of them a hilarious—and exceedingly libelous—parody of society written by the unknown Mr. Anstey, which must be another of Bridgeport's pseudonyms. He had found himself in it, though his fictional counterpart was too funny to take offense. But others would not be so gracious, particularly those whose foibles included greed or brutality. Or those who were stupid, unscrupulous, or rude.

"The man has talent," he admitted with a shake of his head.

"That he does."

The set ended, putting him again at the mercy of matchmaking mamas and Lady Hardesty. Succumbing to prudence—or cowardice, if he were being honest—he left. He couldn't use Diana as a shield again this night without scandal.

Diana danced the next waltz with Charles, then sent him off for an innocuous country set with Chloe. Lady Parker still looked askance on that connection, but had not forbidden it. Yet Diana fretted. How much longer could those two stand the pretense. Their faces came closer to displaying smoldering passion every day. Already she could see it in their eyes. It was only a matter of time before Lady Parker did.

"How could you accept that fribble when Woodvale was available?" demanded Lady Hardesty, sneaking up behind her.

"But he's not available." She looked Harry's goddaughter squarely in her fifty-year-old eyes. "Marriage is entirely his mother's idea. He is not interested."

"No man is. But he has a duty to his title. And whatever his protests, he is here. I am disappointed in you, Diana. You should have grabbed him while you could."

"He cared nothing for me," she said firmly. "But I would not have accepted an offer from him in any case. He is a libertine without heart or remorse."

"He is intelligent, well-read, and enjoys a lively discussion," countered Lady Hardesty.

"He is a fortune hunter despite his recent inheritance."

"And Langley isn't?" Her disbelief was plain.

"Not at all. Like most young men, he has enjoyed London. But he has a core of sober responsibility. Once he decided to settle down, he lost all interest in youthful pursuits. Have you heard of a single liaison—or even a wager—in the last month?"

Lady Hardesty pursed her lips. "I cannot recall any."

"Precisely. Not since he fell in love. He is the most loyal man of my acquaintance." She bit off further words lest she give Charles and Chloe away. The pretense was wearing thin on her as well, but she must maintain her charade of adoration until they were safely wed.

"I am more interested in you, Diana. You don't love Langley. I've seen the way you look at Woodvale—and the way he looks at you, especially when he thinks no one is watching. You belong together."

"Stuff and nonsense!" The woman was too astute, she admitted, suppressing the shudder of lust that hit her whenever she caught Nicholas's eye—or even though of him. But physical attraction wasn't enough, and he was incapable of offering more. She had been serious about his lack of heart. "I have chosen my path. We will not speak of this again."

*Stupid!* she chided herself as Lady Hardesty walked away. That last comment had all but shouted that the woman was right. The connection with Nicholas remained, not that it would do her any good. He had claimed that he no longer wanted her as a mistress, but that would not hold true when she was again free. Somehow, she must find the courage to refuse him one more time.

Nicholas followed Sophia out of the Cunningham ballroom—to keep her out of trouble, he insisted, though he knew it was merely a ploy to avoid Lady Hardesty. His cowardice annoyed him. Others had noticed his maneuvers, shooting his reputation all to hell.

Tonight was no exception. Thrice he had ducked the woman's candidates, but his face had revealed every bit of his disgust. Blue-devils plagued him worse every day, growing so bad this afternoon that he had tried to banish them with a bottle of brandy. But all he had accomplished was losing control of his social mask and setting his ears to buzzing.

Now he had a new problem in the form of Sophia. She had clearly reached a crisis point. Her smile was false. Her melancholy had gotten so bad that people were noticing—and speculating on the cause. Was her brooding undermining her sense? He hoped she was not going to throw herself at Eastbrook. The man would be appalled. Getting caught alone together would destroy her credit and make her a laughingstock, but it would do nothing to dissolve his betrothal.

But his fears proved groundless. She ducked into an empty antechamber.

"Not enjoying the ball?" he asked, quietly locking the door so they would not be interrupted. Too many people were determined to catch him alone with a lady.

"Hardly." Tears glittered in her eyes. She bit her lip, finally bursting into speech. "Everyone will be miserable, and it's all my fault!"

"Suppose you define *everyone*, then tell me what you did to make them miserable," he said gently.

"George. Miss Parker. Charles. Lady Bounty." The tears ran down her cheeks unchecked. "I know you think I'm obsessed, but George can never be happy with Miss Parker. He is already irritated at her unrelenting frivolity. And I know that she can never be happy with him. She loves Charles."

What? There was not the slightest hint that the girl cared for Langley. She'd only danced with him a few times—all since his betrothal. And she was close to Diana, which explained that. "Did she tell you she loved the man?"

"No, but they were embracing in the folly at Harrison Court. By the time I fetched the Parkers, she was gone and he was forced to announce a betrothal to Lady Bounty. Now Miss Parker will never let George go!"

He frowned. He did not for a moment believe that either Langley or Diana was unhappy with their betrothal. They were too relaxed together—too intimate. He had watched them since returning to town. The truth was obvious.

So what had Langley and Miss Parker been doing in the folly? he wondered dizzily. Had Sophia asked Charles to seduce the girl after he himself had refused? It seemed likely. Her admission that she had fetched the Parkers made it more so. But it hadn't worked.

Langley had been paying court to Diana for weeks. If she had appeared in the folly, he would have immediately abandoned Miss Parker. But this revived all his questions about Langley's motives. Perhaps the man was a better actor than he had thought. Was he only after Diana's fortune?

Ice coiled in his stomach.

He was overreacting. No tales linked him with any ladies in recent weeks. And he had been most attentive. No one could maintain that charade day after day under eyes as keen as his.

So Sophia must be reviving her failed plan, hoping to pressure him into separating Eastbrook from Miss Parker. If she could convince him that Miss Parker loved Langley, then he would help her end Eastbrook's betrothal.

She had failed again. Aside from deducing her plot, he had sworn off meddling. Every time he stooped to dishonor, Diana suffered. He was finished.

"But I am well served for my plot," wailed Sophia, interrupting his thoughts, but confirming that she had talked Langley into helping her. "Papa has a new offer for my hand. If I do not accept someone this Season, he will give me to Lord Griswold."

"I do not know the gentleman."

She sniffed. "He is a baron who lives about ten miles from our estate. He is all of fifty, has rotten teeth, and smells. He jumped at Papa's offer, though, for he is in dire need of cash and he has no heir. His former wife left him with three young daughters," she added, cringing.

"He sounds awful," he agreed. "You had best make a determined effort to find someone eligible."

"Never. Honorable men will not want me, knowing I love another—I could never hide such a thing. Only men like Griswold will not care. Talk to Papa, Nicholas. Surely you can make him understand. I must move to my own estate. I can find an acceptable companion. Surely he cannot hate me enough to force such a match."

"He can, and will," he said, shaking his head. Bankleigh might not hate his daughter, but he would not renege on his sworn word. "In your own interest, you must pick a husband, Sophia. At least half a dozen sober-minded gentleman would offer if you gave them any encouragement."

"Hah!"

"It's true. Lord Harold Spencer would take you in a trice. As would Sir Richard Fotheringay, Lord Bankhead, Lawrence Stoverson, Robert Macefield, John Pringle—"

"But I don't want them," she interrupted him, new tears escaping her eyes. "I want George. Or no one."

"Stubborn, aren't you. Which is why you are in this fix."

"Talk to him," she begged again.

"It would do no good—as well you know. You have pushed him too far to expect him to change his mind now. Either you compromise, or you will wind up with Griswold."

"I can't! I can't! I will throw myself off a cliff before tying myself to so odious a husband." Her passion startled him, but it was obvious that she was serious.

A solution was nipping at his mind, one that could solve both their problems. After taking a moment to examine it, he sighed. "If you feel that strongly about it, you might as well wed me. I don't love you, but neither do you love me. We are good enough friends to muddle along together. I can see no way of breaking off George's betrothal, and frankly he seems content with it. As does Miss Parker." It would also get Lady Hardesty off his back. He had reluctantly concluded that the betting books were right. He wasn't going to survive this Season unshackled. But he wanted a little say in who he got stuck with. Sophia wasn't bad looking, and at least she wasn't stupid. Stubborn he could handle.

"You?" she squeaked.

He shrugged. "Why not?"

"Why not, indeed." She stared out the window for several minutes. "Very well, my lord. I will endeavor to make you an adequate wife."

Which was as much as he could expect. He placed a gentle kiss on her hand and led her back to the ballroom, his head swirling worse than before at the suddenness of his capitulation.

# Chapter Eleven

Diana choked on a bite of toast. Motioning the footman out of the room, she succumbed to coughing. An audience was the last thing she needed just now. And not because of embarrassment. Long after she recovered, her eyes stared sightlessly at the *Morning Post*.

Surely she had misread the announcement! But the words would not change. Lord Bankleigh was pleased to announce a betrothal between his daughter, Lady Sophia Prescott, and the Marquess of Woodvale.

*Oh, Nicholas!*

He would regret this. She knew he would. Lady Sophia worshipped propriety and was far too self-righteous to make him a comfortable wife. Her sharp tongue would drive him to distraction, and her willful determination was every bit as strong as his mother's.

*When I finally decide to set up my nursery, I will choose an heiress.* His voice echoed as it had done for ten years. Stubborn, blind fool! Despite the changes in his own life, despite the character of the lady involved, he had stuck to his plan. He had wooed Sophia for weeks, ignoring any hint of her flaws as he secured the biggest dowry in town.

*Damn you, Nicholas!*

Imagining him tied to Lady Sophia forced her to face the truth. She still loved him. Had never stopped loving him. Oh, she had hated him, too. But the pain of his cruelty had lingered only because she also loved him.

Sitting up straighter, she tried to concentrate on his faults. He was not a man who would make a comfortable husband.

He could be as determined as Lady Sophia—which itself hinted that this would be a match made in hell. He was single-minded and ruthless in pursuit of his goals. His raking was legendary and anything but discreet. No marriage of convenience was likely to change that.

Loving him would never compensate for those faults. She would be miserable with a husband who spent his time in other women's beds. Nor would she tolerate a man who would ride roughshod over her. His ingrained selfishness left him oblivious to others' needs and uncaring of any pain he inflicted as he bulled his way through life. Let Sophia have him. They deserved each other.

He had done her a favor all those years ago by refusing her love. And her temporary betrothal to Charles was a true blessing. Nicholas would have had little trouble coercing her into his bed. Intimacy would have made this news even harder to bear. Thank heavens she had been spared that.

She repeated that again and again, until she almost believed it. She must put him firmly behind her. The past was truly gone and could not be resurrected. Her future was set. The transition might be rough, but if she stayed busy enough, she would manage. And she had plenty to do.

Letting out one last sigh, she set the paper aside.

How could Charles and Chloe elope with minimal damage? Would Charles's original plan actually work?

A moment's thought left her shaking her head. Perhaps it might have once, but not now. By moving up the date of the wedding, the Parkers had already triggered gossip. Few believed their excuse. Speculation had ranged from a falling out between Chloe and her parents to misbehavior that left Chloe in an interesting condition. After that, changing the identity of the groom would cause a scandal of epic proportions.

So either Charles and Chloe must actually wed on their secret elopement—the isle of Guernsey was a possibility; like Scotland, it required no license, and it was only a day's sail by packet—or they must elope onto the ship that would take them to Charles's post. But that would work only if he got his orders very soon. So far that hadn't happened.

She sighed. They had best plan for both contingencies. And she needed to protect herself from George and the Parkers. Possibly even the Weymouths. All of them would be furious. George would forgive her once his initial embarrassment faded. He might even admit that he was better off without Chloe. The Weymouths would put the incident behind them once George married. But the Parkers would cling to this grievance forever. So how was she to deal with them and the neighbors they would influence?

Nicholas grimaced as he followed Justin into the hallway behind his theater box.

"Very bad form, Nicholas," his friend chided softly. The first act was in progress, but voices carried. "How could you publicly escort Lady Forester the very day your betrothal announcement appeared in the paper? Everyone in London knows she is little better than a courtesan."

Running frustrated fingers through his hair, Nicholas ignored the condemnation in Justin's eyes. "I did not know about the announcement until half an hour ago," he admitted. "Why the devil did Bankleigh print it? I haven't even spoken to the man."

"You mean you are not betrothed?"

"I'm committed to it, of course. I spoke to Sophia last night, but nothing is settled." And wouldn't be for weeks; Bankleigh had a reputation for hard bargaining.

But he should have expected this. He knew the man was determined to force Sophia into marriage. The moment Sophia mentioned accepting his offer, Bankleigh would have tied it up so she could not back out.

Justin shook his head. "When did you get interested in Lady Sophia? I never would have considered her as a potential wife."

"Be careful, Justin."

"Why? You know my impressions of the lady. We've discussed them before. Is that why you said nothing?"

He opened his mouth, but no words emerged. He had not mentioned his betrothal even to his best friend because it had seemed unimportant. But he could hardly admit that without insulting Sophia. And only now did he recall Justin's earlier words. His heart sank to his toes. He must have been more foxed than he'd thought to have forgotten.

Justin continued. "I don't know what bugaboo is driving you, Nicholas—and I don't want to know. But you need to take a long look at yourself before you destroy every shred of your reputation. Even if you care nothing for Lady Sophia, the timing of this little escapade is abominable. And its blatancy is downright cruel."

"Agreed. It won't happen again."

"See that it doesn't."

He watched Justin walk away, then pressed his hands to his eyes and sighed. He had set up this meeting with Lady Forester two days ago when her flirtatious advances had caught him during a particularly intense wave of melancholy. If he had realized the announcement was public, he would have canceled, but he had risen late that morning, leaving no time to scan the newspapers before meeting with his solicitor.

Lady Forester must have known, though, he admitted grimly. Yet she had said nothing, setting him up to appear as cold as Devereaux, London's most callous rakehell.

*Damnation!*

Had she meant to do it, or was she pursuing some other goal? One of his reasons for escorting her tonight was curiosity. He had recently heard a vastly different tale of her sudden marriage than the one accepted by the gossips.

Jonathan Tindale had been another member of the house party Forester had attended last summer. He claimed that Lady Forester and her family had met the entire company that first night, and that Forester had been instantly smitten—which cast doubts on her reputation for callous manipulation.

Yet Nicholas felt manipulated. She was the one who had suggested the theater. And she had maneuvered him into appearing more interested than he was, brushing against him and all but embracing him. What game was she playing?

He returned to his box, but instead of watching the stage, he studied the other boxes. It didn't take long to understand. Lord Forester was directly across the way, snuggling with a pair of courtesans. But five minutes of watching revealed that he was not truly paying attention to his companions. His eyes kept wandering toward his wife.

Nicholas compared Tindale's claims to his other facts about the Foresters. They had met the previous summer. Lord Forester was heir to an earl and a well-known rake. Lady Forester had been a vicar's daughter two generations removed from the aristocracy. No one was surprised that his eye had chosen the delectable girl to be his summer flirt. And with his history, no one had been shocked that he had convinced her to meet him on the sly. She was beautiful and eminently beddable, but she was too far below him to make an acceptable wife. And she'd had no dowry.

He shivered at the similarities between this tale and his own summer in Warwickshire. Assignations with gentry lasses were fraught with danger—as they both had learned. But he had not been caught with Diana. Forester had not only been caught, he'd been caught with his clothes off. Idiot! A wedding had quickly followed, but neither of them evinced any pleasure in the union.

He nearly laughed as his eyes moved between husband and wife. Only the fact that he was caught in the middle kept him quiet. Forester had been caught all right, but not in dalliance. The fool was in love with her. And he would bet his last shilling that she returned his regard. But circumstances and pride were preventing either from admitting it. Each was using blatant affairs to hide the truth, and perhaps to goad the other into a confrontation. What a farce.

By the first interval, he had attracted Forester's attention with a vengeance. He had moved so close that Lady Forester was practically in his lap, then spent the remainder of the first act whispering in her ear. His eyes alternated between staring down her low-cut bodice and glaring at her husband. When laughter drew all eyes but Forester's to the stage, he let his hand trail suggestively across her bosom and grinned.

It worked. Even as the curtain rang down, Forester was up and slamming out of his box.

Nicholas leaned over Lady Forester's shoulder. "Quit playing games," he whispered into her ear. "Isn't it time for a little honesty? You will never be happy until you tell your husband the truth."

Her eyes widened in shock, but he left the box before she could respond. He cheekily gave the same message to Forester, then pushed him through the door and left them alone. Hopefully, his own performance hadn't blackened his reputation beyond repair.

That hope lasted less than a minute. The next man he encountered was a furious Eastbrook.

"How dare you demean your betrothed and make a mockery of your upcoming vows by entertaining a Cyprian in public on the very day your nuptials are announced?" Eastbrook demanded, hatred blazing from his eyes.

"Not that it's any of your business," he drawled, holding his temper with difficulty, "but I had not expected the announcement just yet."

"What difference does that make?" His eye bulged. "You dishonor Lady Sophia by even thinking of another woman. I cannot understand how so proper a lady could consider wedding you."

"Just one of life's little mysteries, Eastbrook." But something in the man's face kept him from brushing past. Even a self-righteous prig would think twice about initiating such a low-bred public confrontation. So what was driving Eastbrook? Was he so obsessed with propriety that he had assumed the role of society's conscience?

It didn't matter. He had admitted fault to Justin—the complaint was legitimate, and Justin was a close friend. But he'd be damned before he let a suffocating prig criticize him. So he smiled. "Surely you understand marriages of convenience better than that, Eastbrook. I'm hardly going to sacrifice my pleasures for a chit so long in the tooth that her father would promise anything to get her shackled. She knows me well enough to expect no more."

"You mean that you offered for a girl you don't love?" George sounded horrified.

"An odd question coming from a man whose marriage was contracted when he was still in short coats."

George glared. "That is beside the point. Lady Sophia is an innocent who will never be happy with a libertine."

"Innocent?" He shrugged, again letting that smile flirt with his lips. "Virginal, it's true. But she has been out long enough to know the rules. In her eagerness to escape her parents' pressure, she gladly accepted a libertine. Once I get an heir, she can go her own way, though if she wants to live separately, it will have to be on my Scottish property—I need her estate to house a cousin. But she knows exactly what she's walking into. And it is not your affair, in any case."

George was sputtering incoherently, so Nicholas took his leave, furious that a man he barely knew would question his actions.

But the die was cast. His solicitor would begin negotiations with Bankleigh tomorrow. By summer he would be wed, and by Christmas Sophia would be carrying his heir.

So why did his heart feel so heavy?

"How was the theater?" Diana asked as Chloe joined her in the drawing room. Chloe had arrived first today. Charles would be along shortly. Occasionally he slipped in through the back or met them elsewhere. They had worked out elaborate schemes to keep Chloe's visits innocent.

She shuddered. "I nearly told George what a pompous ass he is."

"In front of your parents?"

"I caught myself in time, but I've never sat through such a long evening. I hope Charles gets his orders soon. I can't stand much more."

"What happened?" Surely Chloe was used to boredom by now.

"Lord Woodvale brought Lady Forester to the theater and spent the first act nuzzling her neck. George was furious, grumbling nonstop about libertines thumbing their noses at innocent young girls. But that was nothing to his tirade after the first interval. He must have spoken to Woodvale while he was out getting lemonade, because he went on and on about ruthless lords and marriages of convenience."

"What does he consider his own marriage to be?"

"I almost asked that, but with Mama and Papa there, I didn't dare. George claims that Woodvale plans to lock Lady Sophia away in Scotland or some such nonsense—personally, I can understand him not wanting to live with the girl, but then why is he wedding her?"

Diana offered no explanation. All her energy was focused on keeping her face under control.

"But that tirade was nothing to the one he spouted after Woodvale abandoned Lady Forester to her husband."

"What?" Her pain lightened to hear that Nicholas had not left with the lady. Lady Forester was notorious. Perhaps her husband had decided to rein her in, though his own reputation was little better.

"I thought at first that George was upset because Woodvale left the Foresters in a vehement public argument in his box." She giggled. "Everyone in the house was straining to hear, but they kept their voices down, despite their furious gestures. Forester tried to drag her bodice higher—Woodvale had hardly taken his eyes off her bosom—but she yanked it back, popping one breast out and nearly ripping the fabric."

"Good heavens!"

"But that wasn't what upset George. Woodvale joined the two women Forester had arrived with. They left together during the second interval. George claimed they were courtesans."

"How would he know?" she asked lightly through a wave of anger. *Two* courtesans? Within twenty-four hours of his own betrothal? The man was sick—and she was lucky to be free of him.

"Someone must have pointed them out." Chloe stifled another giggle. "I doubt he ever met one."

"Didn't Forester object?"

Chloe shook her head, looking puzzled. "That's odd. He and Lady Forester argued for most of the second act, but they seemed to reach some sort of accord. They refused to open the door during the second interval, and left together at the beginning of act three."

Diana nodded, realizing that it all made sense. "My maid claims that they sent round notes this morning canceling all their engagements. It seems they are leaving for Paris. They won't be back for a year or more."

"Lucky."

"You'll get your chance, Chloe. So how was the play?"

"I don't know. Between listening to George and watching the other boxes, I never saw it."

Charles arrived to find them laughing.

Turning down the next aisle at Hatchard's Diana nearly ran into Nicholas. Speak of the devil. She had heard whispers about his theater antics at every stop this afternoon.

"Congratulations on your betrothal," she said, grateful that her voice remained composed even though the meeting had been unexpected.

"Thank you." His eyes glittered, but after his performance at the theater, she knew his excitement had nothing to do with his nuptials. He nodded toward her books. "Quite an eclectic assortment."

Her selections ranged from a collection of Coleridge's literary critiques to Peacock's latest novel, an exposé on the cruelties inflicted upon climbing boys, and one of Maria Edgeworth's improving books.

"I enjoy reading," she said calmly. "And I like to challenge my mind."

"So you deliberately search out writing you can disagree with?"

"I'm not above admitting that I am wrong if I find a compelling argument." She added Hazlitt's *Characters from Shakespeare* to her stack. "Have you set a date?"

"Not yet. How about you?"

"The fourteenth of October," she quipped off the top of her head. "What books have you found today?"

She glanced at his titles, a collection just as esoteric as her own. Poems by Keats, a novel by Scott, a treatise on crop rotation, and another on gas lighting. Her comment died when she noticed that he was staring at her bosom, which was resting atop her stack of books.

"Shame on you," she chided him. "Though I suppose one cannot expect a libertine to change."

She tried to escape down the next aisle, but he followed. He was again radiating that blatant masculinity that played havoc with her senses and sent tingles along every nerve.

"Are you running away from me?" he demanded, stopping her in her tracks.

"Why would I?" she countered. "I was trying to finish my shopping before my arms get tired. Books are heavy."

"Oh." He sounded oddly disappointed. "Let me carry those." Before she could object, he had scooped her books into his own arms. His hand brushed her breast in passing.

"There is no need," she protested, clamping down on the wave of heat started by that inadvertent touch. At least she hoped it was inadvertent.

He sighed. "There is if I wish to speak to you."

"Why should you? We'll just end up arguing again. And this place is too public."

"Then forgive me instead."

"We've had this discussion—"

He freed a hand to cover her lips, stopping her words. Its heat burned, instantly drying her mouth.

"No, we haven't. I was out of line at Harrison Court. You

know me well enough to have recognized my determination. Did my pressure drive you into accepting Langley?"

"No one forced me into anything," she declared hotly, letting her anger shield her reaction to his touch. "Your offer was unwanted, but I am capable of deflecting advances without hiding behind a protector. You would be better served by forgetting me and concentrating on your own affairs."

"I suppose you mean that fiasco at the theater last night."

"Actually, I didn't. That fits your reputation so well that I hardly noticed."

He flinched. "I suppose I deserved that."

"You did. Exchanging your original questionable escort for a pair of courtesans the day after you betrothed yourself to yet another lady was cruel, insensitive, and totally selfish. No one believes your vows of distress. Certainly not me."

Anger flared in his eyes. And pain, though she barely registered that through her own. "Actually, I was attempting to reconcile a pair of idiots who were so full of pride that they couldn't admit what stared them in the face."

"Really?" Perhaps that had been the result, but she doubted it had been his intent when he invited the lady to accompany him. All of London knew her reputation.

"You don't believe me." His eyes caught hers and held them.

She tried to close her mind to the jumble of emotions swirling in his head. Whatever his purpose in pressing her, it did no good. Friendship was impossible. Understanding would be worse, for it could only feed her pain.

Wrenching her eyes away, she reached for her books. "My beliefs don't matter, my lord. Good day. I'm sure you have things to do."

But he didn't relinquish the volumes. "Is this all you need?"

She nodded.

"Then allow me to escort you to your carriage."

She could think of no argument against it, though her nerves were stretched to the breaking point by their exchange. And her need for distance would not be met any time soon.

Already this meeting had raised new questions that demanded to be heard. Why was he parading his guilt before her? She had decided his original apology had been made to set up his seduction, but now she had to wonder. This one had no ulterior motive—at least no obvious one. Was he serious? If so, the guilt must be real, which conferred a heart on the man. And gave him a measure of maturity, reviving the admiration she had once felt.

She bit her lip, struggling against tears as she fought to suppress the questions. The only way to function was to forget him and get on with her life. Surely he would retire to the country once he wed. As would she. With luck they could slip into a routine that would prevent them from visiting London at the same time. A few years of not seeing each other should suffice to bury the past.

Nicholas suppressed the urge to bolt as Lady Hardesty made her determined way across Lady Lipton's drawing room. He had nothing to fear from the woman now.

"I'm disappointed in you, Woodvale," she said once she reached his side. "How such a supposedly intelligent man could make such a hash of his life, I will never understand. Given your experience with women, how could you choose such an unsuitable wife? You have nothing in common and can only make each other miserable. Bounty would be disappointed."

"You will keep your opinions to yourself," he said coldly, scowling at his persecutor. It was her pressure as much as anything that had pushed him toward marriage. Why couldn't the tabbies mind their own business? And what was that comment about Bounty? Few people knew of any connection.

"I won't. You need to know more about the girl if you ever hope to get along with her. She is selfish, self-righteous, and determined. Did you hear about that incident in Hyde Park last month?"

"What incident?"

"I thought not. It happened before you returned to town. She all but attacked Miss Jennings, accusing her of immoral conduct, then cutting her dead."

"Your point?"

"Her only complaint was that Miss Jennings had taken a turn about the terrace with Lord Jefferson Janssen during Lady Jersey's ball. All very proper. I was out there myself."

"Surely there was more to it than that," he protested. Sophia was not stupid. And she couldn't be jealous about Jeff. By her own admission, she'd turned him down twice.

"That was all. Nor was it the first time she had taken it upon herself to criticize the behavior of newly presented girls—all of whom were quite proper even in the eyes of high-sticklers like Mrs. Drummond-Burrell." That Almack's patroness was usually the first to condemn any misbehavior.

"Youthful exuberance," he said in excuse. But he knew he would have to discuss it with her. Scenes like the one Lady Hardesty had just described would make her a social pariah.

"Excessive priggishness," she corrected him. "Lady Wharburton ceased inviting her two years ago, especially to her masquerades."

"Why? The only people she eschews are those of questionable morals, but Sophia is far too proper to fall into that group."

"She is far too outspoken to make a comfortable guest. You'd best take her in hand, Woodvale. She is fast becoming a harridan who will soon find herself ostracized."

Having delivered her warning, she withdrew.

Nicholas left the rout soon after, unwilling to wait until Sophia arrived. He had much to think about before he spoke with her again. Lady Hardesty's words had a ring of truth he could not ignore. His own observations should have drawn similar conclusions, but he had not bothered thinking about them.

Sophia was not only self-righteous and filled with her own conceit, she was remarkably shortsighted, never considering the inevitable results of her actions. Her outspoken criticism of accepted standards was already affecting her position in society. As he had once pointed out to Diana, the *ton* did not allow anyone to rip away its facade of propriety.

His mind veered to Diana. Even a passing thought of her raised his temperature. She had been actively avoiding him in the two days since they'd met at Hatchard's, ducking out of rooms when he entered, leaving early if he seemed to be headed her way.

She obviously didn't trust him, which hurt. He only wanted to talk to her. He had abandoned his other schemes when she announced her betrothal, but conversation stimulated his mind. Especially with her.

He sighed. He should never have tried to seduce her. Diana had always been different. He should have known that she would eschew illicit liaisons.

# Chapter Twelve

"That's my limit for tonight," announced Justin, rising from the whist table at White's.

"And me," agreed Shelford. "Luck's out."

Nicholas shrugged, straightening the pile of vowels in front of him. He had joined the game to occupy his mind, too blue-deviled to care if he won or lost. Lady Luck had responded by giving him the best hands of his life.

"Want to try piquet?" asked Langley before Nicholas could rise. "Perhaps I can do better in a different game."

He shrugged again. Langley was ahead on the evening, though not by much. Since he wasn't ready for his own company, he opened a deck of piquet cards. Blue-devils still crowded close, promising another sleepless night. Not even dalliance had been providing relief.

Problems pressed heavily on his spirits, bringing new burdens every day. The week since his betrothal had been the longest of a life that was suddenly racing out of control.

Bankleigh's solicitor was making demands far above what he had expected, and he feared he would be stuck meeting some of them. He had lost leverage when the betrothal announcement had appeared. All he could do to regain ground was to drag the betrothal out for years if Bankleigh got too insistent.

But even that plan was unlikely to succeed. Lady Bankleigh and his mother were already corresponding over wedding plans. Both expected an early marriage, preferably in St. George's at the end of the Season. And his mother had already vowed to redecorate Woodvale Abbey for his bride. His protest that Sophia should have a voice in any changes had been a mistake. Today's mail had announced that she would arrive next week to accompany Sophia to furniture warehouses and linen drapers.

Even worse, both of them expected him to stay at the Abbey from now on. It didn't take a genius to discern his mother's devious manipulation. She had written to Sophia, agreeing that it was London's sordid influence that had driven him to raking and wagering. It was exactly the support Sophia needed to press for a permanent return to the country. In the meantime his mother had offered to move into his town house, since he would no longer need it. Doing so would give him the privacy men desired during the important early months of marriage. Of course, she had no intention of ever vacating it again. With two such manipulative women on his hands, he could see years of strife ahead.

Damn! Contrary to what he had told Eastbrook, he did not plan to keep a mistress after marriage. But neither would he eschew social and intellectual gatherings or renege on his Parliamentary duties. Both required frequent stays in London. And if he wasn't to go crazy from abstinence, Sophia would have to accompany him.

He cut the cards, shaking his head at his own stupidity. What had possessed him to offer for her? Surely he hadn't been *that* drunk. Marrying her far surpassed his responsibilities as head of the family. He had not considered her temperament before proposing—just as he had never considered his mother's before letting her move in with him. And he had regretted it every day since.

Langley dealt the cards, suggesting lower stakes than was usual for White's, but he accepted without comment.

He had known that Sophia was both stubborn and particular—why else was Bankleigh reduced to forcing her into marriage? But he had not considered how that would affect him. After his talk with Lady Hardesty, he had tried to lay down a few rules. He could not afford a wife who was not accepted in society. Even his title couldn't protect her from the subtle snubs of people like

Lady Beatrice and Lady Debenham, who knew everything about everyone and thus wielded tremendous power.

But Sophia was unwilling to compromise. Nor would she consider any opinion but her own. Her criticism already infuriated him.

She hated London—which he had already known—but she expected him to hate it, too. She despised socializing with anyone who did not conform to her standards, which she expected him to adopt. She was appalled to discover that he read novels, Byron's poetry, and a broad spectrum of newspapers, including the Whiggish *Examiner*. The prudishness that made her adopt euphemisms even for kissing signaled that she was disgusted by intimacy, he admitted grimly as Langley won what should have been his trick. Sophia would submit to his touch out of duty, but she would make sure that she never enjoyed it. How could he have been so stupid? Her idea of rubbing along together was that he should become her ideal mate.

"My game," he announced, winning the last trick.

He should have expected it. He and Langley were alike in many ways. Sophia openly despised Langley, so why should she feel better about him? If he changed, he would hate himself. If he didn't, she would hate him.

His mind couldn't cope with that conclusion, turning instead to Diana. Was that why she had chosen Langley? Because he was much like the man she had once loved? But she had also loved Bounty, who was unlike both of them. His lips nearly twisted into a snarl, but he suppressed it.

Langley sighed. "Your luck is better than mine. One more game. But if I lose, I am done for the evening."

"Is this quarter's allowance late?"

"Canceled." He grimaced, obviously annoyed at revealing that, but he followed it with a shrug. "It no longer matters. Everyone will know the truth soon anyway. I've accepted a position with the East India Company. I sail in a fortnight."

"Why would you do that when you are betrothed to an heiress?" The question was out before he had a chance to censor it. Such prying was hardly gentlemanly.

But Langley did not seem to mind. "I refuse to live on her money."

Nicholas knew his face registered surprise, but he couldn't control it.

"I have always meant to support myself," Langley stated, evoking new shock. "But my father refuses to understand me, and my mother throws hysterics at the mere mention of trade."

"Which explains your secrecy." He dealt.

"Leaving before it becomes general knowledge should minimize the scandal." Again he shrugged.

And that was yet another similarity between them. Both had ignored parental pressure, determined to make their own way in the world. He had to admire the man even as his fingers longed to wring his neck.

Sophia must have recognized Langley's determination and known she could never deflect him from his course. But she believed she could control Nicholas. And who was to say she was wrong, he admitted grimly. He had exerted no control over any aspect of his life since his uncle's death. Had she deliberately manipulated him into proposing, taking advantage of his inebriation to win herself a title?

Later. This was not the place for deep thoughts. He recognized the subject's closure, but could not resist one more question. "Will you wed before leaving?"

"Of course. I wouldn't dream of leaving my wife behind. She will love China."

"She actually told you that?" demanded Nicholas, slamming the cards onto the table. Diana loved reading about other lands, but she disliked travel—as she had confirmed only recently. All she had ever wanted was security and a husband she could love. Bounty had given her the first. Did she think Langley would provide the second?

"We haven't discussed the details. I only received the posting this afternoon, but I've no doubt that she'll be pleased."

"If you think that, then you don't know the lady at all! How dare you drag a gently bred female to a heathenish land where there is no society, no intelligent conversation, and where she doesn't even speak the language?"

"What business is it of yours, my lord?" demanded Langley in return. "Do you suggest that I leave her here without protection for at least a dozen years?"

"I would be pleased to look after—"

"I'm sure you would," he interrupted, fury erupting in his eyes. "I am not naïve enough to leave a lamb under the watchful eye of a wolf."

"I should call you out for that," growled Nicholas through the red mist that had engulfed him at the image of Diana alone in a strange land.

"Be my guest."

He opened his mouth to comply, but reason intruded. He was not Diana's guardian. She was no longer an ignorant seventeen-year-old. "Why are you wedding her if you refuse to make use of her dowry and are leaving the country immediately?"

"My reasons are my own concern, my lord," repeated Langley implacably. "As is my marriage. Do you wish to play out this hand or not?"

He nodded, unwilling to insult the man further by refusing a game of cards. He had been out of line with his prying—way out—and was fortunate he wasn't facing a duel because of it.

But Diana's future should have been his concern, he admitted half an hour later as he walked back to Berkeley Square, his need for fresh air outweighing the threat of footpads.

The last ten years again paraded through his head, but this time his perspective was different. He had gone to London after leaving Warwickshire and immediately plunged into indiscriminate raking. Liaisons were nothing new for him, though he had previously chosen his contacts with care. But no more. Every encounter was less satisfactory than the last, leading to such carelessness that he was lucky he had not picked up a French disease or left a string of bastards in his wake. His loss of control should have warned him how deeply his emotions were engaged. But it had not. His only thought had been to put Diana and his dishonorable conduct behind him.

What a bloody idiot he had been.

He had loved her.

He still loved her. Why else had his heart raced the moment he had seen her again? Why else had he returned to raking that very night, fully two years after he had abandoned that life? He was still trying to forget her, still burying his need for her, still failing miserably at both tasks.

His curses grew harsher and more inventive as he strode across the square. He had lost her through his own stupidity. What had he gained in ten years without her?

A title that carried more responsibilities than he had ever wanted. A fortune that eased anxiety, but provided no happiness. A reputation that still raised eyebrows in some circles.

The only thing of real value he had ever possessed had been Diana's heart. But he had rejected it, hurling it at her feet, shattering it and her in the process. Her pride might try to silence that admission, but he would never forget the agony in her eyes when he had left her in that clearing.

It was too late to rectify his errors. Blindness and stupidity had hidden the truth. Even if she were not betrothed to another, it was too late. He had hurt her too badly. She would never forgive him.

*Are you sure about that?* demanded an insidiously tempting voice.

Yes. He knew Diana better than anyone—including Langley. Her betrothal was insurmountable. She would never have accepted Langley if she did not love him. No one forced Diana down any path she did not want. It was a fact she had thrown in his face too often to ignore.

And she would indeed follow Langley to China, if only he asked. Her loyalty was unmatched.

He sighed. He deserved Sophia. For a man who had long traded on his understanding of human nature, he was remarkably obtuse. Not once had he applied his knowledge to himself. A lifetime of Sophia was an appropriate punishment.

*But does she deserve you?* demanded his conscience.

Hope stirred. The girl was young, self-centered, and had shown poor judgment. But she did not deserve the misery she would find with him. He would not abandon the activities he enjoyed. Reading, art, intellectual discussion, London society—

He left out raking. He wasn't enjoying it. Now that he understood its purpose, he had no need to continue. But whatever miseries he must endure for loving a woman he could not have, he would not inflict them on another.

He could not jilt her, of course. That would leave her reputation in shreds. The only possible future she would then find would be marriage to someone like Griswold.

But neither could he wed her. So they would enjoy the longest betrothal in history. There were advantages for them both. He would be free of matchmakers. Sophia could move onto her own estate—he would insist on it—until the wedding. Their betrothal would protect her from charges of impropriety, and living alone was all she'd wanted anyway.

It would work. He could travel for a few years, postponing any marriage until later. A belated grand tour, as it were.

He nodded. And it was a good time to take care of his mother. He had already sent notice to his steward that she was to remain at the Abbey. Before he left, he would move her to a property he owned in Cornwall. A loyal staff would see that she stayed there. Since his dower house was already occupied, no one would question the move. A minor bit of blackmail over the discontinuation of her allowance if she complained to any of her correspondents should remove any potential problems.

Finally feeling in control of his life, he climbed the steps to his house.

As dawn intruded through the draperies, Nicholas gave up on sleep. His euphoria had lasted less than an hour. He had accused Sophia of not considering the effect of her actions, but he was guilty of the same thing. Sooner or later a permanent betrothal would harm her. At the very least her reputation would suffer when he returned to England and did not wed her. Could he take that chance?

Calling for his horse, he headed for the park, turning the question over in his mind.

He couldn't. Even considering it demeaned his title. He lived in a rigid world. The marquessate afforded him power, acceptance, and preferential treatment. But the price was conformity to the rules that governed aristocratic life. Failure to comply could collapse the social order.

In truth, he was insignificant. His estates did not truly belong to him, for the land was entailed to the title. He could neither sell it nor mortgage it. He was merely a caretaker for future generations, enjoying the benefits, but obligated to maintain productivity and improve conditions so that his heirs could do likewise. Ignoring established conventions threatened his heirs with chaos and the loss of prestige.

So he must honor the vow he had already made to Sophia. They would fight many battles until they reached workable compromises, but even a lifetime of misery was better than tarnishing the title he was obligated to respect. It was yet another reason he wished he had never inherited the honor.

A wave of heat shattered his thoughts as he spotted Diana cantering toward the Serpentine. At times like this he did not feel like an insignificant pawn in the game of life. Pushing his own horse faster, he moved to intercept her.

"Good morning, my lady." He chose formality today, both to hide his own feelings and to acknowledge his respect.

Diana pulled her horse back to a trot. She had been trying to clear her mind after another sleepless night. How long would it be before she was free of pain?

Nicholas looked better than ever this morning, with his green riding jacket reflected in his eyes, making them appear darker than usual. Or perhaps it was the circles beneath them that deepened the color. He had probably not yet been to bed.

Blushing furiously at her image of where he had spent the night, she contented herself with a bland, "My lord."

"I ran into Langley last night. He said that he would be leaving for China in a fortnight."

"Wonderful!" In her excitement, she forgot to be distant. "So it finally came through. That was the posting he was hoping for. He has no real interest in India—at least not as a home."

"You approve?" he asked coolly.

"Of course."

"He says you will accompany him."

Only then did she remember that Nicholas still expected her to wed Charles. But she could hardly tell the truth—especially since she need only play out the charade for two more weeks. Chloe would never forgive her if a loose tongue forced Charles to leave without her.

"That is the plan."

"I never thought you would enjoy living in such an outlandish place as China."

"Why should you?"

He frowned. "Do you love him, then?"

A direct question that he had skirted more than once. Why did he care? "That is not your concern, my lord," she managed, though every instinct was screaming *no*. The only person she loved—or had ever loved—was Nicholas. At least as he meant the question. She had loved Harry in the same way she had loved her father. But again she could not reveal the truth without destroying Chloe's happiness.

Besides, Nicholas was betrothed to Lady Sophia. A chill swept her at the memory. Did he love the girl? She could not see how, for Sophia's rigid disapproval of everything Nicholas enjoyed could not possibly appeal to him. But she had never really known much about him beyond gossip, she admitted. Their old relationship had been based on the physical. Reputations often twisted the truth. Most of the personal things she knew about him had come out since meeting again in London.

"I heard you have scheduled your wedding for St. George's the first week in July," she said to change the subject.

Nicholas frowned. Was this another way Bankleigh was trying to pressure him? It wouldn't work. He might have to go through with this farce, but he would do it on his own terms. "Pure speculation. The gossips must have nothing to do. Haven't there been any juicy scandals lately?"

"Besides Lord and Lady Means's escape from the Caribbean last week?"

"Temporary visit," he corrected her with a laugh. "They did not flee for their lives, and will go back this autumn."

"Small news, to be sure. So when *is* your wedding scheduled?"

"It isn't—and won't be until the settlements are completed. Who is handling yours, by the way?"

"I am. The contract is quite simple."

He glared at her. "What about jointures, children's portions, pin money—"

"I am quite capable of handling my own affairs, my lord," she said coldly. "Harry trained me well."

He opened his mouth to respond, but changed his mind. Only after several minutes of silence did he again speak. "I only want you to be happy, Diana."

"I am."

He stared until she continued.

"I have been offered many choices since Bounty died. Some were good, some bad, some merely different. In every case I chose the path that was best for me. Others may disagree, but I am satisfied."

He nodded, sagging into the saddle. She was right. Her affairs were not his business. It did neither of them any good to keep pushing the point.

"If you will excuse me, Nicholas, I must return home. There is much that needs my attention today."

"Of course."

He watched her leave. If she was sailing in a fortnight, she would have plenty to do to get ready.

He wished he could believe that she wanted this change. If only he didn't know her so well. Others would not have heard the false note that had threaded her vow.

Or was his self-interest creating phantoms?

## Chapter Thirteen

Charles lounged in the corner of Lady Riverton's ballroom, keeping one eye on the entrance while he traded quips with a half dozen friends. Tonight their shallow posturing and inane humor annoyed him. Had he really been that vapid, that boringly trite, that pretentiously silly for six-and-twenty years?

"Lady Sheridan is wearing yellow again," observed Lord Barkenton, *ennui* dripping from every word. "Shocking what it does for her figure."

"To say nothing of that sallow complexion. If she reduced her consumption of sweetmeats, it would improve both," said Bradshaw, twirling his quizzing glass.

"At least she doesn't look like a corpse," quipped Lord Philip, nodding toward Lady Oglethorpe. Her face was gaunt and paler than even fashion required, assuming a greenish cast from her emerald silk gown.

Bradshaw chuckled.

"Albright drove Miss Havershoal in the park again," reported Barkenton. "He'll be wed before the summer's out."

"Not likely," said Mr. Mason. "He's ducked his mother's machinations before."

"Ten pounds he's caught this time," insisted Barkenton.

"Done."

"Is Shelford thinking of posting a new record now that Naseby bested his time to Brighton?"

Charles stopped listening. He had spent most of the day with officials from the Company, discussing his new duties. It had prevented him from seeing Chloe. Now he waited for

George. The man always escorted the Parkers to balls, then escaped the crowd and found a quiet place where he could sleep.

It was time to take matters into his own hands. Diana had given up on the Parkers. Chloe had likewise failed to gain a hearing. Neither the Parkers nor the Weymouths were willing to back down. So his last chance to avoid eloping lay with George. Surely the man could not want a wife who shared none of his interests. Even a dullard like Eastbrook must recognize their differences by now.

Ten minutes later his vigilance was rewarded. Eastbrook delivered the Parkers to the door and left. Chloe was immediately swept into a set, so Charles slipped out of the room.

This time George headed for the library, which was nominally closed to the guests. Despite his rigid conventions and determined propriety, George was not loathe to break a few rules in his own interests—which might make this job easier.

He had thought long about his best approach. Since his reputation was wild—at least in Eastbrook's eyes—claiming a personal interest in Chloe would serve no purpose. But his betrothal to Diana might explain his meddling in Chloe's affairs.

"Eastbrook," he said in greeting as he stepped into the library.

"What are you doing here?" demanded George. "The library is closed."

Charles said nothing, but let surprise show on his face.

"Lord Riverton assured me that I would not be disturbed." His voice was frosty.

He should have known that George would never break convention, conceded Charles as he sank onto a chair. Of course the man would have obtained permission.

But that was irrelevant. "I wished to speak privately with you," he admitted. "You are aware, of course, that Lady Bounty is a close friend of Miss Parker."

"A friendship I have never approved," he countered icily. "It will end the moment we wed. Her bizarre ideas corrupt innocent ears and could destroy the very fabric of society if they were allowed to stand."

"You are speaking of the lady who will be my wife." He glared daggers until George dropped his eyes.

"My apologies."

"Lady Bounty cares deeply for Miss Parker," he continued. "The girl has run tame in her home for years. They are closer than sisters. Lady Bounty has been trying to soothe Miss Parker's fears, but in truth the girl is quite unsuited for the life you can offer her."

"I have long suspected that she had filled Chloe's head with nonsense," George muttered darkly. "Which is why I must sever the connection. Once Chloe is removed from her influence, she will be content enough."

Charles fought down his fury. Sanctimonious bastard! But losing his temper would serve no purpose. "I beg to differ," he managed calmly. "I will be blunt, Eastbrook. You know nothing about Miss Parker. Her parents know nothing, either, because they willfully ignore anything they do not wish to believe. Nor have they spent time with her beyond duty visits since she was a child. After ten years in the sole custody of a governess and one more at a strict school, they expect her to be exactly like Lady Parker. But they have never paid enough attention to see that she is nothing like her mother and never will be."

"What possible interest could this hold for you, Langley?" demanded George, angrier than Charles had ever seen him.

"What interests my wife interests me," he replied bluntly. "You are deliberately blinding yourself to what is before your eyes. Miss Parker is an adventurous young lady who craves excitement, revels in society, and longs to travel. Her education already surpasses that of nearly every lady of my acquaintance, and she thrives on expanding it. She can speak intelligently on any subject and hold her own in debates with both males and females. Is that the girl you would willingly choose for a wife?"

George sputtered in protest, but Charles ignored him. "Ask yourself these questions before it is too late, Eastbrook. How will you cope with a wife who has endured her parents' staid country life only because she had neighbors she could turn to for lively discussion? Are you willing to beat her hard enough and often enough to break her spirit? That is the only way you will ever get her to accept your life. You do not impress me as a man who enjoys being a tyrant, but that is the only role that will keep Miss Parker under control, because you can offer her nothing that she desires. And what kind of home will your children find with parents who hate each other?"

George's mouth moved, but not even sputters emerged now.

"Arranged marriages rarely work, Eastbrook. England is littered with aristocratic couples who pretend tolerance in public but live separate lives in private. You need look no further than your own parents. Is that what you want for yourself?"

George's fist jerked, but his face had paled alarmingly.

"Think about it," suggested Charles as he rose to leave. "Her parents are among the few who made an arranged marriage work, so they believe she can, too. They are forcing her to accept you, despite the fact that she has protested against it since she was old enough to understand what they were demanding. They ignored her opposition because they believe that she is incapable of rational thought. But I have met her often at Lady Bounty's house. I recognize intelligence when I see it. Marriage will not change her character. Force might produce surface compliance, but do you really want a wife who despises even the thought of you?"

He left without another word. This was his last chance for an honorable marriage. Had he chosen the right approach? Eastbrook was dense. Anger would slow his thinking even further. He might not calm enough to think rationally for days, and by then it would be too late. Even immediate agreement might not be enough. Would he conclude that the Parkers' force was dishonorable enough to excuse jilting Chloe?

His prospects did not appear favorable—Lady Luck had been a fickle friend of late. Arranged marriages had a long history of acceptance, and George was very traditional.

\* \* \*

Nicholas watched Langley escort Diana off the dance floor. He waited until the man left, then eased closer.

"Are you free for the next set?" he asked.

She jumped. "I did not hear you approach, my lord. You must move like a cat."

Or her mind was too wrapped up in Langley, he thought grimly. But still he wanted to waltz with her. Already his hands tingled at the thought of touching her. He was in worse shape than he had thought. "Would you dance with me?"

"I had meant to sit this one out, for I am still recovering from that last reel." She smiled to remove the sting from the words, though he felt it anyway.

"If you are overheated, then perhaps we could take a turn about the terrace." He held out his arm. "I won't assault you, Diana," he added when she hesitated.

"Very well."

The slight pressure of her fingers on his arm sent shivers clear to his shoulder. Why was he doing this? Proving that they could meet socially was a weak excuse at best. But he could no more avoid escorting her than he could cease breathing. The stark truth was that she would leave England in a fortnight. He wanted to amass as many memories as possible. He would need them in the coming years. So he set himself to be lightly entertaining.

"Did you hear about Miss Uxbridge's fall from grace?"

Surprise filled her eyes, but her quick gasp exploded into laughter. "Rogue! I had forgotten that her mare's name was Grace. She must have been mortified!"

"Why? She only had an audience of forty or fifty high-sticklers when she—"

"—made her Graceless landing."

It was his turn to chuckle. "At the height of the fashionable hour in Hyde Park. She should have remained in a carriage. She has never been a rider."

"But she has been casting sheep's eyes at Shelford for at least a fortnight. Perhaps she thought to impress him with her skills."

"No Corinthian of any note would consider her skillful."

"True, but infatuation so often distorts one's judgment."

As he well knew. He could barely restrain himself from dragging her into the shadows and plundering that sensuous mouth. It didn't help that he could recall her taste as clearly as his own. Nor that tonight's gown made her bosom appear more voluptuous than usual.

"Have you seen the latest exhibit at the Royal Academy?" she asked, deflecting his thoughts. It had to be deliberate, for her eyes bore into his own. She was reading his mind again.

He could only pray that she never saw past the lust to the love that lurked beneath. That knowledge would benefit neither of them. He tried to deflect awareness of the lilac that always enveloped her. Pulling himself together, he discussed the Royal Academy exhibit, comparing it with the one at the British Institution and agreeing that Turner's private sales room often contained better paintings than those he exhibited elsewhere.

From there they compared Richard Trevithick's latest advances in locomotives to Stevenson's newest engine design, and speculated on the impact they might eventually have on transportation; mentioned the recent news that Princess Charlotte was carrying an heir to the throne; and finally discussed the increase in subversive activities that had so many government officials fearful.

Long before he was ready to stop, the set ended, and they had to return to the ballroom. As they turned back, a couple emerged from the folly at the back of the well-lit garden. Eastbrook and Miss Parker. Both were laughing. They indulged in a warm embrace before Miss Parker turned toward the house.

Nicholas stiffened.

"They are betrothed," Diana reminded him, though her voice sounded odd—almost as if she were shocked.

"True." He said no more, but that embrace had been genuine. Thank God he had not let Sophia talk him into interfering. It would only have hurt both parties—and Sophia would still have lost. But perhaps she would now admit that she was following a false dream and turn her attention to making the best of their marriage.

"Guess what!" Chloe had dragged Diana away from the ballroom the moment Nicholas had taken leave of her. Now they shared a tiny antechamber.

"Did you decide George would make an acceptable husband after all?"

"Of course not!"

"Keep your voice down. These walls are thin. I saw you in the folly just now." What had happened? Chloe was so excited that even her assumption had not annoyed her.

"George took me walking during the last set. Your suggestions worked, Diana!" She must have spotted the frown, for she stopped long enough to explain. "Surely you remember telling me to show him my real interests, but do it a little at a time."

"That was nearly a month ago. I had despaired of him responding."

"So had I, to tell the truth. But he sought me out, escorting me outside during the last set. Then he asked me all sorts of questions—did I enjoy living in the country; why did I prefer London; what books had I read, and where had I gotten them? And he actually listened to my answers. He was not overly pleased when I confirmed that you have been teaching me, but in the end, he admitted that we did not suit. I assured him that I agreed. He is going to speak with my parents and his. With luck they will listen to him."

"That is good news, but do not be too optimistic. After making so much fuss about rescheduling the wedding so they could hold it in town, I cannot imagine your parents canceling this close to the new date. Even if the Weymouths agreed, such a breach of propriety would appall them. They will pass the whole thing off as wedding nerves."

"Surely not!"

"I may be wrong, but do not count on it. Have you spoken with Charles tonight?"

The gloom abandoned her eyes. "Only briefly. We're going to China!"

"I know. And the ship sails at dawn on the fifteenth, so even if your parents are adamant, you will be gone in good time." The wedding had been scheduled for the fifteenth. By slipping out during the night, Chloe would be able to escape.

"You have given up all hope of doing this in the open, haven't you?"

"Not yet, but time is pressing. We must be ready for any contingency—and that includes eloping. Can you leave the house without being detected?"

"Yes, but how will I manage the luggage? I can hardly sail to China with nothing but the clothes on my back."

"I have been thinking of that ever since Charles told me the details of his appointment. The easiest way would be to solicit George's help. Since he now agrees that marriage would not suit, he might be willing—once he exhausts all other options. By then he will be desperate."

"I hinted that I had formed an attraction to another gentleman," said Chloe slowly. "He was not pleased, but accepted it. I claimed to have ignored my feelings and refused to name the gentleman. But that gives him more incentive to be rid of me."

"Good. This is looking better. If he is willing to help—and I think he will be by the time we must ask him—then he can collect your trunks the day before the wedding. But instead of sending them ahead to his estate, he can deliver them to the ship. They will contain heavy woolens that you will not likely need in Canton, but I can see no help for that. And you should be able to get silks at an excellent price once you arrive. Is your maid trustworthy?"

Chloe frowned. "No. She answers only to Mama, even when I wish otherwise. I wanted my hair in waves tonight, but Mama said curls, so here I am in curls."

"So we cannot trust her. Charles will find a maid who is willing to travel. In fact, my own maid's cousin might be just the thing. I will speak with him about it."

She would also discuss Chloe's wardrobe and insist on providing funds for several gowns to be made up on arrival. It would be her wedding gift.

They continued their planning until the end of the set. Chloe had already promised the next one, so she headed back to the ballroom, supposedly returning from the retiring room. But it would not do to look like they had been plotting together, so Diana paused at the window to admire the garden.

Nicholas and Sophia were embracing in the shrubbery, less than ten feet away.

Pain knifed her chest. Tearing her eyes from the sight, she fled. So he had not merely been after a fortune.

*Fool!* she berated herself, whipping up fury to drive away pain. She had never wanted a man she couldn't trust, and Nicholas was certainly such a man. He had given no hint that he would remain faithful to a wife. The fact that she loved him wouldn't change that.

Yet a tiny voice had kept hoping that somehow they could be together, that he returned her love, that his courtship during that long-ago summer had been real.

*Idiot!* Based on nothing more than wishful thinking and a love that should never have started and certainly shouldn't be encouraged, she had planned to seek Sophia out and drop hints about Nicholas's real nature. Someone as rigidly proper as Lady Sophia would hardly relish being tied to a seductive rake and profligate gamester. Nor would she enjoy spending every Season in town—and probably the Little Season as well. Nicholas hadn't missed a single one until mourning forced him home. He'd spent summers in Brighton—with one regrettable exception—and autumns in various hunting boxes. The role of a country gentleman was anathema to him.

But if he truly cared for Sophia—and if she returned his regard—then interference could only cause trouble. Love would lead to whatever compromises were necessary to accommodate their differing tastes. She ought to know. If he appeared at her elbow right now and offered her a permanent place in his life, she would follow him to the ends of the earth.

She had to forget him. *Two weeks.* The words echoed in her mind. In two weeks Charles and Chloe would be gone. His elopement would tarnish her reputation enough that no one would be surprised when she left town. She would stay at home until she could meet Lord and Lady Woodvale without pain and without losing her composure. Maybe in another ten years.

Swallowing a burst of nausea, she found her next partner and pleaded a headache. But returning home accomplished nothing. Every time she closed her eyes, she saw Nicholas pulling Sophia into a tender embrace.

# Chapter Fourteen

Nicholas paced the library of his town house. Anger had replaced the blue-devils that had plagued him for the past month. He felt like he had just emerged from a heavy fog. The scenery was shocking, and the future looked grim, but it was time to dig in his heels and address both.

Within moments of returning Diana to the ballroom last night, Sophia had dragged him into the garden. She had also seen Miss Parker and George emerge from the folly.

"How can he care for a bluestocking hoyden?" she had sobbed. "He'll be miserable. She'll force him to town and embarrass him with her antics."

"Maybe he wants a little excitement in his life," he said, refusing to offer any comfort. "Miss Parker is beautiful and eminently beddable—"

"How dare you!" she gasped.

"Because it's true." He pulled her behind some shrubbery to avoid drawing the attention of the other guests. "Love matches frequently involve people who appear very different on the surface. Few people bare their souls to the world. Frankly, I doubt you know anything about Eastbrook beyond his facade. A man who endorses propriety would never reveal his core to a girl not his betrothed."

"You're wrong!"

"Forget it, Sophia. He was never yours and never will be. Accept it and move on."

But her ensuing tirade betrayed her. Far from moving on, she had cultivated her desire into an obsession. Nicholas must use his title and position to build her into a powerful social figure and arbiter of conduct—preferably as an Almack's patroness. She would make George pay for ignoring her. She would miss no opportunity to show Miss Parker up for the frivolous hoyden she was. George would regret his choice every day of his life.

Her rant finally collapsed into tears. Being Sophia, it had not taken her long to control her emotions, though she had let him draw her face against his shoulder to muffle the sobs.

"Feel better?" he asked as the music stopped in the ballroom. He patted her back, then put her aside. "The set is over. You cannot remain out here without drawing notice."

She nodded. "You will help me, won't you?"

"Of course not. I will not be a party to such adolescent foolishness. He clearly cares for Miss Parker. Even if she disappeared, he would find another girl who filled the same needs. Nothing you do will affect him, and I refuse to help you make an utter cake of yourself."

"Why you selfish, sanctimonious—"

"Watch it, Sophia." He was already leading her across the terrace. "Do you wish to treat society to a tantrum?"

She had immediately quieted, schooling her face into an acceptable mask as they had entered the ballroom. But he had felt the rage quivering in the hand gripping his arm. Their next meeting would not be congenial.

Now he paused in his pacing to stare out his library window.

It would be a bigger confrontation than she thought. *Selfish.* It was long past time he considered his own desires. Yes, he had responsibilities to his title, to his dependents, to the future. And yes, he was only a caretaker for most of what he had inherited. But he was also a man, with needs and interests of his own. Hopefully, he could meld all his duties into a tolerable life. If not, his own needs came first. If that made him selfish, then so be it.

Wedding Sophia was clearly a mistake. Only a burst of insanity would have suggested it. She was a harridan who would grow worse with age. He did not want to spend his days with a demanding, disapproving woman who was in love with another man. Nor did he wish to pass his nights with a dedicated martyr.

Yet he could not jilt her. He sighed. No gentleman could do so and hold his head up in public. He still couldn't explain why he had thought that marriage to Sophia would work. He had not known her well, but everything he did know ran counter to his image of a good wife.

*Idiot!*

They would both have to make some serious compromises. And they would have to start now. Neither could afford to walk into this arrangement blind. For himself, compromise meant giving up his belief in marital fidelity. If Sophia wanted children, he would father them, but he could not spend his life tied solely to a martyr.

Sophia would have to give up trying to reform him. Not only must she accept his interests, but she must cease embarrassing him in public. Which meant that she must abandon criticizing accepted practices. And not just in London. If she wanted his name, she could not turn herself into a laughingstock.

Would they live together? It was too soon to say, but he was determined to avoid the nagging that his mother had inflicted on his father. At least Diana would be out of the country, so he could pursue his usual activities without fear of running into her. Constant reminders of what he had lost would destroy him.

Charles sauntered through Green Park, deep in thought. He avoided the more popular paths, for he did not want to speak with people. Too many doubts assailed him.

The image of a laughing Chloe embracing George remained engraved on his soul, having already robbed him of a night's sleep. He knew that she was pretending to get along with her betrothed, but he did not believe that she was capable of such superb acting. That embrace had been genuine.

Myriad questions pounded in his head, none with answers. By the time he'd returned to the ballroom, Diana had unaccountably disappeared. He had already danced his set with Chloe, so he couldn't ask her to explain it. Approaching her a second time would raise suspicions he could ill afford this close to leaving.

George had departed, and not to the library. His fears built. Had his confrontation failed? Had his own feelings shown through the facade of a concerned third party? Perhaps he had pushed George into staking a firmer claim.

He shuddered.

Did Chloe care for George? Had her protestations of love and her willingness to engage in a surreptitious courtship been a ploy to make George jealous? If George approached her with anything like passion, would she respond? She had long been troubled about the prospect of alienating her family and causing trouble with the Company. Maybe her fears had pushed her into accepting the life her parents decreed. But if she was that fickle, could she survive the hardships of months at sea and years in a foreign country? Could she anyway?

The doubts ate into his heart, leaving gaping wounds. What had George done to bring such a carefree laugh to her face?

Yet he loved her. Ever the fool, he still loved her.

Sophia burst from the shrubbery and all but threw herself into his arms.

"Thank heavens you are here, Charles," she gasped. "I need help."

His hands automatically clasped her shoulders to keep her from falling from the impact. "What is wrong?"

"My maid. A dog tripped her. She can't walk, and I fear her ankle may be broken. There was a loud crack when she went down." Tears glistened in her eyes.

"Relax, Sophia." He patted her back. "Where is she?"

"Just down the path."

He had not noted the narrow walk that joined his just beyond a large shrub. It took only a moment to reach the maid. The girl was in great pain. Already the ankle was swollen to more than twice its usual size.

"Dr. McClarren lives quite close. Or would you rather I carried her to your house?"

Sophia appeared undecided. "Dr. McClarren," she said at last. "We have never used him, but I have heard good reports of his skill."

He nodded. Carefully lifting the maid into his arms, he led the way to the doctor's house. A footman was dispatched to fetch Sophia's parents, so he left her in the hands of the housekeeper and took his leave.

But the interlude had done nothing to set his fears to rest. Was Chloe using him, or did she truly love him?

"Did you see that?" demanded Chloe, grabbing Diana's arm.

"Control yourself," ordered Diana. "You are in view of the world."

"What possessed him to make an assignation with Lady Sophia?" Tears trembled in her eyes, but she had resumed a casual demeanor—at least it would appear so from a distance.

"You don't know that he did," she declared stoutly. But Charles's conduct did indeed look suspicious. He had been walking in an unfrequented part of the park and had not seemed surprised to find Lady Sophia waiting for him. She had never seen him walking anywhere in the past. He preferred to ride.

"He embraced her," sobbed Chloe. "In front of the entire world. Has he been trifling with me? Mama warned me that he was a fearsome rake who would seduce and ruin anyone silly enough to smile at him. How could I have been stupid enough to fall in love with him?"

"Lower your voice."

"Dear God! Papa claims he is a fortune hunter. What if this entire tale of the East India Company is false? He may be after my dowry. It is quite large."

"For heaven's sake, calm down. What is the matter with you?"

"I just realized that no one knows about his appointment except us. Maybe he's lying. You must admit that it is odd for a gentleman to involve himself in trade." Tears trembled in her eyes.

"Lord Woodvale knew of it the night before Charles told us." Which itself was quite strange, she admitted. Why would Charles share his secret with Nicholas? He was trying to keep it quiet. His family would be furious when they learned the truth, and he was too busy with his own arrangements to deal with their recriminations. So why tell Nicholas? The men were not close. And why was Nicholas keeping it a secret?

"All right. Maybe I overreacted. But nothing explains arranging assignations with Lady Sophia. I thought he hated her. Did he decide to take her fortune after all? If he doesn't wed me, I'll be ruined—or stuck with George!"

"Enough!" Her sharp command pulled Chloe out of her renewed hysteria. "You are turning one incident into a Cheltenham tragedy. I cannot explain what either of them were doing here this morning, but nothing will convince me that he has been toying with your affections. And nothing will convince me that he has paid attention to Lady Sophia. You will reserve judgment until you learn the facts—and do not forget that Charles and Sophia have known each other most of their lives. Despite having no desire to marry, they *are* friends."

"You are right, of course," said Chloe, but her tone did not sound convinced.

"You are thinking of his reputation, I suppose." Diana sighed. "I suspect your mother made him sound much worse than he actually was—and I do mean *was*. Suggesting that you elope is highly improper, of course, but I cannot blame him under the circumstances. He is more responsible than most of his peers, was no wilder than other cubs, and is too young to be considered a hardened rake. His antics were only the usual sowing of wild oats. Now he wants to settle down, and I am sure he will remain faithful to you in the future—unless you do something stupid."

"What would you consider stupid? Taking a lover?"

"That would go far beyond stupid. I meant jumping to hysterical conclusions every time he speaks to another woman, then nagging him about your suspicions. If you do not trust him, sooner or later he will become so irritated that he will live up—or down—to your expectations."

"Are you implying that I should ignore that scene?" She pointed to the empty path where Charles and Sophia had stood only moments before.

"For now. I suspect he will tell you about it without being asked, because I do not for a moment believe that he would be dallying with Sophia—and certainly not in view of the world. She is betrothed to Woodvale, don't forget."

"That didn't stop him from pursuing me." She giggled. "It does seem rather ridiculous, though. But I love him so much that I cannot bear the thought of losing him."

"Will you see him today?"

"Tonight. We will both be at the Sanford ball, but he has meetings all afternoon."

"Good. In the meantime don't do anything silly. George will be talking to your parents and his over the next couple of days. If they question you, guard your tongue."

Charles was unusually quiet as he escorted Diana to the Sanford ball. Not until they finished the first set did he change, and then only to adopt a painful frown.

"Smile!" she hissed, following his eyes. Chloe and George had just arrived and were talking intently, having drawn far enough away from the Parkers not to be overheard.

"They look so intimate," he choked.

"You two need to talk," she decided abruptly. "Find an empty anteroom. We'll join you shortly. And Charles?" She laid a hand on his arm, looking him directly in the eye. "Love cannot survive without trust."

His brows rose, but he said nothing. Diana went to fetch Chloe, unaware that a scowling Nicholas had seen that intimate gesture and heard her final comment.

"Something is wrong," announced Diana the moment the anteroom door was shut. "Is eloping going to cost you your position?"

"I doubt it. My superiors seem impressed with my knowledge of China."

"Anything new on gaining permission?" she asked Chloe.

"Nothing." She sighed. "George spent the afternoon arguing with Father, but you were right. It did no good."

"*George* did?"

Diana smiled at Charles's incredulity and slipped away to look out the window. Let them work out whatever was bothering them on their own. It would be good practice for the years ahead when they would have only each other.

"We had a long talk last night and agreed that marriage would be a disaster. He will try to convince our parents to set aside the betrothal. So far he has spoken only to Father, but I suspect that his arguments will work no better than anyone else's."

Charles's voice softened. "Is that why you were hugging him last night?"

She giggled. "I suppose that was rather indiscreet. I was so happy that he finally understood that I didn't think."

"Then it worked. I was afraid that I'd made things worse." A long moment of silence must have included an unspoken question, for his next words were clearly an answer. "I spoke with him last night as Diana's betrothed, trying to make him see you as you really are."

"And succeeded. I'm sorry I thanked him so publicly."

"I should not have jumped to conclusions."

Diana glanced over her shoulder. Charles held Chloe in a loose embrace, but Chloe was holding back. "Appearances can often be deceiving—a valuable lesson for both of us, I suspect."

"Meaning?" he asked.

"We saw you and Sophia in the park this morning," admitted Chloe.

Charles burst out laughing.

Diana relaxed and returned her attention to the garden. Obviously the meeting was nothing to fret about.

"I'd been blue-deviled since spotting you with George," he

admitted so softly that Diana barely heard him. "I was trying to walk it off before my first appointment. Then Sophia streaked out of a side path. Her maid had fallen and needed help. I was the first person she ran into."

"Literally." But her voice was again light. "How is the maid?"

"Broken ankle." Fabric rustled as he pulled Chloe closer. "I won't misplace my trust again, love."

"Me, either. Forgive me for doubting you."

Diana closed her eyes and counted slowly to a hundred. Then she let out a long sigh.

"That's enough," she announced softly. "Too many people will see you tonight. If they can tell what you've been up to, we're all in trouble." By the time she turned around, Chloe was checking her hair in the mirror and Charles was smoothing his jacket.

Chloe returned to the ballroom first, for Lady Parker would be upset if she remained away much longer. Diana told Charles the ideas she and Chloe had come up with about luggage and other plans, then gave him a head start back. Even though they were nominally betrothed, she had to watch her reputation.

Nicholas escaped the Sanfords' ballroom. Sophia had been furious when he not only refused to conform to her expectations, but demanded that she modify her own behavior. This was not a battle he would win easily, though she would eventually realize the futility of fighting him. They might never be happy together, but he would persevere until they reached a compromise that allowed a modicum of contentment.

After leaving her simmering in fury, he had meant to dance with Diana—until he had spotted that intimate exchange with Langley. It was not a memory he wanted to keep.

He couldn't stay. Not at this ball. Not in town. He would go down to Meadowbrook until she left. Sophia needed time to think about the compromises he had just demanded.

Half an hour later he finally emerged from the ballroom, having been waylaid several times along the way.

Only two people were visible in the hallway. Diana, who was exiting an anteroom, and a tulip of the *ton*, who couldn't be more than two-and-twenty. Diana's face blossomed with delight as she threw herself into the sprig's arms.

"Jeremy! I had no idea you were in town."

The sprig twirled her around.

Nicholas heard nothing more through the buzzing in his ears. Red haze blocked his eyes. Damnation! Was he to fall apart every time she paid attention to another man? That passionate greeting replayed in his mind—again and again. Was the sprig a lover? What then did she feel for Langley?

His head swirled. Fragments of voices faded in and out, but the only word he heard clearly was *trust*. Which he couldn't. Not her, and especially not himself.

"Nicholas? Are you all right?"

His eyes cleared. She was alone in the hall—and was looking at him in great puzzlement.

"Who was he?" he demanded, raising shock in her eyes.

"Jeremy Reynolds, Harry's grand-nephew and heir to the current earl—not that it's any of your business."

"Is that why Bounty hates you so much? I thought it was because you wound up with his inheritance."

"What?" She saw the accusation in his eyes and drew herself up in icy disdain. "I don't believe this. Of all the low-minded fools I've met, you take the cake. Jeremy is family—and the closest thing I have to a son."

"Son?" he choked, already awash in embarrassment.

She nodded. "Harry paid for his schooling. Jeremy spent all his breaks with us so he could learn about his future inheritance—and to remove him from his father's influence. Now, if you'll excuse me . . ." She tried to push past him to reach the ballroom.

"Wait." He held up one hand. "We need to talk, Diana."

"Why?"

"To prevent idiotic scenes like this in the future." He ran his fingers through his hair. "There is too much between us to pretend that we're strangers, yet we still are in many ways. Questions keep buzzing through my head, but I don't have any answers. I can't stand it anymore."

"So it bothers you, too."

He nodded. "This is hardly the place." Voices proved his point as another new arrival started up the stairs.

"Very well." Gesturing him to follow, she stepped back into the anteroom. "But we haven't much time. Charles has the next set. It would be highly suspicious if I missed it."

He closed the door behind them, then leaned wearily against it. Already he felt lower than a maggot after his unwarranted accusation. *Trust.* Somehow he must regain her trust. He couldn't stand the thought that she would spend her years in China hating him.

"We've been snapping at each other since that first *soirée*. I'm not enjoying it."

She sighed. "Nor I. Debate stimulates, but the barbs are pointless—and painful."

"I do it from guilt—that was no ploy, Diana; guilt has ripped me apart for ten years. I suspect you do it from pain." He paused until she nodded. "I know I hurt you. You refused my apology last time. And you were right. Everything I said and did that day by the stream was deliberate. And unforgivable."

"Why?" Diana stared at the man she loved and would always love. Tears stung her eyes, but she fought them down. She could not reveal how badly he could still hurt her—*was* hurting her. How could he believe that she could have an affair with a boy? Of course, Nicholas had been the same age when they had first met . . .

"I was young—barely down from Oxford. Remember?"

She nodded. Oh, yes, she remembered. He had been so full of life, so cocky that summer. They had taken daring chances. If her father had not been distracted by his illness, it would not have worked. But they had never been caught.

"You thought you could do anything," she said softly.

"So I did. I had my life completely planned. I would take London by storm, use gaming to support myself, enjoy the carefree life for a few years, then lay siege to an heiress. It was a good plan, even the gaming part. But I hadn't counted on you."

She watched a flash of pain twist his face. He paced for a while, then stopped at the window, pulling aside the draperies so he could stare into the garden.

"You dazzled me, Diana, from the moment I saw you. You were peeking out of the forest—so like your namesake with your sunstreaked hair and green eyes. God, those eyes. They have always reminded me of an enchanted glade. I fell in love with you without even knowing your name."

She snorted, prompting him to turn his head and look at her.

"I don't expect you to believe it. I refused to believe it myself. Lust, I insisted. Pure lust. Once I had assuaged it, life would continue as planned. So I laid siege to you. But the more I learned of you, the harder it was to dismiss my feelings as lust. I quit trying to seduce you the moment I learned who you were. But I could not stay away. It wasn't until that day by the river that I understood what I was doing to you."

The day she had admitted she loved him. Diana hid her clenched fists in her skirts. What was the point of dragging this up again? Hadn't she suffered enough?

"The first words that sprang to my lips were *I love you, too.* But I bit them back." His voice broke. "I couldn't admit it, yet couldn't deny it. So I panicked. All my plans were crumbling; fear weighed me down. I was penniless, Diana. Absolutely penniless. I had accepted Gerald's invitation for the summer because it was the only alternative to home. My worldly goods when I arrived in Warwickshire consisted of ten shillings, a first edition of *Othello,* and a horse. I knew that if I set foot in my father's house, I would never leave again. I would have been trapped there for the rest of my life. That was all I had to offer you. Your lack of dowry didn't help any. Do you remember that I hesitated before I answered you?"

She nodded.

"In that instant, I convinced myself that I did not love you, but even then I let panic control my tongue. I chose words that would sting, words that would hurt, words that would guarantee that you never again thought of me with kindness, let alone love. I clung to my plans and threw away the best thing I ever had. I have carried that guilt every hour since."

"I think you need to forgive yourself, Nicholas," she said softly, coming close enough to lay a hand on his arm. "I have long since done so."

"How could you?"

She smiled. "You can thank Harry for that. I told him everything before I accepted him." She met his eyes. "Everything. He pointed out much of what you just said. You would have grown to hate me for trapping you in a life you never wanted. Whatever your feelings, the situation was impossible. So you lashed out when I pressed the issue. If I had been older or wiser, we would not have parted in anger, for I would have known that you were not for me."

"I can hear him saying that."

She raised her brows.

"Bounty was nearly a father to me. One of his estates adjoined ours."

"Sherlock," she said in sudden understanding.

"Right. He found me hiding in the woods when I was eight. I had escaped after an argument with my father. He helped me cool my temper, then began challenging my mind. I saw him frequently after that. He offered me sanity, stability, and excitement. But it was years before I could best him in debate."

"What did he give you?"

"That first edition."

"I thought that was an odd possession for a penniless scamp."

"What did he give you?"

"*Romeo and Juliet.*"

He shook his head. "Damn, but I miss him."

"So do I. But if you knew him that well, then you will know that he was rarely wrong. Thus the way we parted is not entirely your fault."

"I cannot accept that. I was too young to handle what I was feeling, but I refuse to start a new argument," he added, cutting off any response. "You are far more generous than I deserve. And perhaps we can someday meet as friends. We will have time to get used to the idea. I understand Langley expects to spend a dozen years in China before returning."

"Yes, but I will not be with him." The words were out without thought, but she knew now that she could trust him. Her instincts had not lied all those years ago. He *had* loved her.

"You decided to stay behind?" He sounded shocked.

"I doubt his wife would appreciate a chaperon."

"But—"

"I told you once before that I had no intention of remarrying, and I meant it. Charles and I were talking in the folly when the Parkers appeared. Rather than allow them to spread scandal, he claimed we were betrothed. But he knew before he opened his mouth that I would never wed him."

"Then who is he marrying?" he demanded. He had paled alarmingly.

"Sit down, Nicholas. You look ready to collapse." She took a turn about the room before joining him on the couch. "Unfortunately, Charles has acquired a rather rakish reputation, which does not sit well with some of the higher sticklers. He would not be considered an acceptable suitor by the parents of the girl he loves. We have been trying to change that, but one way or the other, he will wed the girl and take her with him."

"Meaning they will elope if they cannot gain permission."

"Exactly. There is one last avenue we are pursuing, but I have little hope of success. Arrangements are already in train to transport her to his ship. I trust you will remain quiet about this."

"If you will identify the girl." His eyes burned into hers, promising help.

She didn't even hesitate. "Chloe Parker."

"My God!" He covered his eyes, pressing his fingers into his forehead as if that might clear his brain. "I thought her reconciled to wedding Eastbrook."

"Never. But why should you have considered her at all?"

"Sophia loves George."

She burst into laughter, guiltily covering her mouth with one hand. "Are you serious?"

He nodded.

"Then why did you offer for her?"

"She is one of the responsibilities I inherited along with the title. Her father is determined to see her wed this Season. Once Langley escaped his net, he found another suitor." He described Griswold. "By that time, Eastbrook not only seemed reconciled, he appeared enamored with Miss Parker."

"So you offered her an alternative. I have no idea of George's feelings, but he does not wish to wed Chloe. He is trying to talk their parents into negating the arrangement—not that I believe he will have any more success than the rest of us."

"I know what you mean. The Parkers are as blinkered as cart horses. As are the Weymouths. They actually pointed out that Eastbrook's signature was affixed to the betrothal agreement on his twenty-first birthday."

"So you have been after them, too. No wonder they are digging their heels in. How can they change their minds after telling half the *ton* they would not consider it?"

"If Eastbrook dislikes Miss Parker, and she is determined to wed Langley, then why were they so friendly last night?" he asked suddenly.

"Chloe has been trying to convince him that she would make him a most unsuitable wife, but he is as stubborn as a mule. Last night Charles finally pushed him into admitting it. George and Chloe had a no-nonsense discussion about what each wanted. She claimed that she loved someone else, though she did not name Charles. George's sensibilities would have balked at freeing her so she could chase after a man already betrothed to another; she didn't want to take the time to explain this mess. Charles had excused his own interest as concern over the distress it was causing me. That was when George agreed to help. If he cannot convince their parents to call off the betrothal, he will transfer all her luggage to the ship."

"As if he were taking it to his estate," he said. "How fortunate that Langley is sailing the same day as Eastbrook's wedding is scheduled."

"That's the only break we've had. For a long time we feared that he would not leave until later."

"Eastbrook will get nowhere with the Parkers."

She sighed. "I know. He was closeted with Lord Parker all afternoon. Without success. The man is impossible."

"He can keep trying. It will keep him out of trouble—and it won't hurt to apprise everyone that he is just as unhappy about this arrangement as Miss Parker. In the meantime I think we can gain their approval, though it will require a radically different approach."

"What do you have in mind?"

"A scandal that will send all parties into shock. I believe I will invite everyone to dinner." His eyes sparkled with mischief. "There are no important balls the day after tomorrow. If I do this right, we may even discover Eastbrook's feelings. Sophia finds him sympathetic, but she hasn't a clue whether he actually cares for her."

"Nor do I. Until last night he was determined to wed Chloe."

"Exactly." Dropping his voice, he sketched out the essence of his plan.

# Chapter Fifteen

Diana didn't bother with her carriage the night of Nicholas's dinner. Charles escorted her across Berkeley Square.

"Do you really believe this will work?" he asked as they strolled toward Woodvale House.

"Nicholas is very good at getting what he wants." She ignored his raised brow at her form of address. "You got the special license?"

"Yes, though we could just as easily have been married at sea."

"But a few days together before you leave would be better. *Mal de mer* would hardly enliven your wedding night."

He laughed. "I had not considered that. I had best brush up my nursing skills."

"How do you know which of you will need them? Have you ever sailed?"

He mumbled something profane.

"Good luck. In the meantime you can use my house. I need to return to my estate anyway. Some problems have recently arisen that need my attention." This last was a lie, but she would have to settle her nerves before facing Nicholas again.

"I hope your reputation will not be too badly tarnished."

"A few months on my estate should mend it quite nicely."

"If you say so." But his skepticism was short-lived. "I don't know how I can ever thank you, Diana."

She smiled. "Name your first daughter after me."

The butler opened the door, preventing further discussion. This was it. Charles lightly squeezed her hand and led her inside.

Nicholas had decided to stage his drama before dinner so they wouldn't have to hide nervousness through two hours of polite conversation and pointless wedding discussions. As planned, Charles and Diana were the last to arrive. The butler led them past the drawing room.

Everything was set, Diana noted, peeking around the almost-shut door. Sophia was playing hostess, giving her more authority than a guest would usually have. Her eyes betrayed an unusual excitement, but she maintained her rigid propriety. The Parkers, Bankleighs, Weymouths, and Langleys were all present, as were Chloe and George. Nicholas was not.

Diana caught Chloe's eye, then followed the butler.

She could easily picture the scene in the drawing room. Chloe's anticipation had made her anxious, so Lady Parker would not be surprised when the girl excused herself to the retiring room.

Within a minute she joined them in the hallway.

"The library is the last door on the right," said the butler, his expression conveying neither approval nor disapproval. "My lady," he added as Charles led Chloe away. Opening the door to the breakfast parlor, he stepped aside so Diana could enter.

Nicholas was already inside. "I have been delayed," he explained, noting her raised brows. "Sophia has put dinner back half an hour in response to my message and will entertain my guests until I arrive." He grinned. "Actually, dinner is not scheduled for at least another hour. Wiggs will occupy everyone by passing around something edible."

"You are a rogue. I wondered how you would get all of us out of the drawing room without raising questions."

"I trust no one told George what was in the wind."

"Of course we didn't. Do you take us for fools?"

"Forgive me." He paced the floor. "Now that we've actually begun, I can imagine too many disasters."

She could understand his fears. The same ones assailed her. The happiness of the others was not all that was at stake. Success was the only way to keep their own reputations intact.

"Do you really believe this will work?" she asked as he stopped in front of her, doubt clear in her voice.

"Trust me. Please?" His intensity gave her pause.

A door opened. "This is quite improper, Lady Sophia," said George his voice clearly disapproving.

Diana grimaced.

But Sophia ignored his tone. "Lord Woodvale particularly asked me to show you the library. He has a book on sheep breeding he thought you would enjoy."

Their footsteps were drawing closer. Despite his complaints, George was complying.

"This won't work," whispered Diana. "Even George is not prudish enough that he'll object to spotting you alone with a widow when we haven't even shut the door."

"But that is not what he will see," murmured Nicholas, sweeping her into his arms. His lips descended.

Shock reverberated from her head to her toes. He had given her no warning, no opportunity to brace for his touch. Surprise parted her lips in a gasp.

Rogue that he was, he took advantage of that opening, sliding his tongue past her teeth to caress her own.

She responded. How could she not? Heat flashed as she parried his thrust, caressing him in turn. Her hands wrapped around his neck, pulling him closer, threading into his hair.

Twin moans resounded through the room.

Nicholas dropped one hand to her hip to pull her tight against his aching groin. He had hoped for a response. Prayed for it. This plot had more threads than she knew. But thought quickly fled. His body screamed for more as he feasted on her mouth. He hardly heard the voices in the hallway.

George gasped. "The c-cad! He's unscru— dast— dam— He is disgusting! As if that scene at Drury Lane wasn't bad enough! How dare he dishonor you so?"

Sophia sighed. "It doesn't matter. One cannot expect fidelity from a rake, and he is better than the alternative Papa offered once Charles snapped up Lady Bounty. I'll get used to his ways in time."

"But that was Lady Bounty with Woodvale!"

"Quite shocking, I agree, but not my affair."

George could only sputter.

Nicholas registered satisfaction in a distant corner of his mind, but most of his attention remained on Diana. Already his groin was ready to explode from her nearness. How could he have been so stupid as to think that money or position or even a roof over his head was more important than her? Every liaison in the past ten years was wiped from his memory as she drew back to nibble at his lips. One of her hands had worked its way under his coat.

"They've gone," she murmured. "Keep your mind on the job." She giggled. "You are right. I've never heard George so incoherent."

"This isn't over, Diana," he swore, plundering her mouth one last time. "But first we must resolve this other matter."

"I suppose."

Hand in hand, they peeked around the doorjamb, then tiptoed down the hall. She stifled another giggle when they reached the library doorway.

Charles had staged a more scandalous scene than even Nicholas had dared. Of course, he and Chloe were on the verge of marriage, Diana admitted. It gave them greater freedom. But she couldn't suppress a spurt of envy.

He was sitting in a wing chair, which he had positioned so that anyone entering the room could tell what he was doing but not see too much. Chloe sprawled across his lap, her legs dangling over the far arm, with Charles's hand well under her skirts. Her near arm pulled her closer while he kissed her.

Diana's stomach clenched, heat again flooding her womb. She could feel Nicholas's hand doing delightful things under *her* skirts—as he had by the stream that last day. His long fingers had glided over her skin, leaving flaming trails in their wake. His manhood had throbbed against her hip. The smell of fresh-cut hay had drifted from a nearby field as robins sang merrily in a thicket of shrubs. His kisses had been deep and frantic, tasting of morning chocolate and coffee.

She stifled a gasp, appalled at the clarity of the memory. *This isn't over* ... To control her blushes, she forced her attention onto George, who did not yet know that she and Nicholas were behind him.

He was scarlet, though whether from embarrassment or fury she was not sure.

"Chloe!" he choked out.

Charles opened his eyes, then slowly helped Chloe sit up. He seemed drugged—as she had been in the breakfast parlor—but he rapidly pulled his wits together.

"Eastbrook."

"Thank you for bringing him, Lady Sophia," said Chloe, making a halfhearted attempt to straighten her gown even as her other hand caressed Charles's cheek. "I could not leave without bidding you farewell, George. I appreciate your efforts, but we've run out of time. I am officially renouncing our betrothal. Charles and I will leave immediately for Guernsey. We can no longer postpone it, as our ship sails next week."

"B-but." George swallowed and tried again. "What of Lady Bounty?"

Charles shrugged. "She doesn't give a fig for me. She only stepped in to keep Chloe's parents from discovering us one day."

"But eloping!" George was shaking his head. "The scandal will ruin you."

"Not if you support us," said Chloe. "We are leaving the country and will be gone for years. If you make light of our change in plans and prevent my parents from following us, it should be forgotten long before we return. I'm depending on you, George. Tell them that we have already set sail. Make them believe it. There is a ship bound for America that leaves on the midnight tide. By the time they discover our real plans, we will be wed, so they can only accept them."

Nicholas banged the door against the wall and entered the library. "There you are, Sophia," he said in jovial greeting. "My apologies for being late, but it couldn't be helped. I got sidetracked. Delightful afternoon."

"Harriette Wilson or Lady Alston?" asked Charles idly.

"Neither. A lively lass just up from the country."

"Beast!" sobbed Sophia, covering her eyes to hide her lack of tears. "And now Lady Bounty. Can't you at least limit your conquests to one a day? Even Devereaux is more discreet."

"I warned you how it would be. You know I offered you nothing but escape from Griswold."

"Surely you can at least pretend decorum in public!"

"If that's how you feel about it, take your puritan principles and run," Nicholas said unfeelingly. "I will not give up my fun for a cold-hearted heiress. There are too many delectable maidens in the world, and my appetites have never been stronger. You're on your own now, sweetings. At least until Griswold grabs you." He slid his arm around Diana and sank into another of those heated kisses. "Mmm. Much better. I do prefer a willing wench."

Diana stiffened.

"Shh," he murmured against her lips. "Remember that I'm a conscienceless scoundrel."

"I ought to bite you," she whispered back, then returned his openmouthed kiss. "And I'll take a knife to certain portions of your anatomy if I come out of this with a reputation as a courtesan."

He winced.

"You can't throw me to Griswold," cried Sophia. "I'll kill myself before allowing that swine to touch me!" Her subsequent hysterics were faked, but George didn't notice.

Nicholas ignored her, sliding his lips down Diana's neck and across her shoulder to nuzzle her gown aside. Somehow, he'd undone the top three tapes.

George choked.

Diana's senses swam, but she kept one eye on the others even as her body melted against Nicholas, her arms pulling him closer. Damn the man! Why could she not ignore him? But she could no more forgo this opportunity than fly. The lovemaking was both public and false, but it would provide memories that could warm her for years.

And two could play the game. Quick fingers loosened his cravat, opening his shirt to expose a patch of dark hair and drawing a gasp.

"Just trying to make this scene more realistic," she quipped, stilling his protest with her lips. But one eye stayed on the others.

Charles was again kissing Chloe.

"Who is Griswold?" demanded George, paling until Diana feared he might swoon. He faced Sophia, turning his back on Nicholas's clever hands and Charles's latest foray up Chloe's leg. The room reeked of passion. The temperature was becoming unbearable.

Sophia uncovered dry eyes, immediately throwing herself against George's shoulder. And just as well. She obviously couldn't cry on demand. "He is odious, but Papa will make me accept his offer. How can I? He is brutal, he smells, and he'll demand an heir. But more than that he wants my dowry, for he is rapidly sinking beneath debts. How will I survive?"

"Was that why you accepted this libertine's offer?" he demanded, stroking her back as he glared over his shoulder toward the tableau by the door. Even that brief look brought a new blush to his face.

Nicholas's mind was back on the job. He was straining to hear, his hands motionless and his arms relaxed.

"It seemed like a godsend at the time." Sophia's fake sobbing was working. George now had both arms around her. "Nicholas offered to save me from the indignity of being sold—which is what Papa's arrangements amounted to—but I find I cannot accept infidelity. I thought I could close my eyes to it, but stumbling over his women in every room is too much." She sobbed louder. "How can I tell Papa I threw over a marquess? Griswold is only a baron."

She wasn't making much sense, but George's sensibilities were too overloaded to notice.

"Don't take either of them, Sophia," he begged. "You would be far better off with me."

"You?" Sophia pulled her head back to stare at him.

Diana could hear the effort Sophia expended to sound surprised, but George was no good at reading people. At least Sophia's eyes were now red. She had been rubbing them against his shoulder.

"Why not? I will treat you far better than either Woodvale or Griswold. And saving Miss Parker from retribution will be easier if I can produce another wife."

Diana nearly groaned. Good God! George was brainless. What kind of proposal was that? She sidestepped until both eyes peeked over Nicholas's shoulder—which was shaking so hard with suppressed laughter that she feared he would ruin everything.

But Sophia was made of sterner stuff. Her voice rang with determination. "I think not, my lord, though your thoughts are kind. I've already accepted one martyr, and look where that got me. Somehow I will find a way to escape Griswold, even if I must run away. After the fiasco of this Season, I have decided to wed no one who cannot offer what I need."

Nicholas was twisting his head in an attempt to see. "Don't move," whispered Diana. "You will distract him." She kept her eyes nearly closed so it would look like she was lost in Nicholas's arms if George again glanced their way. Chloe and Charles were likewise motionless.

"He can't be distracted by what he doesn't see," he whispered back, sliding his hand to cup her bottom. She nearly yelped.

"You'll pay for that!"

"With luck." He was inching her skirt up so he could slide his hand under the hem. Tingles spread from that minuscule movement, growing and multiplying until she was trembling. She nipped his ear in revenge, sending shudders through his body.

George tried to speak, but nothing intelligible emerged.

"God, what an ass," said Nicholas against Diana's throat. "I never thought to hear such a mutton-headed proposal. Whatever does she see in him?"

"I can't imagine."

George somehow found his voice. "What do you want, Lady Sophia? I'm sure I can give it to you. We share so many ideals."

"Like condemning fun?" quipped Nicholas, tracing her ear with his tongue.

"Shh."

"We've both got country estates. Is it a town house you lack? But that doesn't seem like you." He paused in thought.

Nicholas trailed kisses across her cheek. "I wonder if two such prudes can figure out what to do in bed?" Then he had to press her mouth against his shoulder to stifle her laughter.

George cleared his throat. "How about an orphanage for the street urchins you break your heart over?"

Sophia gasped. "How did you know I wanted to start an orphanage?"

"I know you so well." The barest hint of a smile caught one corner of his mouth.

"George?" She again leaned back against his arms, looking into his eyes.

"What can I offer you, Sophia?"

"Not an orphanage. I have the money and estate for that already."

"Then what? I'm no good at mind reading. You need to tell me."

"Dunderhead," whispered Nicholas. "The man's as dense as a post."

"Denser," said Diana, stifling another laugh. "I'm tempted to write him a cue card."

"Why did you offer for me?"

Five people held their breath as George hesitated.

"Come on, George," whispered Diana. "You can do it."

"Let's get this over with," begged Nicholas under his breath.

Even Charles paused to shake his head. Chloe twisted her head to stare at her former betrothed.

George closed his eyes. "I l-love you."

"Then I would be honored to accept."

The sighs of relief nearly fluttered the draperies. Diana sagged into Nicholas's embrace. George was actually kissing Sophia. He must have forgotten his audience.

"Thank God," murmured Nicholas. His tongue dove back into Diana's mouth. She closed her eyes, no longer caring what anyone else was doing . . .

Someone shrieked.

"Gracious!" The new voice was coldly disapproving.

"If this is a joke, Woodvale, it is in very poor taste!" Lord Parker was angrier than Diana had ever seen him.

Wiggs had fetched the couples from the drawing room. Now they crowded into the library, shock and disapproval on every face. The room bulged. Eight parents tried to outshout one another.

"Oh, the scandal!" cried Lady Parker, collapsing against Lady Weymouth as her screeches rose into full hysterics.

Lord Weymouth shoved Sophia aside so he could tower over George. "How dare you court censure with this blatant infidelity?"

"Infidelity!" shouted Sophia, pushing him back and draping her arm around George's waist. "Look at that trollop you tied him to!"

"How dare you preach of infidelity when you've kept a mistress in our own village for years?" demanded George.

"Chloe, you will go home this instant!" thundered Lord Parker.

"She won't," countered Charles, whisking her behind him for protection as he stood eye to eye with his prospective father-in-law.

"Not another scandal!" sobbed Lady Langley. "We barely survived your brother's."

"What?"

"What mistress?"

"I won't allow you to throw over a good match!"

"You're a fine one to talk, Mother! What about your lovers?"

"Lovers?"

"I'll never wed George!"

"Never!"

"—bedazzled you!"

"—seduces innocents!"

"How can you deny it? I heard you, Mother!"

"That's no innocent—"

"My palpitations!"

"He's turned her head—" The veins stood out on Lord Parker's neck.

"—a light skirt!" Lord Langley's fist slammed onto the desktop.

"How many of her children are yours?"

"Dictatorial—"

Nicholas chuckled.

"How dare you judge me!" Lord Weymouth's hands fisted.

"Good heavens," murmured Diana. "There's going to be violence if you don't do something."

"He is—"

"Have you no shame?"

"I won't stand for—"

"—unprincipled libertine."

"Trollop!"

"Lady Debenham will crucify us!"

"—foolishness!"

"Fortune hunter!"

"Enough of—"

"—no dowry!"

Lord Parker sidestepped Lord Langley's fist as George made a dive for the sword hanging above the mantel.

"Quiet!" Nicholas's shout overrode the cacophony. Smoothing Diana's skirt back into place, he set her aside. "This is not a battlefield. There will be no dueling in my library."

A sword clattered onto the hearth. A dozen jaws dropped.

"Why, you—" began Lord Bankleigh, but Nicholas cut him off.

"You will be quiet," he said implacably. "You left us no choice but to stage this charade. I have never seen more pigheaded fools gathered in one spot in my life. Perhaps one of you can explain why eight parents who claim to care for their children have done their best to ruin them?" He glared at Lord Parker.

"How dare you?" Parker demanded. "I will not see my innocent daughter in the hands of a penniless rake."

"You would rather see her die of boredom with a man who will come to hate her as implacably as she hates him?" His glare stopped a response. "Have you ever asked her what she wanted? Have you ever even talked to her?" For the first time since his uncle's death, he enjoyed his position. His rank stopped Parker's objections cold. A viscount did not contradict a marquess. Especially in front of two earls.

"She wants marriage and children, the same as any other girl," stated Lady Parker firmly.

"That is true. But she also wants adventure. She wants to see the world, to enjoy life. Forcing her to live docilely in the country would destroy her spirit. Is that what you want?"

Parker was staring at his daughter as if he had never seen her before.

"This must be another of your jokes," complained Lord Langley, glaring at Charles. "Her dowry will never support you. Where will you live? What about Lady Bounty?"

"Lady Bounty knows my heart," said Charles coldly. "Chloe and I will wed tomorrow—by special license, if she can gain consent. Otherwise, we will catch the packet to Guernsey. Whatever dowry she has will go into trust for our children. I alone will support us. I sail for China next week as a representative of the East India Company."

Lady Langley collapsed onto a chair.

"China?" squeaked Lady Parker, pulling out her vinaigrette. "Heathens! Murderers!"

Lady Langley grabbed her hand to share the restorative, inciting new shrieks.

"It is what I want," declared Chloe.

"And I," said Charles, drawing her closer to his side as his eyes moved from one parent to another.

The ladies' tussle over the vinaigrette sent it sailing across the room.

Lord Parker was staring from George to Charles.

"I don't want her," said George. He recovered the salts and returned them to Lady Parker.

"I want Charles," declared Chloe.

"Lady Bounty?" He looked at her and grimaced. Her hair was falling down, and her dress was still off one shoulder.

"I never wanted Charles," she admitted calmly.

Lord Parker's shoulders sagged. "Come along, children. We will discuss this in private. There is much to do and not much time."

"Try the breakfast parlor. Second door on the right," suggested Nicholas. "My solicitor is in the study if you need help to untangle any settlements," he added as Chloe, Charles, and their parents left the library.

Lady Bankleigh and Lady Weymouth stared at Sophia with identical expressions of horror.

"George and I are getting married," she announced.

"George?" asked Lord Weymouth.

"I tried to tell you that Chloe was unsuitable," said George with a shrug.

"And what of Woodvale?" demanded Lord Bankleigh.

"What of him?" Sophia demanded. "He cares nothing for me and can go his own way with my blessing."

Bankleigh sighed. "Are you sure this time?"

"Very."

"I suppose anything would be better than a libertine," he grumbled, casting black stares at Nicholas and Diana.

"Lady Bounty agreed to help me stage this charade," Nicholas stated coldly. "I had to get rid of the chit. She's far too disapproving for my taste. We would have spent the next forty years trying to kill each other."

"Do you mean that you plotted this with him?" demanded Bankleigh, glaring at Diana.

Lady Weymouth gasped, pulling out her own vinaigrette. "Scandalous!"

Sophia shrugged. "I can only be grateful she did. I would have made the best of it, but we would not have suited any more than George and Miss Parker."

Diana saw the fear deep in her eyes. George was not completely stupid. It would not do to let him suspect Sophia's complicity in this farce.

But George was made of sterner stuff than they had expected. He straightened. "Thank you, Lady Bounty. Your selflessness has benefitted all of us." He turned to Lord Bankleigh, his face hardening. "I am appalled that you would force Sophia into so unsuitable a match. And I am incensed that anyone could threaten to sell his own daughter to a man like Griswold. Not once have you considered her best interests. All you care about is your own consequence. But making her choose between Griswold and a libertine demeans you far more than having an unwed daughter!"

"I told you it wouldn't work," said Lady Bankleigh, turning on her husband.

"But it did," Bankleigh insisted stoutly. "Girl's finally off our hands. Thought I'd never get rid of her."

"Of all the cold—" began Nicholas, but Diana stopped him.

"Don't start a new fight," she whispered.

Lady Weymouth was again waving her vinaigrette. Lady Bankleigh stared. Sophia burst into genuine tears.

"It's all right, love," murmured George. "We still have each other."

Nicholas shook his head as he led Diana away. "We will leave you to discuss this in private. Might I suggest an immediate wedding and no public announcements until both marriages are official? If you present society with a *fait accompli* and a united front, there will be less scandal."

Weymouth nodded, then turned back to his son. Lady Bankleigh had collapsed onto a chair as far from her husband as she could get. Lady Weymouth offered her the vinaigrette as Nicholas shut the door.

"You should not have jumped in to defend me," Diana chided him when they had reached the drawing room. "Learning that Sophia set him up will give George a grudge he will not forget in a hurry. She will have enough trouble accepting her father's indifference."

"I realized that a moment too late. Fortunately, Sophia covered the gaffe. But I could not allow them to believe you were conducting an affair with me."

"Why not? That is precisely the image you were projecting to George."

"True, but only to trigger his chivalry. I knew he could never watch me make a fool of Sophia without interfering."

"I gather he objected to your performance at the theater." She giggled. "I thought he would swoon when he saw Charles and Chloe. But right up to the end, I had doubts that this would work. I know those people too well. Even your loftier title should not have carried the day. We should have—"

His lips cut off her voice. "Diana . . ." This kiss was even headier than their earlier ones. "God, I want you," he gasped at last.

She froze. "Heartless rogue! You can't keep your mind out of bed, can you?"

"That just slipped out."

"Right. When had you planned on mentioning it? After dinner? Am I on the menu as dessert? You undoubtedly expect gratitude for extricating me from that betrothal without tarnishing my reputation."

"No!"

"Do you really expect me to believe that?"

"Diana—" He squeezed his eyes shut and drew in a deep breath. "It's true that I want you, but that wasn't where I meant to start, because it raises the wrong images. I never should have offered you *carte blanche*."

She glared silently until he met her eyes.

He sighed. "You're right. I'm heartless. I've been heartless since I left Warwickshire. When I hurled yours back, mine went with it. It's been in your keeping ever since."

"What game are you playing now?"

"The most important game of my life. The prize is marriage—and a lifetime of fidelity. I love you, Diana. More than ever. I never stopped, you see. Everything I've done in ten years has been a fruitless effort to push you out of my mind. But you are more firmly lodged than ever. I can't live without you, my love. Can I please quit trying?"

She bit back tears. "I don't know, Nicholas. I truly do not want a husband."

"I've no designs on your fortune. You would still be financially independent."

"You couldn't touch it anyway." She explained the trust.

"Good for Bounty. He was a wily one. So what is troubling you?"

She said nothing.

"Talk to me, sweetheart," he begged, settling on the couch with her in his lap. "Why are you so determined? Was marriage to Bounty so frightful?"

"Harry?" She was genuinely shocked. "No. He was the kindest man I've ever known. I loved him dearly, though like a father. He knew Papa was dying before I did, and he knew what Uncle Raymond would do once he had me in his power. So he agreed to take care of me. That's why he set up the trust."

Remembering Harry brought a tear to her eye, but Nicholas was still stuck back on Uncle Raymond. "What would your uncle have done?"

"Sold me to the meanest, most lecherous rogue he could find who was willing to pay." She inhaled deeply, letting the breath out slowly. "But not until he tired of using me himself. He always had a penchant for young girls."

"I'll break his neck!" The growl sent shivers down her spine.

"Shh." She loosened his fingers before they could bruise her arm. "No need. His horse already took care of that—before Harry died, thank God. I'm not sure even Harry's arrangements could have kept him away."

"I wish I had known."

"You had no right to interfere. And he did me no lasting harm. He stalked me more than once, but he never caught me.

The closest he ever came was cornering me in the barn one day—I would have been about fourteen. But Papa arrived immediately, and I was able to escape. He was scary, but I didn't understand his purpose until much later. Harry took me away before Papa died, so I was never in danger."

"Then what is wrong?"

"Nothing. At least not in the sense you mean." She rose to pace the room. "I am just so tired of men's lies, of their games and their mysteries. I won't tie myself to another one. Even Harry had secrets, despite pretending to be so open. He never explained your friendship, for example. I often wondered why he refused to take me to Sherlock—I knew why he kept me away from London, of course; I couldn't risk running into you." She shook her head. "Papa was secretive about everything important—and not just with me. Few people knew of his financial woes. His illness had raged for two years before he told me about it. All that time I was sneaking around with you, I could have been with him. I'll never forgive myself for the missed memories."

"It's not your fault he died," he said softly. "And be honest with yourself. If we had not met, would you have known about his illness any sooner?"

She started to answer, but bit her lip instead. Would she have known sooner? Even before meeting Nicholas, she had seen her father only at occasional dinners. The dining room had been a cavernous place that was impossible to light properly, so his sallowness and even his lost weight were not apparent.

"Probably not," she admitted. "But he should have shared something that vital."

"He did not know you as well as I do," he murmured, again pulling her into his lap. "You are strong and can handle the bad as well as the good."

"Nice speech, but you've never been open with me, either."

He sighed. "Ten years ago I did not know what I wanted. It is difficult to share thoughts you don't understand yourself. That, at least, has changed. Now I can safely promise that I would never again keep secrets from you, my love. And I won't ever lie."

"I can't—"

But he cut her off. "You can't give me an heir? That doesn't matter. I already have a perfectly good one."

She stared. "That isn't what I was going to say. I'm afraid, Nicholas."

"Of marriage?"

She shook her head.

"Of intimacy?" he tried, shocked when she agreed. "Why? You have never shown the least hesitancy at my touch. Did Bounty frighten you?"

"He couldn't."

It took him a moment to work it out. He should have known it earlier. Despite the passion that flared so easily between them, she still retained that air of innocence. And Bounty had been like a father—not a lover.

A tear rolled down her cheek. "He was so ashamed of his lack. He taught me so much—about life, about love. But he could never teach me that."

"Shh, darling," he murmured soothingly in her ear. "He was a wonderful man, whose worth was in no way impaired. And you needn't fear I would ever mention it," he added, reading her eyes. "Is that why you never wanted to remarry?"

She nodded. "I've had offers enough—of both kinds."

"And turned them down out of loyalty to Bounty."

"And because they weren't you," she admitted at last.

Nicholas tightened his arms. "I will never again hurt you, Diana. And I will honor Bounty forever. He kept you safe for me. Do you love me?"

"Yes." Tears shimmered in her eyes. "I never stopped. Something that powerful doesn't go away, does it?"

"Never. So, please. Marry me."

"Yes."

"Soon," he murmured, kissing her under her ear. She had always been particularly sensitive in that spot.

"Very soon," she agreed, laughing. "We haven't much choice.

I offered Charles my house until he sails. It looks like Doctor's Common will be doing a brisk business in special licenses."

"I already bought one."

"Arrogant, arrogant." But love threaded her tone.

"We'll wed tomorrow, then stay here until Charles sails. You will want to spend time with Chloe."

She nodded.

"But I don't care to attend any balls," he added, kissing her face. "I'm not ready to smile while Lady Hardesty gloats."

"She has often sung your praises—even while she shoved other men at me," murmured Diana. "I wonder if Harry said something."

He threw back his head and laughed. "That rogue! No wonder he never mentioned his wife to me—we kept in touch, and I last saw him only two years before he died. You told him everything. He must have recognized that I'd fallen top over tail in love with you, so he arranged to push us together after he was gone."

She joined his laughter.

"Dinner, my lord," said the unflappable Wiggs from the doorway. He was gone before Diana could rise.

Nicholas helped her up, then pulled a ring from his waistcoat pocket. "The Woodvale betrothal ring," he confirmed, sliding it onto her finger. "I should accompany this with a speech—which I will treat you to later. But it occurs to me that the luckiest break of my life was when you declared your love that summer."

"Why is that?" She busied herself fixing his cravat.

"I had pushed my control too far that day," he admitted, pinning her hair back in place. "In another minute or two I'd have had you, right there. Only shock at your words pulled me back. I would have married you, of course, but we could only have lived with my father. Bitterness would have turned our love to hate. It's been lonely these past years, but we can now look forward to a lifetime of happiness—together."

"Amen."

Linking arms and exchanging one last kiss, they headed for the dining room where twelve satisfied guests awaited them.

SIGNET REGENCY ROMANCE (0451)

# *TALES OF LOVE AND ADVENTURE*

☐ **SHADES OF THE PAST by Sandra Heath.** A plunge through a trapdoor in time catapulted Laura Reynolds from the modern London stage into the scandalous world of Regency England, where a woman of the theater was little better than a girl of the streets. And it was here that Laura was cast in a drama of revenge against wealthy, handsome Lord Blair Deveril. (187520—$4.99)

☐ **THE CAPTAIN'S DILEMMA by Gail Eastwood.** Perhaps if bold and beautiful Merissa Pritchard had not grown so tired of country life and her blueblooded suitor, it would not have happened. Whatever the reason, Merissa had given the fleeing French prisoner-of-war, Captain Alexandre Valmont, a hiding place on her family estate. Even more shocking, she had given him entry into her heart.

(181921—$4.50)

☐ **THE IRISH RAKE by Emma Lange.** Miss Gillian Edwards was barely more than a schoolgirl—and certainly as innocent as one—but she knew how shockingly evil the Marquess of Clare was. He did not even try to hide a history of illicit loves that ran the gamut from London lightskirts to highborn ladies. Nor did he conceal his scorn for marriage and morality and his devotion to the pleasures of the flesh.

(187687—$4.99)

Prices slightly higher in Canada

Payable in U.S. funds only. No cash/COD accepted. Postage & handling: U.S./CAN. $2.75 for one book, $1.00 for each additional, not to exceed $6.75; Int'l $5.00 for one book, $1.00 each additional. We accept Visa, Amex, MC ($10.00 min.), checks ($15.00 fee for returned checks) and money orders. Call 800-788-6262 or 201-933-9292, fax 201-896-8569; refer to ad #SRR1

**Penguin Putnam Inc.**
**P.O. Box 12289, Dept. B**
**Newark, NJ 07101-5289**
Please allow 4-6 weeks for delivery.
Foreign and Canadian delivery 6-8 weeks.

Bill my: ☐ Visa ☐ MasterCard ☐ Amex _____ (expires)
Card#_____
Signature_____

### Bill to:
Name_____
Address_____ City_____
State/ZIP_____
Daytime Phone #_____

### Ship to:
Name_____ Book Total $_____
Address_____ Applicable Sales Tax $_____
City_____ Postage & Handling $_____
State/ZIP_____ Total Amount Due $_____

**This offer subject to change without notice.**